THE CHOCOLATE DEBACLE

"While reading *The Chocolate Debacle* I felt like one of the dogs Trey Barkley, the accused killer, walks! The story pulled me along with the sights, smells, clues, and characters, which demanded my immediate and full attention. The book was by my side even when I had to take care of business…. Did Trey kill Flo Loughton? I thought I knew, then I didn't, then I did…sort of. Much more than a whodunit, the characters are real people dealing with extraordinary, unimaginable and yet commonplace circumstances involving serious mental illness. Mentally ill persons who kill are in the headlines. This book tells a very real story of what happens when mental illness and murder cross paths."

—Xavier Amador
author of the international bestseller *I Am Not Sick, I Don't Need Help!*, a regular forensic contributor to CNN, and psychologist on the Unabomber, 9/11 hijackers, Jared Loughner, Elizabeth Smart kidnapping, and many other notorious homicide cases involving persons with serious mental illness

"*The Chocolate Debacle* is more than a mystery novel. Its plot explains schizophrenia and its symptoms, and challenges stereotypes that lead to rushes to judgment. It is a reality that many individuals and families affected by mental illness face."

—Mary Giliberti
executive director of the National Alliance on Mental Illness

"*The Chocolate Debacle* combines mystery and compassion in its portrayal of a young man whose mental illness makes him a target of the police in a murder investigation. So rarely do we see persons with acknowledged mental illness as protagonists that it was not until I picked up this book that I realized this to be true. Told in winning prose with a sense of humor that is striking when it hits, much like *The Tale of a Dog in the Night*, this book is a must read for anyone who likes a good yarn and a main character you cannot easily forget."

—Lisa Rojany Buccieri
publisher and editor in chief of New York Journal of Books

"*The Chocolate Debacle* is a superbly crafted suspense novel—but it is also much more than that. As social commentary, it unveils the stigma that affects people with mental illness and their families, as well as the inherent fallibility of our criminal justice system. As a work of literature, it explores a deep contradiction of human experience: although we are intrinsically connected with other human beings, we remain isolated in a world of our own thoughts and perceptions. Whether mentally ill or not, we all face the same fundamental problem. As Schwartz's characters struggle to overcome their isolation and to discover friendship, love, respect, or mere acceptance, we are at times amused by their awkwardness but always deeply moved by their humanity and by their courage to persist and to live life as best they know how. In the end, we have a murder mystery without a villain, which is quite in keeping with the author's gift in portraying flawed human nature with insight, empathy, and warmth."

—David Kaczynski
executive director of
Karma Triyana Dharmachakra Buddhist monastery
and brother of Theodore Kaczynski, a.k.a. the Unabomber

THE CHOCOLATE DEBACLE

Also by Karen Winters Schwartz:

Where Are the Cocoa Puffs?:
A Family's Journey Through Bipolar Disorder
Goodman Beck Publishing, 2010

Reis's Pieces:
Love, Loss, and Schizophrenia
Goodman Beck Publishing, 2012

THE CHOCOLATE DEBACLE

Nov 29, 2014

For NAMI Virginia,
Enjoy this book with a cup
of cocoa!

a mystery novel by
Karen Winters Schwartz

GB

GOODMAN BECK PUBLISHING

GOODMAN BECK PUBLISHING

PO Box 253
Norwood, NJ 07648
goodmanbeck.com

The characters and events in this book are fictitious. Any similarity to real
persons, living or dead, is coincidental and not intended by the author.

ISBN 978-1-936636-13-6

Library of Congress Control Number: 2014948917

Printed in the United States of America

Dedicated to the memory of my mother, Dot Winters,
who sadly never had the opportunity to read this work.

ONE

It was very tough for Trey Barkley when he turned right onto Fennel Street rather than left. But he did so nonetheless. He'd promised himself when he'd opened his eyes that Thursday morning that this would be a right-hand-turn day; a promise was not something he entered into lightly. Even Hector seemed uncharacteristically on edge. Maybe it was the right-hand turn, or maybe it was the fact that Trey had picked him up early that day, but it wasn't until they had proceeded up Fennel and past the P&C grocery store (Trey just couldn't accept that it was now a Tops) that both Hector and Trey began to relax.

The plastic grocery bag, which unfortunately sported the Tops logo, rattled in the summer breeze, and Hector's shit, safely sheathed, banged gently against Trey's upper thigh as they walked. Strange, but the noise and the gentle tap on his thigh was somehow a comfort, so when little Caleb Rossiter came screeching out of the old P&C and screamed further with delight when he saw Hector, Trey clutched the handles of the bag of shit tighter and was more or less prepared when the boy assaulted the two of them. Caleb's face was painted with slimy brown chocolate. He pushed what was left of his treat out to Hector before Trey had the chance to detour the candy bar. It was gone and down Hector's throat in a heartbeat.

Hector was delighted with his acquisition and wiggled his small body with glee as Caleb proceeded to smear the remainder of the chocolate into Hector's fluffy white coat. "Dammit, Caleb," Trey complained. "You're getting him all dirty."

Then suddenly Mrs. Rossiter was there. She grabbed Caleb's greasy little hand. "Caleb, don't you ever run away from me like that again." She dragged the boy away without a glance, smile, or word thrown Trey's way.

"I'm going to have to bathe him," Trey mumbled, perhaps not loud enough for Mrs. Rossiter to heed, and just like that, Trey's right-hand-turn day was fully wrecked.

Trey went toward Mrs. Loughton's house with trepidation. He never liked to enter unoccupied houses when he walked his clients' dogs, greatly preferring to simply open the door, call the dog (or dogs), snap each leash onto each collar, and continue on his way. His clients almost always left their doors unlocked, but he insisted that they leave a key hidden somewhere in case the door had been inadvertently locked. He hated the idea of not being able to do his job, the poor dog stuck miserably inside a locked home.

Oddly, when he'd picked up Hector twenty minutes prior, Mrs. Loughton's door was in fact locked. But then everything about the day was turning odd. He'd had to pick up the bright yellow flowerpot that sat to the left of the door. He'd then bent down and flicked off a small slug from the house key, which was slightly eased into the mud under the pot. Then he'd picked up the key and used it to open the side door near the garage, after which he'd replaced the key, neatly realigning the pot so that it looked totally undisturbed.

And now, twenty minutes later, once Trey reached the gate that led to Mrs. Loughton's side yard, he stopped and reconsidered. He really did hate to enter his clients' unoccupied homes, but he couldn't just shove Hector's little ass through the side door and walk away. What would Mrs. Loughton think upon coming home from her job as a lawyer in Syracuse only to find her little dog all soiled?

Hector was looking up at him with adoration, a nasty brown smear down his back, his curly tail pushing the hot summer air about. Trey had to smile down at him, pick him up, and then press his nose into the fluff of the little Maltese's face. "You are a sweet baby. I love you." Hector licked with enthusiasm. "Such a sweet baby." And then he realized how ridiculously effeminate that sounded, and how absurd it must look for a twenty-six-year-old man to be pressing a white puff of a dog to his face while professing his love. Trey set the dog against his shoulder and looked up and down the street, relieved that no one was around.

Mrs. Loughton lived on West Elizabeth, which was a couple of miles north from where Trey lived with his parents, on West Lake Street. Much smaller than his parents' home, her house was nice enough—lived up to Skaneateles standards. The grass was cut tight and neat with minimal weeds. The house was white with green shutters and had recently been painted. The gardens in the back were a little unusual—a jumbled mass of vegetable plants with not a flower to be had. The white picket fence had also recently been painted, but the garage was in need of a major scraping and painting; Trey imagined it would be remedied soon enough. Maybe if the painter let her down then he'd offer to paint it this fall. Not that it really mattered. Not that every garage had to have a fresh coat of paint. It wasn't like he or his parents were patronizing elitists. In fact his parents worked quite hard to prove just the opposite, seemingly embarrassed by their wealth. And this seemed to be the general aura of The Village—down-home

America with a subtle shitload of cash dangling from Talbot- and Henri Lloyd-clad asses.

He laughed. *He* certainly wasn't wealthy. No Henri Lloyd on his sorry ass.

All this discreet pretention boded well for him. Just as most of the Skaneateles residents hired painters and housekeepers and nannies and gardeners regularly, they also needed to hire someone to walk their dogs. It was just standard operating procedure.

The Village, which should truly always be capitalized, sat on the north end of Skaneateles Lake, and other than his time at Brown University, Trey had spent his entire life there—in The Village. His mother would say, "I live in The Village. West Lake Street. Not right on the lake, but we have a lovely lake view." And then his mother would laugh and add, "Near the country club." Her hand would go out and tap whoever's arm she might be chatting with. Then she'd quickly change the subject to something philanthropic and worldly.

As much as Trey liked to make fun of the place, he loved The Village and its little foo foo dogs and its big designer dogs and the way it should always be capitalized. He loved the Americana summer concerts in the gazebo—how many musicians could one cram into a gazebo? He loved sipping on his strawberry fruit smoothie as he perused the books at Creekside. He loved watching the kids play in Austin Park and the ladies jog along the path with their dogs or their strollers—their breasts tightly secured in their ISIS sports bras. He loved sitting by the lake and watching the Mid-Lake Boat Tour leave the dock, the tourists excited to get onto the water, sip their wine, and hear who owns which massive home that sprawled along the shores of Skaneateles Lake. He loved the antique boat show that came in the summer and the world-class musicians who played during the Skaneateles Festival; and nothing—*no, nothing*—did he love more than the role he played as the Ghost of Christmas Present in Dickens Christmas, a magical street production of *A Christmas Carol* that consisted of dressing up in vintage clothing and talking all *thee* and *thou* and *hither* and *hath*, which went on every weekend between Thanksgiving and Christmas. Having played Tiny Tim from ages four through seven, Trey lobbied hard to win the role of Ghost of Christmas Present after his return to Skaneateles six years ago from his two-year stint at Brown University. He felt, in spite of his small stature, that he was a natural for the part. He feared his mother's financial contributions may have been a factor, but he didn't like to think about that, and regardless, he'd earned his place the last six years.

He'd spent a lot of time perfecting his green robe, decked with white fur. The fur was fake, but quality fake. Every year he re-made his holly wreath, which he wore upon his head, using real holly. Unfortunately, he'd come to find that real berries tended to fall off, so he carefully wired each of the individual holly berries he'd purchased from Michaels into the prickly leafed wreath and then glued a few thin, high-quality plastic icicles, improving the wreath's credibility. He spent hours oiling the leather of the scabbard he'd found in an antique store, making sure he did it at least once per month throughout the year. He'd made the torch, shaped like a horn of plenty, out of an oak branch he found in the woods of Austin Park. The Dickens' committee members refused to allow him to fill it with oil and light it with real fire, so he'd spent a considerable amount of time one summer outfitting the torch with battery-powered flames made of thick, clear plastic. When he moved the torch just so, there wasn't a soul dead or alive who could tell that it was fake. Yes, it had taken some doing, but he'd made the Ghost *his* Ghost.

He had a certain reputation to uphold, so he was relieved that no one saw him smooching with this pooch, because pretty much everybody knew everybody, and when there wasn't some function or festival or high school sporting event or charity luncheon or wine tasting at the Sherwood or town meeting to discuss the unnatural and insufferable noise those motorcycles made as they drove through The Village (was there a way to ban them as they'd banned the semi-trucks?), then there was not a whole lot more to do than talk about one another—but only in the nicest, most private, and most unpretentious sort of way. Trey preferred not to be the subject of such talk.

Trey kept Hector in his arms as he glanced once again up and down the street, then he opened the side gate, made his way to the side door, turned the door handle to Mrs. Loughton's house, and slipped inside. The air conditioning was on; Trey hated air conditioning, and the hairs on his arms immediately stood to attention. He took off Hector's leash and hung it on the hook next to the door. Hector squirmed in his arms and gave one sharp, piercing bark that echoed through Trey's head, but still Trey would not release the dog. He made his way into the kitchen, the dog pressed into his chest.

Trey had only ever been in Mrs. Loughton's kitchen; he'd walk from the side door to get there, and once there, he'd sit at the kitchen table and wait for Mrs. Loughton to write him a check in her no-nonsense sort of way, a tight smile along with a little awkward chitchat. Of all his clients—he had fifteen in total—Mrs. Loughton was the only one who was a complete conundrum. She had a shitload of rules: Hector was never to be walked with another dog; Hector was to get only one of the biscuits shaped like little cats that Trey always had in his pocket (the treats all the dogs loved so much, the treats he procured from Aristocats & Dogs and spent 0.82 percent of his weekly income on, the treats that made even the most standoffish dogs fall in love with him); Hector was never to be walked more than, or less than, a half mile (which had been one of Trey's concerns with his right-hand-turn day); Hector was never to be allowed to jump up on anyone or anything; Hector was never to be allowed to sit down and lick at his "personals" in public—it just wasn't proper! (Trey had had a hard time keeping a straight face for that one); Hector was never allowed to start after a squirrel or even look one's way if it could be avoided; Hector was not to be talked to in a condescending manner—he was especially not to be demoralized with baby talk (Fuck it. Trey was guilty of breaking this one); Hector was to avoid all avoidable dirt, mud, leaf debris, vegetation, puddles, animal feces, large stones, hot asphalt, yellow snow, CATS, et cetera, et cetera. But with all her rules, she had never once criticized, chastised, or treated Trey with anything but the utmost respect. She paid him better than any of his other clients, always gave him a large holiday bonus, and had even visited him once when he had been hospitalized briefly, bringing him a box of Girl Scout cookies—Thin Mints. And yet in two years she'd almost never, until quite recently, offered an openly kind word. She'd really offered very few words of any sort, penning out his weekly check on Friday evenings when he asked all his clients to pay him, passing it his way wordlessly as if he were a problem best dealt with hastily. She could have easily left the check taped to the side door as most of his clients did; and she certainly didn't need to invite him into her kitchen and push toward him, in a put-out sort of way, a plate of whatever pastry or confection she might have housed in her pantry—as the normal offerings were certainly not home-concocted. Then they'd fallen into the habit of just sitting there, Trey eating and Mrs. Loughton watching him eat, rarely speaking. Sometimes she'd glance through the newspaper and comment on a thing or two. Sometimes he'd tell her something Hector had done on their walk. Almost always they were silent, but over the last few weeks this had been changing. Mrs. Loughton was falling into chatting him up. And it was odd and a little annoying and a little…well…it was a little nice. She'd even had him to dinner, just the night before, which had been quite interesting. But he'd never left her kitchen.

The kitchen was neat and clean, free of counter clutter. He glanced at brownies left over from his previous night's dinner with Mrs. Loughton, which sat covered with plastic wrap on the counter. He was tempted, knowing that Mrs. Loughton had made them for him. He could certainly, seeing that he was already *in* the house, help himself. But he resisted the urge to pull out a chunk of the chocolaty goodness and instead concentrated on the task at hand.

He could easily wash Hector in the kitchen sink—he was absolutely kitchen-sink-cleaning size—but he could not locate liquid dish detergent around the sink area. When he opened the cabinet under the sink and dug around momentarily, finding nothing but Ajax Triple Action, he worried about toxicity of such a concoction on Hector's pink skin. That's when he decided that Hector most likely was never bathed in dish detergent, but bathed and then conditioned with only the best of products. The logical place to look was the bathroom.

It felt weird as Trey made his way up her steps—Hector whining in his arms—and onto the second floor of the house. The upstairs hall was painted a soft yellow and dotted with family photos. Trey paused a moment to take them in, remembering Mr. Loughton and how he had just up and died one day, three years prior at the age of fifty-six. He'd never heard exactly why he died. Trey skimmed quickly over the photos, and sure enough, there was Mr. Loughton on the wall much as Trey remembered him, only slightly younger. The photo must have been over ten years old. Mr. Loughton looked to be near fifty when it was snapped, athletic, tall and thin, a golf club in one hand, the Country Club in the background—not that much different than Mrs. Loughton had once looked. But now with Mrs. Loughton easily pushing sixty and a widow and all, she had let herself go just a bit recently. There were photos of other people he did not know—family, he presumed—old shots, some black and white, stern faces from the past, sitting up rigidly straight. There was a shot of Mr. and Mrs. Loughton on their wedding day, Mrs. Loughton looking younger and rather pretty as a bride, but no more animated than if she were being photographed for the local garden club. He lingered a moment on another old photo of Mrs. Loughton. She was laughing, the sun in her eyes, her hair blowing back, the blue waters of Skaneateles Lake sparkling in the background, and she was hanging from the trapeze of the sailboat, her ass dangerously close to water; she looked surprisingly good—damn good.

Hector squirmed from his place under Trey's arm. Trey shifted the dog slightly, pulled his attention away from the photo, and considered the five doors. The doors of the two rooms to the left were open, and he could see that they were bedrooms—probably guestrooms, given the fact that they were small and tremendously neat. He stepped down the hallway and peered into the room to the right at the end of the hall. Sure enough it was a bathroom, but a quick search found nothing but a bark-like green piece of soap on the sink. He headed back down the hall and opened the next door, which proved to be a closet crammed full of an impressive mass of stuff. A few items actually sprung out with enthusiasm, causing Trey to jump back and Hector to give one quick, sharp bark that echoed through the hall. A colossal closet slob. He loved it! He struggled somewhat as he tried to keep hold of Hector and replace the old musty pillow, stringless tennis racket, and bent lampshade, throwing the pillow in last and pressing his back against the door before anything else might escape. He glanced up, his back still pressed against the closet door, and there she was: Mrs. Loughton looking all sexily at him, the water in the background, her ass fine and tight, almost kissing the water. And right next to her: dead Mr. Loughton.

But it wasn't until he stepped into the master bedroom that he really felt creeped out; and let's just say it: paranoid as hell. He almost, right there and then, scrapped the entire endeavor. And it wasn't until much later that it occurred to him that that moment, right there and then, was the moment that might have changed what was to come.

Mrs. Loughton's bedroom was painted deep blue with bright white trim. The floors were light, polished wood. Small Oriental rugs with a dominance of blue were thrown here and there. The bed, to which Trey's eyes were naturally drawn, was king-sized, hastily thrown together and lonely—only one of the sides having a look of disturbance. A lone light green robe was draped across the right-hand corner of the foot of the bed. He could picture her lying there, her graying hair resting on the pillow, her hand going out now and then to the neat side of the bed. He felt a punch of some deep longing of his own, knowing, no matter what, that this was his future—graying hair against his pillow with his hand finding no one. And even though his bed was unlikely to ever be king-sized, it would surely feel as large.

Hector began to wriggle more forcibly from his spot under Trey's arm. Trey shifted him once again to his shoulder and turned away from the bed in search of the master bath. The door to the bathroom was open, and Trey stepped into its interior like a thief, stealing a quick glance at a wadded-up washcloth that sat on the space between the twin sinks, a lone toothbrush, a tube of mascara, and a soft, light purple summer gown that hung from the hook on the wall. Off in the corner, near the walk-in shower, sat a silky pink pair of undies on the floor, dropped as she had stepped into the shower—the fibers of the bathmat still indented by her feet, the air still damp, the odor of her primping still present. Then she was everywhere, and Trey couldn't open the shower fast enough and grab the tubes—one shampoo, one conditioner—snatch the moist blue towel draped below the gown, and withdraw.

Hector growled and struggled to get away as Trey stepped back through the bedroom, but Trey tightened his hold and pressed his hand holding the towel and the shampoo and the conditioner against the doorframe to balance his retreat. The conditioner fell. Hector barked again. Trey's breath started to come out in little spurts as he shoved the tube of shampoo into the back pocket of his jeans and shifted the towel so that it fell across his arm. Then, as he leaned over to retrieve the conditioner, he thought he caught some unfathomable image—so fast, so quick, that it could hardly be real. Then the very real reality of his body and the very real need to get away and save his body caused him to drop everything—including Hector—and flee from the house.

TWO

When Flo Loughton woke up one morning to find herself a widow, she couldn't clearly see right then and there the benefits of such a situation. So when she turned over to the quite dead form of her husband, crying at that moment seemed to be the only logical response. And as short-lived as it was—she was totally composed by the time the paramedics arrived—the tears were genuine and heartfelt. There was nothing they could do; Frank's heart had just decided to stop at some point while they slept. Had there been something? A small sound? A movement? A stirring as his life had eased away? Something that should have caused her to wake? Surely a normal person wouldn't sleep through such a thing.

But Flo didn't linger long on guilt; there had just been so much to do. Her husband wasn't nearly as organized as she'd have liked him to be, and his death gave her the perfect opportunity to whip his life into order. And there was her law practice that really couldn't stand on its own without her, and her committee chair for the Skaneateles Festival (being a transplant Skaneateles-ite and not a native, she'd fought for that appointment), and her tennis partner depended on her, and it wasn't like she was going to just stop going to yoga at Mirbeau.

Life had continued, without her husband, in much the same manner as it always had. Her sight was sometimes clouded by the vast number of people telling her how sorry they were, how horrible it was that her husband should just up and die without any sort of forewarning, and that she was going to be okay—which was strange, because even in her darkest moments, she had never doubted that she would be okay, having found all her life that *not okay* and *okay* were very hard, if not impossible, to differentiate.

Growing up in a small town in New England was perhaps a contributing factor to her n'importe quoi attitude, but really it was more that she'd learned pretty early that crying was good for not much more than stuffing up her nose, making her face blotchy, and making her already tiny eyes disappear into the folds of her despair.

But it was undeniable that there were times late at night when she did indeed long for him, and although she didn't bother crying again, it was at these moments that the benefits of living alone—not having to worry about what someone else might want for dinner; knowing that any mess to be found in one's house was of one's own making; going to bed whenever one was tired, without the added complication of *Is sex necessary?* running through one's head—seemed to be selfishly petty when compared to these rare moments of insatiable loneliness.

Perhaps it was not her husband she longed for, but something more abstract, something more agreeable. Not that Frank had been the least bit disagreeable; it's just that he'd been so…agreeably Frank. And she resented the notion that she should carry around the cross of widowhood. That look, that smile, that gentle hand that would come out and squeeze her arm. "How are you, Flo?" And she knew the answer should have been, "Just fine. I'm holding up just fine." But what she said, what put people off, was,

"And how should I be?" Then she'd smile her best smile and attend to whatever task was before her. It didn't take terribly long for people to just stop asking, which was just fine by her.

It was at some point within the first six months of Frank's death that Flo ventured out of Skaneateles to Camillus. She'd been walking between Marshalls and Dick's Sporting Goods, on her way to shop for a new yoga outfit, when she happened to glance in the pet store window. There, sitting perfectly proper, while all its other puppy-pen mates were leaping about, sat a little white puff of fur that strangely reminded her of Daniel—the first boy she'd quite possibly ever loved, the first boy ever to be allowed to explore all her intricate crevices, the first and last boy to ever break her heart. So naturally she was drawn into this pet store. As she opened its door, as she was hit by the odor of puppy poop and wet guinea pig shavings, it occurred to her that she hadn't been in a pet store since she was a child. She'd never had a dog or even a fish, never coveted a kitten or kept fireflies in a jar. But when the girl with the ring through her right eyebrow and the snake tattoo on her neck lifted the little white puff and placed it in Flo's arms, her whole life shifted to something softer and slightly more vulnerable. Then she had almost recoiled, set the dog down, and walked out of the store without a second glance—but she never got the chance, because what was soon to be known as Hector stretched out his tiny little neck and licked at the smooth tan skin of Flo's face, sending a little shiver of something not quite definable, but something definitely worth investigating.

She later sat at her kitchen table and stared at the little dog, its eyes looking up at her with such trust, and she thought, *What now?* Because truth be told she'd never truly been in love, at least not like this, and it was disconcerting—already feeling some deep sadness from the knowledge that someday Hector would be dead and she'd be left to carry on alone. All dogs were fleeting little things. She stood up, determined to remove him from her home. Sure that she'd made an awful error, she swept him up along with her handbag, which held the pet store receipt, and walked with grave determination out her front door toward her car parked in her short driveway, only to run smack into that strange young man with the sandy flop of hair and those sad, weird eyes. His face immediately turned into something affable as he took in the little dog in her arms. He stopped. The large black dog he'd been walking immediately sat down near his left leg, looking up at him with obedient anticipation.

"I, um. You, um, you have a new dog," he said.

"Well—"

Then he was reaching out his hand toward Hector and stroking his fur, and before Flo could respond, Hector was in the young man's arms, both dog and man sharing an envious, admirable moment—something she was quite sure she was more than capable of giving and receiving, so when the young man asked her if she needed a dog walker for this new young pup, she'd had no choice other than to remove Hector from his arms and invite the young man into her home to discuss the details. She had apologized immediately, having to admit that she'd forgotten his name; even though she knew him and had seen him walking dogs for years now, his name had escaped her memory. "Trey Barkley," he told her. Then the memories became even more clear—the history of this odd young man. His mother, some sort of artist, had been on the Festival Board briefly, his father was a well-known thoracic surgeon in Syracuse, and his older brother was in his last year of surgical residency at Johns Hopkins. But Trey, the youngest of the boys, had returned home suddenly after a couple years of college; there was something wrong with him…some mental issue… something just not quite right.

Trey looked down as he spoke his own name, self-consciously

petted the big black dog's head he'd been walking—some sort of pain crossing his face—and said, "I have references."

"Oh, I'm sure you do, and I will most certainly be calling them, but tell me, Trey Barkley…how *does* one go about housebreaking a puppy?"

THREE

By the time Trey Barkley walked into the Aristocats & Dogs early afternoon on Thursday, he was feeling better. Still shaky and slightly uncertain, but it was under control. It wasn't like his freak-outs were something unusual or something that he wasn't used to dealing with, but still. So it was not absurdly surprising that he jumped when Mrs. Simmons hailed a hello from behind the counter, or that he couldn't quite remember where the dog treats shaped like little cats were kept, or that he fell into wandering around the store, running his hands along the plush stuffed animals, tapping the cat toys so that they tinkled gently, picking up the shoe-shaped rawhide and giving it a little sniff, and pulling the cans off the shelf and carefully reading the ingredients, then making another pass through the small store while fighting that feeling of panic until Mrs. Simmons finally came to his rescue and handed him the box. "Is there something else you need, dear?" she asked, and he shook his head and pulled out the eight dollars and forty-three cents from the front pocket of his jeans, handing her the money quickly lest she see him tremor.

"Thank you," he said, giving her a quick smile, then retreating from the store. He'd finished with all his morning walks—each dog, each house. Several he walked at the same time—those dogs that were easygoing and took a liking to a walk-buddy. Now it was time to head home for lunch before his afternoon shift started. Same dogs, same walks, but he liked it that way. He had it all mapped out perfectly so that the first dogs he walked were owned by clients who left early and arrived home before 5:00 p.m. For those clients who worked normal hours, their dogs were walked in the middle shift. And for those who worked ridiculously crazy hours, like Mrs. Loughton, their dogs were walked early and at the very end of the day.

Trey almost always went home for lunch, preferring not to drag a packed lunch around with him all morning, and even though his parents' home was about a mile from the center of The Village, he liked to walk—he walked all day—and a mile was nothing, especially in the summer. As he walked down the main drag of Skaneateles, with the little shops lining both sides of the street, people nodded to him and smiled. He smiled back, cautiously at first, but by the time he reached Doug's Fish Fry, where a cute little girl looked up at him and grinned between licks off her after-lunch ice cream cone, he was feeling pretty much back to his old self.

Trey smiled at the little girl and was then moved to take thirteen steps back so that he was standing in front of the display window of his mother's favorite shop. He glanced at his reflection in the window, adjusted his baseball cap slightly, then let his eyes focus on the week's featured items. Heads of white manikins adorned with bright summer hats, light silky scarves, and colorful baubles stared back at him. Trey shifted his eyes and examined the smattering of commercial artifacts laid out at the base of the heads. His eyes landed and then stayed on a tiny black ceramic box. Black—his mother's favorite color. On its lid sat a perfect ceramic orange rose—his mother's favorite flower. Twenty-nine steps later he was back out of the store, the ceramic box safely swathed in zebra-striped tissue paper and housed in the store's black checkered signature bag. As he walked back toward his home, he removed one of his carefully folded, unused plastic shit bags from his jean pocket and placed his little surprise inside.

The line of shops stopped abruptly as Trey crossed a small bridge that passed over the outlet of the lake. There were a couple teenage girls sitting on the steps of the gazebo, their hair odd shades, their tattoos apparent—most definitely from out of town. Old people sat on the benches under the trees or leaned against their canes and peered at the lake. Both the Mid-Lake tour boats were docked against the long pier, which was crowded in an average sort of way with tourists dressed in polos and khakis and fluttering floral prints. Children splashed and squealed in the small swimming area, which was portioned off with white ropes and small red buoys. The lake was especially blue and shimmering, and Trey could see a few sailboats moving slowly in the slight breeze, along with a handful of motorboats out on a Thursday. He passed a pretty girl close to his age who glanced up at him and smiled, causing him to stop in his tracks. He turned around, and sure enough, she glanced over her shoulder and smiled again. Weird. Pleasantly weird. He couldn't remember the last time a girl had given him a second look.

It was then he decided (incorrectly as it turned out) that in spite of the earlier evidence to the contrary, the right-hand turn had been critical to positively changing his life. It had caused a shift. The pretty girl looked a lot like Stephanie. If Stephanie had occurred once, she could reoccur; it was just a matter of something as simple as right over left.

"Feel that?"

"Feel what?" she asked lazily.

"That." He rubbed the fingers of his right hand again across the top of her left.

"I feel your fingers. They're rough."

"That's from that chemical burn last month in chem lab. But that's not what I mean. Feel harder."

Stephanie laughed. "You're so weird."

He shook his head. "Close your eyes. Feel. Feel the million microbes skimming the surface of who we are."

"Ew. Trey!" She pulled her hand away. "Cut it out!"

Trey was quiet for a long time, resting his head against her pillow, his thoughts jumping through the dorm room. "I've been thinking a lot about it recently."

She sighed softly, settling more deeply into the bed. "What's *it*?" she finally asked.

"The addition."

"Huh?"

"You know…the summation. What we add up to."

She closed her eyes tight as if to wish him away.

He sat up straighter. "Seriously! This is important. Thirteen. I think it's significant."

Stephanie used her left hand to pull a few long black strands of hair from her eyes and took him fully in. Her dark eyes drilled at his soul. "What is *wrong* with you? Seriously? Thirteen?"

"Look, this is important. Try to stay with me here." He smiled, not wishing her to sense any disdain for her ignorance. Without ignorance education would be impossible. They were, after all, in an institution of learning. He took both her hands in his. "Stephanie has nine letters, right? Trey has four. Four plus nine is thirteen. Right?" She nodded. "Don't you see? Thirteen is central—critical to sacred geometry. It reflects patterns that exist in nature, in the heavens, in man." He let go of her hands and ran his fingers along her naked body. "Thirteen major joints in the human body." She shivered under his touch. "Thirteen lunar cycles. Thirteen degrees of lunar movement across the sky…each and every day." He leaned in and kissed her forehead, which was still slick with sweat. "Thirteen is the attracting center around which all elements focus and collect." He leaned away and touched the center of her forehead with his right forefinger. "Thirteen," he whispered. He ran the tip of his finger slowly down from her forehead until it rested momentarily on her left nipple, then he gently rotated his finger over her areola thirteen times. "One…two…three…thirteen reduces to four…five…," he counted until she purred.

Thirteen and right-hand turns: life-changing.

He watched the pretty girl until she'd walked thirteen steps away from him. He turned his head back toward home and began to walk again. He counted thirteen steps, and then another thirteen steps. Then, as he finished his third set of thirteen—thirty-nine steps total now—Trey began to feel better than his old self and actually began to whistle, which really in itself was quite strange.

By the time he slammed through the screen of the side door of his parents' house, he was singing, quite loudly, "She Likes the Weather"—so loudly, as a matter of fact, that his mother stepped out of her studio, brushing the powdery clay from her hands, and looked at him with concern. "Trey?"

He mimed the perfect base guitar, his head bobbing with the beat, his hair taking on a life of its own. "All of the flowers I've raised came up a little cloudy! Life is bitter! Life is cheap!"

His mother's eyes narrowed slightly, and then she shook her head and laughed. "Okay…. So I guess you had a good morning?"

"Everybody shat! Always makes for a good morning." Trey shifted the bag with his mother's gift slightly to his side so that it was not within her direct line of sight. He wandered off toward the kitchen as she followed. He'd give her the gift right after lunch. Maybe just leave the plastic bag hanging from the handle of her studio door. Not say a word. Just drop it and run.

the chocolate debacle

"La dada, la da," he sang as he rummaged through the refrigerator, pulling out a package of pink boiled ham and thick-sliced Swiss cheese. "Dada, dada, dum."

He turned from the fridge and saw her still watching him, her head cocked to one side, a piece of her short blonde highlighted hair falling forward into her eyes, the slight wrinkles on her face exaggerated, and suddenly he felt naked and irritated. "DA DA DUM!" he yelled, and she turned away.

Trey sighed loudly, stuffed the bag that held the tiny ceramic box roughly into the front pocket of his jeans, and made a mental note to himself: *Remove the lumpy mass from front pocket and reappropriate its contents before taking off for afternoon shift.*

FOUR

Annette Barkley always wanted children. When she was pregnant with her first baby, all she could picture was a boy— blonde and blue-eyed. In the pre-birth dreams that filled her nights, he was always smiling up at her, deep dimples, peeing out of his little baby penis while she laughed, Annette wiping the sweet baby pee from her eyes, his fat legs pumping the air. So when her older son, Samuel, was born, and he was exactly as he was expected to be, it was only natural that she'd want to repeat the process. It was only natural to want to create another little being who was the perfect blend of her husband and herself, except, she hoped, without her husband's offensive habit of sucking on his teeth for a good half hour after every meal and her inclination to be utterly annoyed over such tendencies.

Her second son, Trey Barkley, came into the world with blonde, peachy fuzz on his head, fat little legs, a smile that swelled your heart, and a disposition that surpassed that smile. So when he looked her in the eye twenty-six years later and said, "DA DA DUM!" in a most vile way, it was more than just an aural slap; it was a punch of pain somewhere untouchable, except by him—and that spot was raw. Right then, right there, at that very moment, she hated him, and wanted more than anything for him to disappear, for him to never have been born, for him to be anywhere but in front of her, in her kitchen, eating her food at twenty-six years old and messing up her otherwise perfect life. She turned from him and headed back to her studio.

Annette Barkley, who was originally Annette Fisher, never really met her future husband; Jack Barkley was just always there. She remembered him standing at the bus stop with his bright blue snow boots, his nose bright red. She remembered him leaning his head back on her desk and peering at her with upturned eyes until Mrs. Rowan, their first grade teacher, snapped him back to attention with a quick slap to his hand. She remembered his bloody nose when he fell off the jungle gym during recess. She remembered how slow he walked from the batter's box when he struck out with the bases loaded and two outs. She remembered walking past him in the halls of junior high as he had Sheila Miller pressed against the wall, his tongue in Sheila's mouth. "Disgusting!" she'd said to her friend. So when people asked her how she met her husband, she was moved to say, "Well, I never really did." But if she'd been asked, "When did you fall in love with him?" she could tell them the exact moment, the exact second. It was that second right after she'd said, "Disgusting!" when he removed his tongue from Sheila's mouth, looked her way, and blushed. And if she asked Jack, which she still often did, "When did you fall in love with me?" he would smile, bend his head her way, and say, "Now. I'm falling in love with you now."

Sure there had been many other Sheila Millers and, of course, Annette's version of Sheila Millers, through junior high and high school, through their college years—she at Le Moyne studying art and Jack at Syracuse University studying biology—and even, but less so, through Jack's med school years at Upstate; but it was from that very second in the halls of junior high that she knew she would marry this man.

They married on a summer day in the gazebo in the park looking over Skaneateles Lake, all their friends and family looking on, both families long-time residents of Skaneateles—her great grandfather had even been mayor back in 1943 through 1949. A giddy, happy day. Forgotten were all those nights crying because Jack was out slipping his tongue into someone else or those nights she was defiantly slipping her tongue around some loser of a guy just to prove a point. It was a happy marriage. Then Samuel was born just eleven months in, Trey a year later. Perfect, happy little boys. A perfect, happy family.

As Jack's medical career advanced, so did Annette's artistic diversification and experimentation. She tried watercolor, flirted around with acrylic, and painted the acrylic over with oil and then another layer of oil, creating massive shades of brown-colored squares that lacked the soul she was searching for. They littered the back of her studio like flattened waffles. She tried enamels, batiking, etching, silversmithing, and then welding with large chunks of metal, which she liked. But when Jack complained about the large metal structures taking over their yard and then their garage, she switched to drawing first with pencil, then with charcoal—sweeping deep lines across the paper until all she could see, smell, and taste was black. She invested in a potter's wheel only to find the wobbling wet clay made her dizzy. Used now only as a workstation, it sat in the far corner of her studio. But she found the texture of clay soothed her—its silky pleasure slipping around her fingers, the sensation of stiffness as it dried around her fingernails, its earthy taste and smell that filled the room. Smitten, she bought a kiln and filled it with hundreds of tiny, sculptured Aztec figurines. What was left of them watched her with eyeless eyes as they collected time and knowledge and red-clay dust from their spots on the windowsills of her studio.

the chocolate debacle

As the years went on, her clay work grew larger and more abstract. Clay was delicate and ephemeral, so she took a bronzing class, learning how to turn her clay into something fixed and unyielding, creating abstract pieces of sweeping movement or dramatic, looming human figures only suitable for great halls. Only no great halls seemed to want her work; the pieces were strewn throughout her home like permanent disappointment.

But regardless, her studio was her space, her place, her salvation from nothing particular other than perhaps the very thing she was trying to create. It was only natural for her to withdraw back into her space that Thursday morning and shut the door. She was annoyed for the thousandth time. She was not really annoyed with Trey as much as she was annoyed that she'd let him get to her, that she'd withdrawn, that she'd let him DA DA DUM! her right out of her own kitchen. Annette went straight over to her newest clay figure, a woman-like structure standing ten feet tall, and considered, quite seriously, reaching up and freeing from the figure the burden of its head. She even took two steps upon the ladder and narrowed her eyes, staring into its empty features for a full ten seconds, before she laughed and felt better for that laugh, so she laughed again, sat down on one of the rungs of the ladder, and cried.

FIVE

When Trey Barkley approached Mrs. Loughton's house late that Thursday afternoon, it was with creeping dread. He was quite late, almost two hours late, which was totally contradictory to everything he believed. Even though Hector hadn't left his mind all day, Trey's actions directly contradicted his guilt. Instead of manning up to his failure and attending to what needed to be done, he'd been snarky to his mother, dawdled languorously over lunch, dawdled enthusiastically with every dog he walked, and now, somehow, two hours late, he was still hoping he wouldn't need to face the fact that he'd allowed a little freak-out to occur, causing him to leave poor Hector totally unpresentable to his owner. He made his way to the side gate next to the garage, but before he had the chance to lift up the gate latch and swing open the gate, before he had the chance to make his way to the side door, open the door, and call the dog, his heart was already beating faster than what was acceptable. He knew he had to re-enter the house and wash the dog, but he was terrified—terrified of another freak-out. He paused, took a few deep breaths, and bent down, his hands on his knees.

His freak-outs. He could remember a time when he was freak-out-free, when Stephanie's hair had shifted through his fingers, when his brain ticked with precision, when his parents swelled with pride, when his brother would punch him as an equal, when the residents of Skaneateles would coo over him as he limped down the sidewalk—his Tiny Tim crutch seemingly all that was keeping him from tumbling into the earth. "God bless us, every one!"

And now a Ghost: "You have never seen the like of me before!"

"Look upon me!" Yet they look away.

He pulled that thought out of his head and took more deep breaths.

"It's the trying that counts." Once his father had gotten over the anger, these were the words he had offered Trey.

Trey drew in a deep breath and then, keeping his eyes closed, dove down until his hands blindly searched the rocky bottom. Ripping free as much of the slimy weed as possible before the need for oxygen brought him back out into the sunshine, he opened his eyes to the perfect moment when his brother resurfaced. Trey's aim was pure. The green mass of goo hit Samuel in that ideal spot: above the eyes and right below the hairline. Much to Trey's delight, Samuel's concurrent assault missed its mark and sailed over Trey's head, landing safely in the water behind him with a soft plop. Trey cackled as Samuel slipped back under the water, resurfacing without further ammo and his head weed-free. "Asshole," Samuel called.

They'd been at it for a while now. Slime-weed-battle weary, Trey was relieved when his brother—looking much more like a man than a boy with the thick eruption of light brown chest hair and an envious definition to his arms and chest—stretched his arms back and floated on his back. He'd be leaving Trey soon, heading off for his first semester of college in just a few short weeks.

"Are you ready?" Samuel asked.

Was he? Was he ready to be alone with his parents?

"I guess so," said Trey.

"Hey, Dad. We're ready," called his brother, and Trey realized he was talking about their yearly swim across the lake and not the fact that Trey would soon be alone. It had become a yearly tradition for the last five years, ever since Trey had turned eleven and Samuel twelve.

"You boys be careful," his mother yelled from her spot in the lawn chair underneath the large maple, which stood in front of the lake cottage they rented for a week every summer. It was one of their parents' friend's places, on the south end of the lake, away from The Village, which was a whole different world to Trey and his brother—at least when they were younger. Now rather than ghost stories around a family campfire, Samuel spent most evenings in town with his friends.

His dad manned the rowboat as the spotter. They started out slow, pacing themselves for the one-mile swim. They were side by side, the boat behind them. As always, it was Samuel who set the pace. The water was warm, as it was nearly August. The surface was slightly choppy but manageable. Trey was feeling good. This year was going to be different. Unbeknownst to Samuel, Trey had been training all summer, getting up in the early dawn to swim and swim and swim. He was as ready as he was ever going to be.

It was at the halfway point that Samuel paused mid-stroke and grinned Trey's way. Trey's heart, which was already beating fast, took a little leap just as his brother put his head back in the water and kicked forward. In a few strides, his brother was ahead. One deep breath and a few strokes later Trey was right back at Samuel's side.

"You boys still have a long way to go," Trey heard his father warn over the swoosh of water.

Then there was nothing but the water and his movement, which was smooth and fluid, and the knowledge of his brother's closeness—so close, so in tune, that the water seemed to part in unison for both of them. Trey was soaring with energy and the oneness and the success of each stretch of his arms and each kick of his legs. The force was surreal and godlike and drove them both on and on until Trey was seized and then struck down.

He grabbed his left calf with both hands, sinking under the surface. His eyes opened to tiny, shimmering bubbles. He sank further until the bubbles were gone and the thin, wavy lines of the thermocline wiggled around him. Then he let go of his leg and reached upward toward the rolling brightness of the sun.

"Trey, get in the boat," he heard his father say as soon as his lungs had refilled.

Trey sucked in more air, rubbed at his eyes, and noted his brother was still moving. He shook his head. "I'll be fine," he gasped. He rubbed hard at his calf, which was still seething with pain, the water splashing in his face, some of it getting in his mouth and nose. He coughed and wiped at his eyes with his left hand, his right firmly kneading his calf.

"Dammit, Trey! Get in the boat."

"No." He looked forward only to see Samuel glance back, smile, and continue with an easy crawl. Trey let go of his leg and stretched it out, the pain creeping up to his thigh. He began to swim on only to have his leg knot up again. He sunk under the water, clutched his leg, and let the wetness take him in, relishing the momentary silence. He resurfaced to a small wave that flooded his eyes and his nose and his mouth, causing him to sputter and gasp and take in more water, followed by more coughing. Samuel was now significantly away.

Suddenly a motorboat passed too closely, its wake cutting the space between Samuel and Trey. "What the hell are you doing?"

his father shouted at the driver of the boat. "Can't you see we have swimmers here?" Trey treaded water, the pain easing up a bit in his calf, and watched as his father looked at Samuel and then at him and then back to Samuel.

"Sam!" his father yelled into the wind. "Turn around!" Then he turned to Trey, put out his hand, and screamed, "Get in the fucking boat!"

The wake of the passing boat hit Trey, filling his nose and mouth once again. His father fell to his knees, his hand still extended toward Trey. Trey was suddenly exhausted. He treaded and coughed, finally giving in to his loss. His father's hand was close now. Trey didn't pull away; he was actually relieved when his father's fingers dug tightly into the skin of his forearm. Then Trey was safely in the boat, breathing hard, rubbing at his calf, forcing himself not to cry, trying to ignore his father's angry glare. The boat lurched forward as his father took up the oars and rowed with all he had, trying to catch up to Trey's brother, who was now nothing more than a splash of water on the far horizon.

And right before they reached his brother, his father's words: "It's the trying that counts."

Trey felt his heart slow to a deep thump. His breathing slowed. He stood up slowly and reached for the gate. Even though Mrs. Loughton would be home in less than an hour, and he might not even have time to get Hector walked, washed, and dried, it was a matter of integrity. But as Trey's right hand touched the gate, something made his eyes stray to the one-car garage, which was just a short breezeway away from the main house. He rested his hand on the fence, leaned forward just enough to see through one of the small garage windows, and was immediately given a reprieve. Mrs. Loughton was already home. Home early. Her car was snug in the garage. And since it was clearly too late to remedy the chocolate debacle, and apparently unnecessary to walk Hector at this late hour, Trey Barkley made the decision to slink away from the door, slip behind the bushes next to the garage, ease himself into the neighbor's yard—out of sight from Mrs. Loughton's front windows—work his way up the street, and simply head on home.

SIX

Detective Seth Wooley entered the house at precisely 9:42 a.m. Friday morning. He tapped on the screen of his new iPhone just to be sure, making a quick note on the memo pad, holding it a little longer than necessary, because, come on, his new phone was awesome. Dr. Maddy Hatcher, the new deputy chief medical examiner, was directly in front of him, having met him in the entranceway of the home as he stepped up to the front door, and he could smell her no-nonsense odor of formaldehyde and something enviably feminine—something akin to an after-sex tang. Just a couple of years younger than Seth, she was in her early thirties and sexy as hell. "You like?" He waved his new phone her way.

"Nice."

"Check this out." He quickly swept at the small screen, and within moments he had a shot of the house—the house they were now entering. "This is where we are in the world."

"Cool," she offered, but he could tell he'd lost her, that her mind was not on his impressive new equipment. He popped the phone back into his pocket, ran his hand through the spastic dark curls that cursed his head, and sighed. He didn't know why he tried. It was pretty obvious that Maddy considered him like most women considered him: with indifference.

Indifference.

It was an emotion he hated and coveted. He supposed indifference was as critical to a medical examiner as it was to a cop, helping to keep that objectivity. But indifference gone unchecked could mean leaving things too quickly, losing that edge that makes us human. And it was being the object of indifference that he'd struggled with most of his life.

"Take this!" he'd cry, standing near the couch, the brim of his hat low, his eyes pinned on his target. Whipping both guns from the belt, he'd empty both barrels into his sleeping father. "Bam! Bam!" His father would slowly open his eyes, grunt, and then, without the passion of death, die slowly as he fell back to sleep.

In spite of the indifference, truth be told, Seth loved and respected his dad—always had. But what seven-year-old didn't love and respect their dad? So it was possibly this, the fact that the memory of his father was forever stuck in a seven-year-old's perspective, that had saved him—laid down the path to the work he loved.

"Damn, this sure is a pretty little town," he tried, glancing at Maddy, then looking up and down the street. "Hard to imagine anything bad happening here."

She shrugged.

"I guess bad things happen everywhere," he added rather lamely.

Perhaps if his father hadn't drunkenly and fatally taken on that tree—freezing that seven-year-old's perspective forever—Seth might easily have gone the other way.

It was really the work that saved him. Ever since he could remember he'd wanted to be a cop. He'd never been able to figure out where that desire came from. So many people on the force came from a long line of cops, but his father had spent most of his life on quite the opposite side of the line. The obvious answer was rebellion against his father, but he'd dressed in his black hat with the star in the middle, his dark curls pushed toward his eyes, his holster low on his hips, his legs spread in readiness, way before he was old enough to understand what his father was.

It was the puzzle part he loved the most. Which is why he always wanted to be a detective, and now that he was, it was all he wanted to be. He had no aspirations to move up in the force. Detective was just fine by him. It wasn't just the puzzle of putting the pieces of the crime together. What he found much more intriguing was the people part of the puzzle—what motivated someone to steal, to sell drugs, to mistreat one another, to drink themselves into abusive behavior, to drink themselves to the point of tree assassination, to love only to murder…. *The* story. *Their* story. He was intrigued by the stories.

Even though he'd like to stretch this threshold moment, try his best to illicit some sort of emotional response from Dr. Maddy Hatcher in order to get to the people-part of who she was, it was time to get to work and figure out Mrs. Florence Loughton's story. He set his face to detective mode, stepped more fully into the threshold, scanned the parts of the house's downstairs interior that were immediately available to him, and asked, "Upstairs?"

She nodded.

He smelled it immediately, and as he ascended the staircase it grew stronger, reminding him of walking across his mother's lawn on the first hot day of spring with little thought of where he was placing his feet, only to be assaulted by the most brutal aide-memoire as his feet slipped through the winter's deluge. "Dogshit?" he asked Maddy.

"Yup."

He nodded. "So there's a dog?"

"Yup. A very sick dog."

the chocolate debacle

Seth moaned. "Maddy, I hate that sort of thing. Couldn't you have taken a picture or something? I mean, dammit. Kill anyone you want, but please, just keep the animals out of it. A dog. Really?" He rubbed his hand across his face and appealed to her.

She shrugged that annoying Maddy shrug—the one that made him want to shake the haughty right out of her or press her up against the wall and fuck the compassion right into her. "I only just arrived a couple of minutes ago," she said. "I wanted you to see it before we shipped it off to the vet."

He just sighed and continued up the stairs. He could hear the photos being snapped and the trod of the ETs, and as he grew closer, he could hear the soft pant of discomfort.

He saw the dog immediately. It was small and white and lying just outside the threshold of one of the bedrooms, panting. Seth could see its little body rising and falling. "Oh man. Just have someone take it to the vet, will you?" But he walked a few steps down the hall and took in the scene. Blue towel lying in a heap, a tube of conditioner—both near the dog—piles of runny, stinky shit and foamy vomit dotting the light wood floor of the bedroom, along with what looked like bloody dog prints. There was a large dark smear across the dog's white back.

"Is that blood on the dog?"

"Chocolate."

"Chocolate? Are you sure?"

Maddy shrugged. "Yeah, I don't know. I have that unfortunate history of mixing them up."

"Okay. Let's just get this poor thing to the vet." He pulled his eyes off the dog. The ETs were done snapping photos and were just getting started with dusting the bedroom for prints. There was one rookie officer standing in the hallway who looked like he might give a shit and needed to get the hell out of there. "Hey! Randall!" Seth called. "Take this pup to the vet, will you?" Then

Seth sighed heavily, stepped carefully over the dog, and frowned Maddy's way. "Okay. So, show me. Show me the body."

SEVEN

Flo Loughton was a corporate lawyer, and as a corporate law-yer there was a certain order to be maintained, a certain dignity to uphold, a certain respect given to the very word: corporation. And it was necessary to extend that same dignity, order, and respect to the rest of one's life. Therefore, marriage, love, and sex—often filled with sticky uncertainly—was not something she coveted, longed for, or sought. So when Frank, in his very Franklin-esque way, dropped to his knees one month after they'd both graduated from New England Law, she immediately told him to stand up. But he shook his head, kissed her left knee with determination, and said, "Floie, life's just too short to make it so damn straight. You need a curve every now and then. I'm your curve."

And so he was.

They'd moved to Skaneateles shortly after getting married. Frank had taken a job at the Syracuse legal clinic and accepted a part-time teaching position at Syracuse University Law School. He was determined to do some good for mankind by helping those he felt were in need and by instilling curves of morality into those young, soon-to-be lawyers. It became necessary to obtain a house. Neither one of them was especially keen on the outlying suburbs of Syracuse, so they made further and further forays away, until one crisp fall day they stumbled upon this village by the lake, turned to each other, and smiled. Skaneateles had in some way reminded Flo of her childhood town in Massachusetts, and the lovely, unpretentious West Elizabeth Street had in some way reminded Frank of the street where he grew up in a suburb of Boston. And the nice tree-shaded house had reminded Flo of her grandmother's home in Martha's Vineyard. The house was within walking distance of the only grocery store, the two drug stores, and the charming center of town, which was laid along the shores of Skaneateles Lake and crammed with gifts shops and decent restaurants. It was one of the loveliest towns Flo had ever set her eyes on. Determined, these two transplanted New Englanders infiltrated this little town and eventually infiltrated its selective infrastructure of wine and cheese affairs, of book clubs and progressive dinners, of yoga at Mirbeau and tennis dates, of chats in the park and committees, of after-work boy beers in the tavern and monthly card games.

Flo, in need of her own career-bolstering endeavor, in a no-nonsense sort of way, rented a small office space in downtown Syracuse and just simply made herself indispensable to the smattering of small corporations that still existed in this mid-sized Central New York town. As she worked to build her law practice, she went about establishing a certain controlled presence as a married woman in Skaneateles. She'd gone into her marriage with absolutely no intention of having children; she'd made this point of negotiations nonnegotiable. Every possible precaution was taken, short of restricting the act itself. But as the years went on—Frank throwing curves her way and her newfound committee ladies talking nonstop about their toddlers' newest exploits—she got a little sloppy; then all caution was thrown windward. Then, as each year passed with her mindless indiscretion proving fruitless, it became a desperate thing. Then it became sad. Then it became very sad. Then the fact that something which was never quite diagnosable was fundamentally wrong with her reproductive abilities and that neither one of them were willing to undergo the technological heroics necessary to become parents became just another fact of life.

As she watched other people's children grow, she watched her career grow and her garden grow each summer and her husband grow older and herself grow older and her marriage grow older. And it was all perfectly acceptable. She took special pride in her ability to produce the most satisfactory tomatoes. Even during the most difficult of summer weather—even when everybody else was plagued by the blight or blossom end rot—her tomatoes thrived. "They're afraid not to grow," she overheard one neighbor say to another after she'd shared some of her bounty. And instead of feeling hurt as she walked away, she smiled and made a mental note to bring them both some of her exceptional red and yellow bell peppers.

But the summer that Flo Loughton fell head-over-heels in love, her tomatoes did indeed suffer. She watched with what could only be described as adoration as Hector scampered through the grass of her backyard or growled at a potholder that had fallen to the floor of her kitchen or cocked his head at the sound of her brisk *hello* into the phone. Then there was the entry of Trey Barkley into her life—this strange, soft-eyed young man who, like her, suffered to smile, and, like her, was, when it came right down to it, not the least bit intimidating to tomatoes or dogs or small children but nonetheless took a small amount of pride in that misapprehension.

"So this is the thing," Trey had said to her, "puppies just don't get it. They just don't understand why they can't just piss or shit." He'd paused there, looked at her quickly, then, deciding she'd not been the least offended, went on. "So they just go. But there are some crazy, great things dog owners have going for them. Dogs want to make you happy, and they're total creatures of habit. And they don't really like to shit where they lie." He narrowed his eyes her way and said, "Confinement: that's the key." Flo Loughton interrupted Trey and went to fetch a pen and pad of paper. As he outlined basic housebreaking and early training, she took elaborate notes, interrupting him just once more to drop some Pecan Sandies onto a plate and offer a glass of milk, which she pushed his way without a word. Hector whined slightly from his place between their feet on the floor at the odor of the cookies, but both Trey and Flo ignored him, other than she stroking his soft white fur with the sole of her foot, which she had some time ago freed from her work pumps. Trey's feet, well housed in his green sneakers, stayed perfectly planted under his chair; his only movement, other than his mouth as he talked and chewed, was the occasional rise of his hand as he brought her offering to his mouth. Neither one of them smiled, and neither one of them laughed, yet Flo felt more at ease than she'd felt with anyone, other than her husband, for as long as she could remember.

Maybe it was only natural that she found herself thinking about this young man, and that she found herself spending a little extra time in the cookie aisle at Tops, or that it sometimes took her a little longer to find her checkbook on those Friday evenings when Trey sat patiently at her kitchen table waiting for his weekly payment. And nothing ended her week on a better note than those rare times when he might linger a bit, bestowing on her some especially endearing Hector tale, which he told with indifferent flatness, which contradicted, in every way, his words that so truly portrayed his love for the dog. And if this was the only thing the two of them had in common, it was enough.

It was when she was contemplating a package of Oreos at Tops that she overheard Betty Snyder say to Maryanne Fowler, "Yes,

I heard he's at Hutchings Psychiatric Center. Took him in last night." Maryanne made a *tisk tisk* sound. "You know they live right down the street from me. I just don't know why Annette lets him just hang around, doing nothing but frightening people."

"Well, he's been doing pretty well. It's been a quite a while—"

"I heard he was wandering around the park, screaming for no reason." Betty leaned in toward Maryanne as she added, "Naked. I heard he was naked."

Maryanne laughed a bit at this.

"I mean, shouldn't he be in a group home somewhere? You know…don't they have places that might…you know, a place where he might be…better off?"

"Oh, I think he's harmless—" offered Maryanne.

"He's scary! That's what he is!" said Betty. "He doesn't live on the same street as you. You don't have to worry about making sure all your drapes are pulled tight."

Maryanne caught Flo listening to this exchange and frowned an apology her way. Then Betty looked at her too; Flo knew she was remembering that Flo was one of Trey's clients. The tiny flash of contriteness that might have flicked across her face was overcome by bolshie self-righteousness. Betty turned back to Maryanne, speaking a bit louder than necessary. "I like Annette, really, I do, but I just think, considering her son's mental issues…well, there just ought to be a better place for him to live other than in The Village, that's all. Somewhere safer for all involved."

Flo put back the package of Oreos she'd been holding and made her way to the checkout counter. Then she stopped at the card table that she'd noted as she'd walked into the store and bought that box of Thin Mint Girl Scout Cookies from the cute little girl in red pigtails, because, after all, they were so much better than Oreos.

EIGHT

Trey turned the corner onto Elizabeth Street at exactly 10:09 Friday morning. He was running late, and it wasn't just because he was a little anxious about the whole Hector fiasco. Mrs. Loughton always left for her office by 8:10. The most he'd have to deal with was a terse note. He was running late because he hadn't slept well, which made him oversleep a bit, which made him groggy and disoriented, which made him drink an extra cup of coffee, which made him jumpy, which made him disorganized, which made him late in getting out of the house because he couldn't seem to find his favorite baseball cap.

He was thinking about Mrs. Loughton as he turned the corner, remembering the crunchy goodness of those Thin Mints and how she'd been sitting straight-backed in one of the green plastic chairs of the dayroom as she watched him come in, her cool, small eyes finding his, her lips pressed against each other in perfect familiarity. He was feeling a bit better by then, sane enough to realize the fact that he'd fucked up, but not quite well enough to care—yet. He'd been somewhat surprised when he'd been told he had a visitor—expecting his mom or maybe his dad and not particularly looking forward to the exchange. He'd shuffled into the room only to find Mrs. Loughton grimly clutching her box of Thin Mints. Trey sat in a yellow plastic chair and scooted it across the tiled, dull green linoleum floor, the chair legs scraping as he moved until he was within cookie-reaching distance. Her lips went slightly up as she handed him the box.

"Is there milk somewhere for you to have with those?" she asked.

"Um, sure." He cradled the box, tilting his head toward the other side of the room. "In the fridge. But I'm cool."

She nodded, then watched as he slid his finger under the tab of the cardboard, opened the box, and pulled out a sleeve of the cookies. He used his teeth to rip apart one end. He tilted the cookie sleeve until the mint chocolate wafers fanned outward, careful not to allow one to escape to the floor. Trey offered the first one to Mrs. Loughton. She smiled, taking his offering between her flawlessly groomed index finger and thumb, the pearly pink tips of her nails digging slightly into the chocolate coating. "Thank you," she said.

He smiled then. "Thank you."

An orderly came into the room, nodded in a friendly way, and made his way to the fridge where he pulled out two small boxes of juice and left without a word. They both watched as he left, Trey pulling out his own cookie and putting in it his mouth, the whole thing hanging from between his lips. He took a small bite and caught the remainder of the cookie as it fell away. "I'm sorry," he said, studying the crumbly brown edges of the cookie that his teeth had left behind. "I'm sorry about not being there, you know, for Hector."

"He misses you." She licked some wayward chocolate free from the tip of her finger.

"Yeah. Same here." Then there was silence, the both of them munching on their cookies. Trey leaned back and stretched his feet her way. He offered the sleeve out to her again, and they both helped themselves to another cookie.

Mrs. Loughton leaned back too, her foot coming close to his, the munching companionable. After a while, she said, "You know, it's rather pleasant here."

"Yeah. It's not too bad." He popped the last bit of his second cookie into his mouth, and after it was totally chewed and swallowed, with any significant teeth-leavings dealt with, he said, "And it's especially pleasant now that you're here."

So it was this conversation that was on his mind as he turned the corner onto Elizabeth Street at exactly 10:09 on that Friday morning and was immediately confounded by the cop cars, an ambulance, and people milling about, swallowing up this tiny tree-lined street. "What the fuck?" he said, coming to a stop and taking in the scene. "What the fuck?" he repeated and made his way closer. He reached the first small group of neighbors and said, "What the fuck?" which they ignored, so he walked further until he was in Mrs. Loughton's yard, uncomfortably close to a cop, and said just loud enough for the guy to hear him, "What the fuck?"

The cop looked over, narrowed his eyes, and said, "You need to move along."

"But this is Mrs. Loughton's house," Trey insisted. "I need to walk Hector."

"Son, you need to move along."

Trey shook his head with confusion. "I need to walk Hector."

The cop stood a little taller, his right hand naturally coming out just above his holster. "Son—"

"That's Trey," someone offered. "He's Flo's dog walker."

Then there was the distraction of movement by the front door. All heads turned that way and watched as the EMT stepped backward and helped ease the wheels of the stretcher over the threshold. A small crowd covered the apparatus, but it was obvious as a gasp went through the crowd, as cameras snapped, as the cop took a step closer to Trey, as someone uttered, "Oh my dear God!" as Trey felt that he might explode, that something horrible was going down, and that this was not, unfortunately, one of Trey's many misperceptions of reality.

NINE

Jack Barkley was just snapping off his surgical gloves when his personal cell phone, which was set on a metal shelf above the sink, sang out its familiar tune: *Aaahoo! Werewolves of London! Aaahoo!* He picked up the phone and saw that it was his wife. *Aaahoo! Werewolves of London. Aaahoo!* Then he felt that unsavory pulse of adrenaline.

He'd just completed his second lobectomy. He'd started off the morning with a tough esophagogastrectomy, so he was tired—damn tired. Although that surge of preparative adrenaline was certainly necessary, it was nevertheless greatly resented. When was the last time he'd received a phone call from his wife in the middle of a surgical day that hadn't caused trepidation? Six years and five months—the *before* part of his life. And now he was in the *after* part. He remembered that first phone call like a reoccurring toothache—sharp and stabbing with a lot of denial: *It's going to stop any minute. It's really not my tooth that's hurting; it's just a head-ache gone rogue. I don't care what the dentist said last month; I don't need a damn root canal.* "He's been taken to the ER," Annette had tearfully said into his ear, six years, five months ago. Even though Trey's odd behavior had been simmering away for quite a while, it was still just at the simmering stage, still just an unusually difficult and prolonged adolescence. No, nothing was boiling over.

"We need to go," she had continued. "We need to get to Providence. To the ER. Should we fly? Would driving be faster? Jack, what are we going to do? Driving, right? How fast can you get home? I'll need to call Sharon. Make sure she can take care of the dog for the next few days. I guess we'll take your car. Jack?" And he had just stood there, tiny drops of blood decorating his scrubs, unable to utter a word—not one damn word while she rattled on—when all he'd wanted to do was flip close the phone and cut into his next patient.

Then getting there seven hours later and finding your youngest son was no longer your youngest son, but something altogether different and unrecognizable. "Schizophrenia. We believe your son may be suffering from schizophrenia." "No. The tox screen was clean." "Yes. It was repeated—twice." "Well, no. We can't be sure. It could possibly be bipolar disorder. It's really too soon to say." Trey was bent over himself in the hospital bed, incoherent and inconsolable. Annette cried silently at his side, while Jack couldn't shake the feeling that this must be something surgical—something that he could just excise. *A brain tumor! Yes! That was it!* "No. We haven't done an MRI." "Well, do one, dammit!" And that was when *before* became *after*—while he was looking over the clean scan, while his wife was huddled in a corner of the waiting room, while Trey was being transferred to the psych ward, while his hands were itching to cut into his son, when his brain clicked over to: *And what now?*

What now? was exactly what was going through his mind as he tapped the answer button, six years and five months later. *What now?*

He brought the phone to his ear. "Annette, I have another surgery. They're on the table waiting," he said, as if being rude to his wife of twenty-eight years could somehow change the reason she'd called.

"Jack, Flo Loughton is dead."

"What? Who?"

"Flo Loughton."

"Who? What? She's dead?"

"She's one of Trey's clients. On Elizabeth Street. The police found her this morning. Trey's a mess. I don't know what to do. Should I call his doctor? I'm really worried how he's going to take this. He was there when they, you know, brought her out. Jack, I'm really worried. Maybe if you could talk to him. You know how it's always easier for him to talk to you. Jack? Do you think you could call him? Or maybe come home a little early. He's encamped in his room. Jack?"

Jack closed his eyes. He wasn't sure if he was relieved or irritated or gearing up toward worry. But regardless, this didn't appear to be an emergency situation. His wife: always willing to leap toward catastrophic conclusions. "Of course he's upset. A woman just died. I'd be worried if he wasn't upset. I'll call him. I'll call him a little later."

"Thank you. Thank you, Jack." But he could hear that little bit of sarcasm.

"I'll skip evening rounds. I'll be home early." His wife sighed. "What? What do you want me to do? If it'll make you feel better, call his doctor. It's not like we haven't been through this crap a thousand times."

"Jack. He's been doing very well. For a very long time," she said quietly. "I just don't want that to change. Preemptive measures—that's all I'm asking."

Jack rolled his eyes and was happy his wife wasn't there to see. "I'll call him. Just as soon as I'm done with this next surgery."

"Thank you. And please don't roll your eyes." He laughed and then so did Annette. "I know you Jack Barkley. I always have."

"As I you." And he ended the call.

TEN

Detective Seth Wooley sat at his desk and studied the preliminary reports and lab results. He looked again at the photos. At some point today they'd have to hold a small press conference—let the press know that this was not just some normal death. "Foul play has not been ruled out," was all that he'd been willing to say to the smattering of press that had been there in the morning when they'd brought the body out. But it had been obvious, from the onset, that this was a murder—a murder in a town that hadn't had a murder in— Well, as far as he knew, they'd never had a murder in the village proper. Population of around two thousand five hundred. Low crime all the way around. Skaneateles, New York, would be rocked by this unsavory news.

He'd spent a couple of hours at the crime scene, taking it all in, getting the feel of the place, getting to "know" the victim. His officers had questioned the neighbors, thoroughly swept the house and property, interviewed coworkers and close friends, and talked with the local police department, which was a great department but way too small to handle a murder investigation without the resources of the state police or county sheriff's department. Seth was pleased they had called in his department; he loved a good murder investigation, especially one that didn't appear to involve drug dealing, spousal abuse, or prostitution. Now he just needed the hard evidence to try to put it all together.

In a town like Skaneateles, this murder was almost certainly done by someone the victim knew; Seth really doubted this was a random violent crime. There were no signs of forced entry. Of course this meant nothing in a town where no one locked their doors. There were minimal signs of struggle. The exact cause of death was still pending. He shuffled through the photos again, stopping at one of the dog. Again, he wondered: *What was up with the towel? That fancy tube of conditioner? And where was the shampoo that almost always accompanied conditioner?* He'd looked up the brand online; it was thirty-five dollars a tube and only available through salons. Sure enough, it was sold at Arabella Salon in The Village, and Flo Loughton was a client there. The salon's computer had a record of her purchasing both the shampoo and conditioner less than three weeks ago.

He studied the photo of the little dog. He rubbed his face, looked up, and scanned the small room he shared with the other Onondaga Sheriff detectives. "Randall! Where's Randall?"

"Still at lunch, I think," was the answer he received.

"Anyone know how that pup is doing?" he asked, waving the photo. The other officers in the room either ignored him completely or shrugged. Was he the only one who gave a shit about the dog? "Murraco!" he barked. "Find out where Randall took the pup, call up the vet, and see how it's doing." Murraco looked up from his paperwork and, in spite of his rookie status, had the nerve to narrow his eyes Seth's way. Seth met his look. "Seriously?" Seth used his best gangster argot. "You really need me to come over there and beat the shit outta ya?" Murraco laughed and shook his head. Seth noted with satisfaction that Murraco pushed aside the paperwork and reached for the phone.

"Hey, Wool. Take a look at this."

Seth turned to see Zukerman hoofing his way toward him. Zuke was a big, red-headed, beefy guy who'd joined the Onondaga Sheriff's Department ten years ago at about the same time as Seth. He was the only one Seth let call him Wool, because he was the only one Seth wanted to let call him Wool—their relationship being as it was, which was tight. Somewhat of a bromance, perhaps, but the intimacy was nice. But Zuke was Zuke to the entire force, so it wasn't a total bromance.

"Very interesting," Zuke said as he dropped the report on Seth's desk. "We have a match for fingerprints. Someone already in the system."

"Really?"

"The dog walker. That Trey Barkley dude who was there this morning. He has priors. A lot of priors."

Seth looked at the computer printout. "Nice." He smiled up at Zuke. "Very nice." He stood up from his desk and called across the room, "Murraco! Forget the dog! Get me everything you can dig up on this Barkley guy!"

ELEVEN

The room was dark—as dark as it could be on a sunny Friday afternoon. Trey had the blinds and curtains snuggly closed. He'd already gotten up twice from his bed and tugged a little, adjusted here and there, cutting that slice of light in half. He had the undeniable urge to tape black paper over the windows. He was sure he had some left in his desk. But then his mother would totally freak. He just didn't need that. And she didn't need that disappointment.

Mrs. Loughton's foot had pressed into the bathmat. Had her toes wiggled? Just slightly?

He got up again, tugged at the curtain, and paced around a bit.

Had her pink panties dangled from those toes mere moments before they were dropped, never to be picked up by Mrs. Loughton?

He stopped in the middle of his room.

Hector. Where was Hector?

Trey opened his bedroom door, slammed it on his way out, made his way as quickly as possible down the stairs, grabbed his Mets baseball cap, and slipped out the front door just as he heard the squeak of his mother's feet on the old floor boards. Then he jogged back to Mrs. Loughton's house.

The place was all but deserted: one cop car still parked on the street, the yellow tape stretched across the yard, someone snapping pictures of the house, a neighbor sitting on the steps of her front porch looking sadly his way (Trey couldn't remember her name), a cop standing by the door, a decked-out woman with spiky high heels, primping her blonde hair while the cameraman swung the camera her way. "Are we ready?" the cameraman asked. The woman licked at her lips, cleared her throat, and nodded grimly.

"I'm reporting from Skaneateles, New York, where this morning one of its residents was found dead in her home. The body of Florence Loughton, Syracuse attorney, was found this morning by the local police after concerned coworkers called the police when she'd failed to show up for work for the second day. The police have yet to rule out foul play, and the Onondaga Sheriff's Department has taken over the investigation. The deceased has no immediate relatives in the area—"

Trey turned from the reporter and skirted the tape, getting as close to the house as it would allow. "Hector!" he called. "Hector!" The cop turned his eyes on Trey. "Hector," he said a little louder, a little more desperate, his voice choking just a bit. Trey glanced at the neighbor as she stood up. The cop took a step away from the house.

The reporter said, "Cut!" slashing her hand across the front of her chest in an exaggerated way.

"Hector!" Trey called again.

The cop was close now, not exactly hostile, but Trey had to force himself not to turn and run. "Can I help you with something?" the guy asked.

He was young, not much older than Trey, but bigger and taller with that I'm-a-fucking-cop-so-don't-mess-with-me stance that bothered the hell out of Trey. What was it about a uniform that turned a perfectly decent guy into a...a cop? Trey pulled on his Snoopy T-shirt, took an involuntary step away from the tape, and studied the red laces of his green All Star Double Tongue Converse. "I just want to know where Hector is," he mumbled. He looked down at Snoopy hanging sadly over his doghouse and read the words upside down, which were printed above the dog's head: *I don't think that's an unreasonable request.* Trey glanced up from his T-shirt, then back to his shoes, and said, "I don't think that's an unreasonable request."

The guy narrowed his eyes, glanced at the T-shirt, and then back to Trey's face. "Hector? Who is Hector?"

"Mrs. Loughton's—" Trey's voice caught in his throat and he swallowed. "Her dog," he managed to get out, swallowing again and blinking his eyes.

"I don't know anything about a dog."

"Can I look?" asked Trey. The cop just shook his head. "Can *you* please look? Maybe he's hiding somewhere. Maybe he's hurt."

"The house has been thoroughly gone through. There's no dog in there."

That's when Trey began to lose it. He'd been pretty together up until then—proud of himself—but this was really unacceptable. And what was worse—worse than the fact that he was about to take on a cop—was the fact that he was now crying in earnest, which made it very hard to try to take on someone, especially a cop with a gun. When Trey's cell phone suddenly burst into life in his pocket, he was almost relieved. But there was still a moment where he stood there, staring down the cop, tears running down his face, the cop staring stubbornly back, the notes of his cell phone (his favorite song: Passion Pit's "The Reeling") cutting at the silence, before he turned away and pulled the phone out of his pocket.

"Hello," he said into the phone. Trey took a few steps away as the neighbor stepped up to the cop.

"Trey," his father said. "Where are you?"

Trey glanced at the cop and the neighbor, who were talking quietly, and felt his chest tighten. *They're talking about me.* He wiped at his eyes.

"Trey?"

Trey strained to listen to what the neighbor was saying, wanting to get closer but afraid. She was telling the cop a bunch of shit—that was fact.

"Dammit, Trey! Where are you?" his father repeated.

"I don't think it's an unreasonable request," Trey said loud enough for both his father and the cop to hear.

"What?" his father said into his ear.

That's when Trey looked up and saw the camera pointed his way, that bitch of a reporter staring at him. She took a couple of steps toward him, her face in a patronizing, predatory snarl—the red light glowing on the camera, recording everything. *Everything.* And then everyone would see and think: *Hey, look. It's another crazy, wacked-out loser.*

"Holy fuck," Trey whispered into the phone. He turned, wiped at his tears, dropped the phone back into his pocket, and ran like hell.

TWELVE

Jack Barkley was able to check up on his post ops and get out of the hospital by 3:00 p.m. He was home by 3:42 p.m. Annette was waiting for him as he came through the door, her face drawn, her body covered with a fine white dusting of clay. "He's in his room," she said, not bothering with a hello or peck on the cheek. *That's fine*, he thought, but then he took a step her way and kissed her lightly. She responded by wrapping her arms around his neck and pressing her body into his. He closed his eyes and lingered there, the odor of dried earth and paint and cinnamon filling his senses, making him hungry and sad at the same time. He pulled away.

"How's he doing?" he asked.

Annette shrugged. "Not sure. He won't talk to me. Says he needs to be alone."

Jack nodded. "Well, maybe he does."

"Maybe." But she said the word with accusation. Always the conflict: he wanting to give the kid space and she wanting to devour him fully.

"He was quite fond of Flo Loughton, Jack."

Jack nodded. "Do you know how she died?"

Annette shook her head. "Remember how her husband died quite suddenly too? Maybe it's something with the house," she whispered.

He smiled. Annette was always latching onto some sort of mystical-power bullcrap. "Like what? A carpenter curse? A pissed-off ghost of grouting past?" He laughed.

She hit him lightly. "Jack, it's not funny. I know you didn't really know her. And sure, she wasn't exactly warm and fuzzy, but she meant a lot to Trey."

"Yeah." He frowned and looked toward the staircase. "I'll see how he's doing."

Jack knocked lightly on Trey's door. He waited. After a long moment, he knocked again. "Trey?" he called through the door. Another long moment went by, and Jack was considering whether he should reach up and retrieve the stretched-out, large paperclip he had squirreled away on the upper ledge of the door trim for just such emergencies. Then he heard his son's thin voice come through the door.

"Dad, I really can't talk now. Okay?"

Jack leaned a moment on the closed door, sighing quietly. "Okay, Treyman. We'll talk later." He waited, then closed his eyes. "I'm sorry. I'm sorry about Mrs. Loughton." He stood there another long moment.

"It's okay…. Thanks."

Jack hated this door. He hated standing in front of it. He hated knowing the door was locked, even if its unlocking was as simple as a quick insertion of a straightened-out paperclip. He hated the unlocking, never knowing what he might find. It had seemed that all of this hatred was behind him; it had been so many years since he'd stood there contemplating the straightened-out paperclip that the feelings shouldn't be so fresh and strong—the fear so raw—the image of Trey standing on his chair, slipping the noose around his neck so vivid. Trey staring at him blankly as he opened the door, then kicking the chair away with one quick jerk of his feet, his son dangling there for the one split moment of shock before Jack took those three quick steps into the room, lifting Trey's slight body against the earth's gravity and screaming, "Annette! God help me! Annette!" Five years, eight months, and twenty-seven days ago.

"Trey?" Jack said through the closed door.

A long wait.

"Yup?"

"I'm really sorry."

"Yup."

THIRTEEN

Flo Loughton started looking forward to Fridays. She wasn't sure why she enjoyed this quiet young man—why she felt the need to sit him down and feed him. Maybe it was because he was so thin, his face narrow, his cheeks sunken. She enjoyed his eyes; they betrayed the seriousness of his face. She enjoyed his laugh, which was rich and infrequent. She enjoyed his unabashed love for Hector. She enjoyed another human in her home.

"Do you eat dinner with your folks?" she had asked one Friday evening as she watched him finish the last bit of a Keebler Chips Deluxe.

"What?"

"Oh, nothing," she said, withdrawing the question with a brief pass of her hand. He'd acted truly shocked by the question—but not as shocked as she'd been from asking it.

"Dinner? Do I eat dinner with my folks?"

She affirmed his questions with a quick nod.

"Um. Sometimes."

She nodded. He removed another cookie from the carton, chewed it carefully, and drank a sip of milk. Then he put down the glass, set down the remainder of the cookie on the white paper napkin she'd provided, and looked her way. "Do you cook? I mean, do you come home from work and cook yourself dinner?"

Flo felt an uncomfortable emotion well up inside her, blinked her eyes with annoyance, and said, "Rarely. I usually pick up something somewhere on my way home."

"Yeah." He nodded. "That's what I do. Doug's Fish Fry or Johnny Angel's. Never Valentine's."

"Really? I rather like their salads," offered Flo.

Trey picked up the remainder of his cookie. He looked at her and said, "Risky."

She smiled slightly.

"Risky," he said again, then went back to eating, she back to watching.

Flo had only been on one date since the death of her husband. It had been just slightly shy of the one-year mark of Frank's death when she'd agreed, reluctantly, to go to dinner with a man. She really didn't know this man. A habitué of the coffee shop she frequented, she'd seen him for years. He was always tapping away on his laptop—some sort of writer, she presumed. She'd enter the shop at 8:40 a.m., and he'd always look up from the keys and smile. He did have a nice smile. As if sensing her sudden singleness, he'd fallen into asking her repeatedly to have dinner with him; for nearly twelve months she'd refused. Why exactly she had said yes to him on that one particular day was still a mystery. It was an unmitigated error on her part and an unmitigated disaster on his.

They'd gone to an innocent-enough Italian bistro. It was a new place that had just opened up on the west side of Syracuse. It had been a Thursday night, so Flo had simply met him after work, her power-bitch suit slightly wrinkled from an over-enthusiastic day, her makeup in need of a quick spruce-up. It was later in the harsh fluorescent lights of the bathroom of the ER that she noticed the faint smearing of her mascara under her eyes and how the deepening lines around her mouth were caked with makeup. She'd wanted simply to go home after having deposited her date safely at the ER, but she was afraid to appear too crass. What was the standard protocol for a first date? Was it really necessary that she see this through?

Stanley seemed acceptable while he was typing away at his computer in the coffee shop. In his early seventies, he looked younger than his years. She'd found out pretty quickly during dinner that he was indeed a writer. A poet. An unpublished poet who taught part time at Onondaga Community College to stave off starvation. He was gray-haired and bearded in an almost artsy way, although the few stray hairs of his bread and the bushiness of his eyebrows pushed him toward odd. But Flo had never had a problem with odd, especially in appearance, so she sat at the dinner table with a mild sort of interest. As the evening wore on, however, the way the red pasta sauce dotted the gray of his beard, the way his eyebrows threatened his corneas when he concentrated on a thought, the way his hands flew about as he talked, the way he talked of nothing that she found especially interesting—all of this began to grate at Flo. So when the waiter came with offers of dessert, she'd politely refused, hoping to put an end to the offending evening. But Stanley had insisted that they order the flaming Italian custard. The resulting disaster was nobody's fault other than Stanley's restless hands—the waiter carefully placing the three aflame custard balls on the table only to have them suddenly take flight. The one that landed on the tablecloth only caused a slight scorch. The other two ill-fated flaming concoctions landed squarely on Stanley's lap—his pants going up in a glorious mixture of rum and cheap polyester. Quick work on Flo's part minimized the damage, dousing the flames with water from their goblets followed by a frenzied patting down with her napkin, but the ER trip was still unavoidable.

Flo realized that this was a tale that would be entertaining if given to the right teller. But to her it was simply a disaster not worth sharing. And there she was in the ER, overhearing the medical staff joke about flaming balls, wishing only to go home, deciding right then and there that dating was not a thing she needed in her life. After that she'd been forced to find a new coffee shop, which, sadly, was never as good as the old one.

Flo had never really had friends. She had tennis partners and business partners and bridge partners. She had secretaries and hairdressers and yoga instructors. She chatted amiably with her mechanic about the funny noise her car was making. She asked the teller at the bank how her baby was doing. She smiled pleasantly when a child stopped her on the street in order to pet Hector. She enjoyed the occasional ladies luncheon. She was exceptionably tolerant when her fellow Skaneateles Festival Board Members chatted on about their teenagers or husbands rather than the important matters at hand. She loved giving gardening advice to her neighbor. She went out of her way to bring tomatoes to the local nursing home. She laughed when laughter was appropriate. But she never really had friends, other than her husband, Frank, and now, seemingly, this odd young man named Trey Barkley.

Flo watched Trey dip the edge of his half-eaten cookie into the milk and capture the drip with the tip of his tongue as he brought it toward his mouth. "So what do you usually order at Doug's?" she asked. "The fish?"

He shook his head, wiping at his mouth. "Fried scallops. Always fried scallops."

"With coleslaw?"

"That's right." He smiled. "Extra coleslaw. And fries. With lots of ketchup."

Flo nodded. "I like ketchup too."

FOURTEEN

Trey was taping thick black construction paper to his tall, narrow bedroom windows when he heard the front doorbell of his parents' house ring. He didn't think too much about who might be at the door, concentrating instead on the task at hand and squelching the soft murmurs of discontent that were going on in his head. He'd found a nice thick stack of the paper in the back of his desk drawer, hidden under a stack of old *Dog World* magazines. That was one of the problems with summer: it stayed light for a crazy long time. Here it was nearly six in the evening and still the sun was intense. If he kept his door shut and locked, his louvered blinds down and pointing up, and his curtains drawn, then maybe his mother wouldn't notice the blacked-out windows. She just never *got* the incredible significance of darkness. "You only get like this when you're not doing well," she'd say, wringing her hands and hovering. "Can't we just uncover one of your windows?" she'd ask, her face squishing inward, her eyes blinking away. "Just one?" As if having only one of his windows obstructed would make him only half crazy or something. But the fact was that the dark room calmed and eased his symptoms, the darkness quelling the sharpness of the voices that rattled on in his head.

That's what his mom didn't seem to get: stress conjured up his tormentors; darkness and quiet sent them back to a controllable hum.

He was up on his desk chair stretching upward, his sunglasses on, his baseball cap pulled as low as it could go while still allowing him to be visually functional. He felt the wheels on the bottom of the chair slip just a bit. His body shifted toward the glass panes. His arms came out quickly, bracing himself against the window jamb, lest he go sailing through the glass and into his mother's rose garden. The tape fell, the sheets of paper fluttering to the floor. "Fuck," he muttered, sucking in a breath to keep from crying again. He lowered himself slowly, now sitting in the chair and resting his head in his hands. The most persistent of his tormentors laughed loudly, causing him to press his fingers deep into flesh that surrounded his skull. "Shut up, fucker." He squeezed tighter and the laughter stopped.

He needed to keep it together. He just needed to keep it together.

His mantra: keep it together.

And this was exactly what he'd said, over and over again, while tromping across the campus of Brown University six years and six months ago. "Keep it together. Keep it together. Keep it together." He was not this crazy fucker. He wasn't. He was a student at one of the best schools in the country. He belonged there, studying chemistry, which he loved, delving into math, which was beyond fascinating. It was science that moved him. He had plans—important plans. Sure things hadn't been going as smoothly lately, his heart still smarting from Stephanie, his body weak from his second bout with the flu in two months—it was no wonder that his mind might be confused.

Fact: when your heart is crushed your body suffers too.

It was a fortuitous and auspicious but ultimately heart-crushing rash that had brought him to Dr. Tondej for the first time early in the fall semester of his second year at Brown. A week later, he'd sat impatiently in the crowded waiting room of the university health center waiting to see Dr. Tondej for a recheck, even though he knew he had no right to be impatient. The receptionist at the student health center had told him he could be seen faster by the PA, but Trey had no intention of seeing anyone other than Dr. Tondej, even if it meant doing the one thing he hated the most: waiting. He hoped he wouldn't die waiting. People always said that kind of thing without meaning it, but Trey knew waiting was sometimes terminal.

There was a small sound that escaped from the girl to his right, pulling his eyes her way. She wiped at her face with the ragged end of her sweatshirt sleeve. Her cheeks were blotchy; her eyes were cast down. His movement seemed to cause her shoulders and head to curve in toward her chest. With a slight shake of her head, her long dark hair slid forward in an unsuccessful attempt to mask her unhappiness. She shifted slightly away.

Trey frowned. He leaned her way. "What are you in for?"

An infinitesimal stirring was the only acknowledgement he received.

He moved a little closer. "Me?" He smiled. "It's just a follow-up. You see, I have this rash."

She glanced up and looked around the full waiting room as if searching for somewhere else to sit.

"No." Trey touched her arm slightly then drew it away. "It's not contagious. Nor, thank God, is it any place embarrassing." He was encouraged when she almost laughed. He pulled up the sleeve of his light purple Express shirt, carefully folding the cuff under so that the fine, dark purple stripes remained aligned, and showed her his rash. "See?" She looked at his arm with mild interest. "Gross, right? Dr. Tondej thinks it's from chem lab." Trey pulled the sleeve of his shirt neatly back into place, buttoned the cuff, and leaned back against his chair. "Damn, he's one hell of a nice guy. I hope you get to see him for…you know…whatever you're in for. I'm certain he's not just a rash guy. He appears quite diversified."

"I hope so too." She smiled sadly. "I need someone nice. The last guy I saw here was a total dick."

Trey nodded. "Well, known fact: the biggest dicks on campus are right here in this very building."

At this she laughed. "Good to know."

He tilted his head and smiled. "Seriously. You'll find none bigger. Anywhere." Just then the nurse called his name. He glanced at the nurse and then back at the girl. He grabbed the girl's hand and stood up. "No," he said to the nurse. He attempted to pull the girl from her seat. "You take her. Give her my spot. Her need is critical. I insist."

The nurse frowned. "Mr. Barkley—"

"Nope. Not coming with you." He tugged the girl upward. "You're taking her."

"I don't have her chart. I don't even know who she is…."

Trey turned from the nurse and looked at the girl. "Who are you?" he demanded.

"Stephanie." She allowed him to drag her forward. "Stephanie Fios."

"Excellent." He pushed Stephanie toward the nurse. "Here you go, Nurse Ratched. I'm quite certain that you'll find the chart for Stephnie Fios right there in your thingamajig." Trey pointed to the row of charts lined up on the desk.

The nurse sighed and signaled Stephanie to follow. She quickly located Stephanie's chart midway back, then placed Trey's chart behind all the others.

Stephanie turned as she walked away, smiled, and mouthed a

thank you.

A week later his rash was gone and she was his girl.

Then just two short months of bliss later: misery. Then shortly after that: the self-guided emergency trip to the campus health center. He'd been doing nothing more than sitting in Chem Lab 204 waiting for his 2-indanol to crystallize, thinking about how the relationship between binary numbers and hexadecimal digits was really representative of the coupling of humans—simplification, reduction (1+1=1) while making it more intangible—when his chest began to tighten. Just like that—out of nowhere—he couldn't breathe. He was convinced he was having a heart attack. "Your heart is fine," assured Dr. Tondej, who he'd gotten to know quite well over the last seven months. "You seem to have experienced a panic attack. They're very common."

But nothing about the way he'd been feeling lately seemed common. "Keep it together. Keep it together." Then less than a week later he was knocking into fellow students as he shoved his way through the narrow sidewalks of Brown, the heavy late winter snow on the quad shrinking the available avenues. "Watch it, asshole!" Someone gave him a little shove. But Trey ignored the insult. "Keep it together. Keep it together." Another collision. "Fucking freak!" came out of some girl's mouth. "Keep it together!" he yelled back. She retreated in fear. "We just have to keep it together." Then he stood perfectly still, the throng parting around him. "KEEP IT TOGETHER!" But everything and everyone was shattering apart. "It's a simple concept," he insisted. "Together: a multifunctional unit. Jellyfish, man. Think jellyfish. Run us through a sieve if you will, but give us a moment and we'll reassemble. Reassemble. Reassemble!" But no one was getting the importance of his instruction. "Dammit, fuckers! Reassemble!"

He remembered someone shoving him, or maybe he was shoving them. He remembered the sudden anger he felt, and then the fear. He remembered their faces and how their words jumbled with the wind and the bells of a nearby church. He remembered the seizing of his own words and then the further disassemble—everyone and everything breaking apart. He did not remember how he ended up in the snow, but he was there lying faceup, the pieces of the university swirling above him. "He's seriously shrooming or something." "Fucked up." He remembered being cold—and scared. "Better call someone." "No, man. He'll get in trouble." He remembered the intense blue of some girl's eyes. "He'll die out here in the cold." He remembered parts of the policeman standing over him. "Son. Son?"

He'd never felt such deep fear, and this was the kind of fear that was settling in around him now—six year and six months later. Something was happening. Something was circling. Some sort of iniquity was baring its teeth. And it had nothing to do with the fact that he had been diagnosed with a mental illness. Nothing.

Trey leaned down and began to pick up the scattered sheets of construction paper, dropping a few sheets again as his hands shook. It was when he was doing his best to form them into a nice neat stack that there was a light knock on his door—his father's knock. He hesitated a moment, then set the pile, still in disarray, on his desk and went to unlock the door. He opened it up a crack, letting just the left side of his head become visible. "Dad."

"Trey," his father said, "this is not a big deal."

Right away Trey knew it was a lie. Every time his father started a conversation with those words, it was in fact a big deal. It was always one big fucking deal. Trey considered, quite seriously, slamming the door in his dad's face, but he knew that doors were just barriers to inevitable truth, so he stepped back into his room and let his dad enter. "Close the door," he said quickly, glancing back at the pile of black construction paper and then back at his dad. He saw his father follow his glance, then frown as he took in the half finished window. "Don't tell Mom," Trey begged.

His father sighed. "Trey, now listen. The police are here. Turns out that Flo Loughton—" Trey flinched at the casual way his father used her name. "Well…it appears that there may have been some sort of foul play…." His father stopped and rubbed at his face. Trey stood stock still. "They just want to ask you a few questions." Trey started shaking his head. "It's no big deal." Trey shook his head harder as his father continued. "They're talking to everyone who knew her. You worked for the woman. You were at her house—yesterday, today. Of course they want to talk to you…and look around your room a bit. It's really no big deal."

"They're not coming in my room."

"Well, see, here's the thing—" And that's when Trey finally grasped how truly freaked out his otherwise calm father was. "We don't exactly have a choice. They have a search warrant, you see." He rubbed his eyes. "Of course, you can refuse to talk to them—that's your right. But as far as your room…this house…well…."

Trey's entire body was shaking—shaking hard. His father stepped closer and put a hand on his shoulder as if trying to quell the quaking, but it only made it worse. "It's no big deal," his father whispered. He put his other hand on Trey's other shoulder. "It's going to be okay."

Trey leaned into his father's hands on his shoulders and once again found himself crying, but this time with the enthusiasm of a child.

FIFTEEN

Detective Seth Wooley waited in the living room of the fine old house. He sat on the plush, mahogany-colored leather couch, which squeaked slightly as he shifted. It looked quite new. Zuke stood off to the side next to a large, abstract sculpture with sweeping arms. Seth watched as Zuke took in the sculpture and then moved several feet away. The Skaneateles chief of police was also present. Higgins was his name. Higgins was a decent-enough guy. Seth had worked with him in the past, and there hadn't been any issues.

Higgins sat across the room in front of another massive sculpture that was no less intimidating than the one near Zuke. Seth noted smaller metal and clay pieces scattered throughout the room. Weird. Had Barkley's parents actually paid for those? Maybe they were of their son's creation. They looked like something a murderer might come up with. Even his own ma, as unmotherly as she'd been while he was growing up, had plastered the refrigerator with his lousy artwork.

Higgins was sitting next to Barkley's mother, the two of them talking quietly. He was apologizing all over himself, trying to diffuse some of the tension, which was fine by Seth. Mrs. Barkley was small and lean with funky blonde hair that stood up in interesting little peaks. She wore a baggy, long floral T-shirt and black capri leggings, no shoes, her toenails painted black—the word *artist* might as well have been tattooed across her forehead. Nope, not Barkley's stuff. He'd bet his next beer that she was the one who'd created these monstrosities.

Seth tried to relax, tried to appear as if he had all the time in the world, but the truth was he was jumping with anticipation. He was dying to eyeball this guy. He'd spent most of the last three hours reviewing Barkley's records. Four arrests. The first was when he was a teenager and involved the illegal possession of alcohol—no big deal. But then there was a series of small but sticky incidents: disturbing the peace, second-degree assault, and, most recently, public indecency along with another disturbing-the-peace charge. The man had a well-documented history of mental illness and instability. The local police were well versed on Trey Barkley. Although Higgins seemed to think murder was a stretch, Seth was feeling pretty good about it being a strong possibility. He had physical evidence all over the crime scene, a history with the victim, and a guy who was obviously prone to volatility. Yes, he was feeling pretty confident.

He looked up to the sound of the squeak of the stairs, which were just visible through the living room door. Dr. Barkley was one step behind his son on the stairway, his hand resting on his son's shoulder, each step from his son an obvious effort. As they approached the threshold of the living room, Seth was immediately disappointed. This dude was a mess—nothing the least bit sinister about him. He looked like a murderer about as much as Tweety Bird looked like a murderer. Skinny and five-foot nine at best, he was pale and shaky, his light brown hair in a tangle of discord, his lips and chin covered with a spotty three- or four-day-old sandy-colored beard, his eyes—which never left the floor—

red and puffy. He wore a Snoopy T-shirt (of all things), his shoes bright green, the brim of his Mets baseball cap pulled low. But Seth knew that looks did not make a man innocent—or guilty. Facts: those are what made a case. And he already had some of those. Now he just needed to gather and line up his ducks.

The two entered the room. Barkley immediately went to the far corner of the room, where he sat down on an old wingback chair, placed the sunglasses he'd been holding in his hand on his nose, then tucked his face into his chest. He pulled his baseball cap down so that it fully covered his eyes and most of his face, then wrapped his arms around his body. Dr. Barkley stepped near his wife, who was looking up at him with apprehension. Dr. Barkley was tall and straight-backed, and nothing like his son.

Dr. Barkley crossed his arms across his chest. "My son has chosen not to speak with you at this time. I'm sorry. He doesn't mean to be uncooperative; it's just that the death of Flo Loughton has been a terrible shock. You may proceed in searching his room or any place else you feel necessary. We're just going to stay right here." He sat next to his wife with finality.

"Okay…." Seth glanced at Zuke who shrugged a *whatev*. "Well, then we're just going to take a little look around. Maybe Mr. Barkley would be willing to talk to Chief Higgins while we're gone. There are really just a few things I'd like to get straight. You know, just so I can put the last two days in some sort of order of events." Seth stood up, and he and Zuke walked out of the room. "Let's take a look upstairs," Seth said to Zuke. He noticed another sculpture dominating the curve of the wooden staircase.

"That's a pretty messed up piece of metal," Zuke said as they passed near the sculpture. He drummed his fingers on what appeared to be the abdomen. "Yup, metal. You think the son makes these things?"

"My guess is the mother," answered Seth as they made their

way upstairs.

"Some fucking weird shit."

"No kidding."

There was no question which bedroom was Barkley's. One was obviously the parents—the larger of the four, the bed neatly made, minimal clutter. The second bedroom must belong to the brother that Higgins told him about—neat and lacking inhabitation, but boyish. The third bedroom was made up in a unisex, guestroom sort of way—a tartan print of light and dark greens on the double bed, all the drawers of the dresser empty other than sheets and linen, no clutter of any kind. The fourth bedroom was a train wreck—Barkley's. "Oh man!" Zuke exclaimed. "You could hide a fucking corpse in here—not be able to see it or smell it."

"No kidding. What is that smell?"

"Not sure I want to know. My guess: last month's leftover tuna sandwich with a heavy dose of sweaty sneakers, moldy shirts, wet dog, and the result of *a lot* of serious wanking," Zuke said as he began a slow walk around the periphery of the room.

Seth chuckled as he stood there a moment trying to take it all in. The room was a decent size—twice the size of the room he had growing up. Off to the right was a twin bed with its bedding in total disarray. To the left of that was a desk muddled with debris. The desk sat between two tall-paned windows. One of the windows was totally clothed, its blinds down, the curtains drawn. The curtains and blinds were open on the other, but its panes were half covered with black construction paper. The floor was hard to appreciate as it was almost entirely covered with stuff—not just clothing, but books and newspapers and dishes and CDs and old towels, a set of downhill skis, an old guitar. Atop a pile of clothing lay a large, purple stuffed porcupine or hedgehog—the sort one might win at a fair. It was on its back, its short legs sticking up toward the ceiling. There was a pile of mismatched shoes, old empty soda bottles, prescription pill bottles, another stuffed animal of some sort.... It just went on and on.

Zuke cussed under his breath as his foot was caught on an old backpack strap. He looked up at Seth. "Really? I mean, fucking really?" He reached down and untangled the strap.

"There's not going to be anything in here," Seth said. "And even if there were—" That's when his eyes hit the dark pink tube. He took a step toward the small pile of clothing on which it sat, slightly covered over with a T-shirt. He used his shoe to push the T-shirt aside. "Well, what do we have here?" Seth pulled out a pair of latex gloves from his pocket, put them on, and carefully lifted up the tube. He turned it over to read the brand. "Kerastase, or however the hell you say it." He looked at Zuke. "Do you know this shampoo sells for thirty-six ninety-nine at the local Skaneateles salon?"

Zuke stopped and turned his way. "Nope."

"Yep. And did you know that conditioner of this same brand was found on the floor of Loughton's bedroom?"

Zuke tilted his head to the right and smiled. "I believe I do."

Seth read the label. "Kerastase Bain Miroir 2 Shampoo protects color-treated hair while transforming each hair fiber, revealing a mirror-like shine."

Zuke shifted his head the other way. "Hmmm...."

"Is Barkley's hair reminiscent of a mirror?"

"Nope."

"Yeah. I don't think so either." Seth removed a plastic bag from his other pocket and carefully dropped the shampoo into the bag. He then pulled out a larger bag and carefully placed each of the articles of clothing that had been near the shampoo into the bag. He noted the several different shades of small brown smears on the light-colored T-shirt. Chocolate or blood? Or both? He smiled at Zuke. "I think we've got enough."

Zuke smiled back. "I think you might just be correct."

SIXTEEN

Annette Barkley was trying to find her center. She was lightly grasping Jack's arm and attempting to slow the beating of her heart in her chest. She drew in a deep breath through her nose—her tongue pressed lightly against the roof of her mouth—held that breath for a long seven seconds, then blew out long and steady through her mouth. She repeated the process, closed her eyes to the image of Trey pressed against the back of her mother's old wingback chair, and attempted to push back the noise of the footsteps up above and the soft rustle of papers that David Higgins held in his hands. She was also trying to clear her mind of the words that had passed between Jack and the detective.

"Why would the court grant such a thing? What right do you have to search our house?" Jack had asked the moment he'd been shown the search warrant. "Are you searching everyone's house who worked for the woman?"

"We have reason to believe your son was at the scene yesterday—the day Mrs. Loughton was killed," Detective Wooley had answered.

"Well, of course he was there. He walks her dog twice a day."

"We have reasons to believe that he was in areas of the house that are suspect."

"What? What reasons?"

Detective Wooley had slipped his hands in the pockets of his trousers, the gun on his belt shifting slightly, then said, "That's all I'm willing to say at this time."

Annette had watched as Jack's eyes narrowed, his hands tightening to fists. He then turned to her, his face tragic, and suddenly he was that little boy—that little boy who had walked defeated from the batter's mound—and she loved him, but especially hated him because, dammit, he was supposed to fix this! She had put her hand to her mouth and turned away.

Trey shifted in his chair and moaned almost inaudibly, causing Annette's eyes to reopen, her controlled breathing thwarted. David Higgins hadn't moved from his spot on the chair, nor had he attempted in any way to get up and talk to Trey as Seth had suggested. His eyes turned Trey's way, his face unreadable. Annette had known David for years. He was just two years ahead of her in school. She and Jack had pushed hard for his appointment as chief of police. She remembered the first time Trey was arrested at seventeen. David had brought him home personally from the football game. They'd entered the house together. "I'm sorry, Annette. The school's pressing charges. If it hadn't been on school property…well, I could have just taken the beer away. But, you know, they have zero tolerance for alcohol. Just bring him by the station tomorrow. We'll do what we need to do." That was the first time Trey was arrested—way before things fell apart for her son.

When Annette Barkley had first heard the word schizophrenia in the ER six years and six months ago, she really had no idea what that meant. She knew the word shot slivers of fear through her body; she knew that the word schizophrenia came from the Greek roots schizo, meaning "split," and phrenia, meaning "mind." Therefore her son's mind must be split and fragmented. She thought right away of the book *Sybil* and pictured all the many disturbing personalities Trey had yet to manifest. She thought right away of what she must have done to cause this. Was it that time she'd turned her back too long to admire that silky red scarf and he'd slipped away? It had taken a terrifying thirty minutes to find her three-year-old son, dazed and shaken in a heap under one of the clothing racks. Was it that one time she'd lost her temper and shook his little four-year-old body while he cried, as she screamed, "Stop it! Stop it, do you hear?" Then there was the time she'd dropped him when he was just a baby, his wet slimy body slipping from her grasp, his tiny head banging against the hard plastic edge of the bathing tub, his little face slipping beneath the water, his eyes looking up at her with terror. Maybe it was because no matter how hard she tried to feel otherwise, she enjoyed—maybe even loved—her other son more. Or was it the fact that she was bitterly disappointed when he was born a boy? She'd decided at some point in her third trimester that she so wanted a little girl. Had she not hidden that fact well enough? She'd not been made to be a mother; it was obvious to her. And even as she was asking the ER doctor, "So you're saying he has a split personality? He's split?" these random thoughts were pulsing through her mind: *I have done this! I should never have been a mother!*

The young psychiatry resident had been kind when explaining that schizophrenia was not a split personality—that split personality was an extremely rare condition called dissociative identity disorder. Schizophrenia was a thought disorder, a brain disorder—typically chronic. Those afflicted have trouble processing information. There were signs called positive symptoms, which included hallucinations and delusions, although Annette could not fathom why they'd be called "positive." There were also what the doctors called negative symptoms, which included things like: trouble socializing, a decrease in the ability to show emotion, the inability to feel pleasure…. Then there were the cognitive symptoms: trouble with concentration, poor working memory, processing issues…. Annette started longing for split personality.

"What causes this?" she'd asked, tears running down her face, Jack silent near her side. He hadn't said a word since the MRI had come back clean.

The young man shook his head and shrugged. "Genetics, environmental…. A combination of the two. Maybe a virus, use of street drugs, trauma…." He shrugged again. "We just don't know."

We just don't know.

Then Trey's first psychiatrist, a young female resident at Upstate, had changed the diagnosis to bipolar disorder. That particular diagnosis had stuck until psychiatrist number three. Then it was back to schizophrenia. By psychiatrist number four, it was schizoaffective disorder with panic disorder and OCD. Then after Trey's third hospitalization, it was changed to bipolar disorder along with generalized anxiety disorder. And now, over six years later, Trey no longer allowed psychiatrist number seven to talk directly to Annette; therefore, she wasn't sure of the present diagnosis.

She'd educated herself greatly over the past six years and was a bit of an expert on mental illness. She'd gotten involved with NAMI (National Association on Mental Illness), had taken their twelve-week Family-to-Family education classes, had read almost every book on the subject, had talked to any psychiatrist who would talk to her, and had spent hours online searching and chatting with other family members of people with the these disorders. And even though she still didn't know how or why this terrible thing had befallen her son, she'd long ago let go of the denial, the guilt, and the anger; she thought she was over the despair. But now it was all hitting her again. She'd let her guard down; she'd let herself become complacent.

He'd been doing so much better—except for that one little slip over a year ago after the death of one of his favorite dogs, when he'd become so depressed that he'd failed to manage his meds or his stress level, bringing the noxious part of his mental illness back to life. This eventually led to that unfortunate, and for her, terribly embarrassing, arrest in the park. He'd snapped back from that one quicker than she had. It was months before she stopped believing that her naked son in the park wasn't still at the top of the gossip list. Now, with this newest crisis, she felt every bit as raw and worried as she had the very first time she'd heard the word mental illness in association with her son. If he'd barely been able to handle the death of one dog, what sort of devastation would this cause?

Annette turned her eyes from David and on to her husband. Jack was staring straight ahead. His arms were resting on his knees, his legs spread slightly apart as if he might leap up at any moment, but his face was a mask of indifference—coldness even. As much as she wanted his face to look a different way, she totally got it, because all she really wanted to do was get up, walk past her troubled son, go back into her studio, shut the door, forget the cops were searching her home, and forget she even had a son or a husband. In fact…maybe she'd skip her studio altogether and just go right upstairs, pack her bags, and take that trip to Paris she'd been putting off for so long.

It was as she was daydreaming about Paris that the two county detectives descended the stairs. They didn't glance her way as they entered the room. They walked right up to her son and told him in the most matter of fact of ways that they were taking him in for questioning. And still Annette held on to the image of the Montmartre, stubbornly unwilling to let go of this indulgence, even as she watched her child shrivel up until he was as small as a boy, until he was so small that he didn't even matter, even as she watched Jack sink back into the couch, even as she felt the tears run down her face. She opened her mouth to protest, but all that came out was, "Cher Dieu."

SEVENTEEN

Flo Loughton spent her early childhood in a small, fenced-in yard that belonged to a small house on busy South Street in Northampton, Massachusetts. Even in the dead of winter with snow blown up and over the chain-linked fence, she was swathed in wool and cotton and rubber and shoved out the door to do what children do when thrust into the hugeness of their own world. And it was limitless—the piles of endless snow, the naked branches painted against the grayness of a winter sky, the forever sound of traffic off South Street, the lines of airplane vapors splitting the gray, the laughter of her little brother as he rolled across the yard, his bright red hat the only splash of color. But they could go anyplace and anywhere with just a word and a thought. The utilization of a broken branch and they were propelled into a world of kill or be killed. A line drawn in the snow, a push, a laugh, a well-aimed snowball, a slight scratch on a cheek…this might elicit a harsh warning from the house, their mother looking up from her typewriter near the window, that perfect sentence she'd been about to create pushed from her mind, her newest novel now in jeopardy. "Kids! You're going to be the death of me! The death of me!" she'd yell through the window. So almost never was their world interrupted until it was time for lunch or dinner. In the summer, when fireflies dotted the darkness, the yard took on a whole otherworldliness of spooky shadows and eerie reverberations; there were all sorts of other battles to be fought. Then there was the crunchy welcoming of fall—bright colors, pumpkins orange against the fence, crows squawking from above. She also loved the soft odor of an early spring—mud and earthworms, winter rot, and renewal. She marveled over that first dainty crocus and then the bright yellow daffodils. She relished the promise of fireflies and flashlight tag. Thus her childhood continued rather unremarkably until the confines of her yard became unreasonable and she ventured into the reality of formal education and societal expectations.

Flo Loughton skated through her primary school. Learning was never the issue. The issue, if there was an issue, was more with her role in that society. Not a particularly pretty little girl—quiet and reserved in her demeanor—her company was not especially sought after. It wasn't really that she was judgmental or felt that she was better than her peers; it was simply that she was, in many ways, better than her peers. She was, from a very young age, a self-sufficient little girl. If there was any major childhood trauma that caused retrospective ache, it would be the loss of her brother. Not by some awful tragedy such as a car wreck or his small body tumbling down a ravine, but by the simple fact that he was an attractive, charming little thing; it wasn't all that long before he was totally swept away by the adoration of his peers, leaving her quite alone in her aloofness. This, sadly, continued for the remainder of Flo's life.

Her mother's temperamental writer's persona annoyed Flo, causing her to soundly reject the more artsy aspects of life, preferring instead cold, hard, measurable facts. Her father was an electrical engineer. Although he died suddenly of a heart attack when Flo was a sophomore in high school, he was still a major factor in her final career choice, instilling in her the need to make a reasonable amount of money. Watching her mother struggle both financially and spiritually as a moderately successful novelist knocked this fact home all the more. Mathematics was always a passion, as was physics, but these were generally difficult careers in which to succeed. Teaching was something that held no interest to Flo. Engineering was seriously considered, but as Flo made her way through her years of education, she began to picture herself with a little more people power. She rather liked the idea of telling people what to do—and get paid for the telling. Corporate law was the perfect marriage of math and people pushing, of solid calculations and manipulation, of money and prestige.

Frank had tried to talk her into opening a practice with him, but he had a different sort of lawyering in mind—the sort that didn't suit her. He longed for too much *people* and not enough power, too much benevolence and not enough remuneration. The downtrodden and unfortunate really didn't suit her. For the most part she dealt with the nonhuman side of a corporation, but she did okay in her no-nonsense way with most of the people she dealt with. Sure there were a few enemies she'd procured over the years—would-be corporate crooks she'd had to rein in, a few underhanded individuals she was forced to unearth and present to the boards of some of the companies she represented. But that was just part of the job—the people-power part.

It was one of these crooked individuals who was on her mind that Friday evening, six weeks before her untimely death. She sat watching Trey break a piece of cookie in two and dunk it into his glass of milk while Raymond Watson, whom she'd managed to unearth just that day, slithered through her mind. Raymond Watson was not a nice man. And as if reading her mind, Trey looked up shyly from his glass of milk and asked, "Do you like your job?"

"My job?" She thought about her answer before saying, "I like growing tomatoes." She paused. "I like the fact that the job allows me to have a place to grow my tomatoes."

Trey nodded. "You can grow tomatoes in a patio pot."

Flo laughed before she gave it much thought, the noise pushing from her throat in a burst of surprise. But she had no chance to be embarrassed by this outburst, because Trey was also laughing as he said, "Or you can even grow them hanging upside down. Which seems totally contrary to the rules of the world. And no doubt frustrating for the tomato plants."

Flo laughed. "That's true. That's very true." She peered his way, enjoying the mirth of his face, before she shrugged and said, "I like my job okay. Sometimes there are irritating issues, unsavory characters…."

It was really the accounting department of one of her clients, a mid-sized public relations firm, that had brought Raymond Watson to her attention. Before that he'd been nothing more than a name on a few documents that had passed under her radar, but it didn't take long for the slight irregularities in Mr. Watson's expense account to lead her to deeper, more disturbing findings. As vice president of the company, spending a few extra thousand dollars on what turned out to be an extramarital affair was no big deal—it could have been easily handled as an internal slap on the wrist. His activity crossed over to criminal, however, when her probing uncovered the fact that significant funds were being funneled to an assortment of outside accounts. The company, not wishing the ensuing public scandal, chose only to fire the man. Due to the sticky legal issues of Raymond Watson's contract, that firing had fallen on her. Her mind flashed to the unpleasantness of earlier in the day, remembering how angry Raymond Watson had been when they had escorted him from the building. "You're a fucking bitch!" he'd screamed her way. She'd barely flinched, but now the thought of his words—his look—sent a shiver along her spine.

"I imagine walking dogs is rather pleasant," she said, eager to shift the conversation.

"It's fine, unless you're terribly opposed to patio-pot tomatoes. It's not like you could *live* on picking up dog crap or anything." He shrugged. "I like the dogs." At the sound of the word *dogs* Hector sat up from his spot between the legs of their kitchen chairs and cocked his head. "Dog?" Trey asked Hector, who responded by standing on his hind legs and pumping his front legs Trey's way. "Come on." And then Hector was in Trey's lap, baby talk coming from Trey's mouth. "You're a baby, aren't you? Yes. A sweet little baby." Flo narrowed her eyes and pursed her lips. "My sweet little man." Trey looked up from the dog, his eyes growing wide when he saw the look on her face. "I'm sorry!" he said. He removed Hector quickly from his lap. He stood up. "I'd better be going. I still need to collect from the rest of my clients."

And even though Flo was rather sad to see him go, she was not sad to have put a stop to the ridiculous debasing of Hector.

EIGHTEEN

Jack Barkley stood momentarily suspended by the front door. He was aware that his wife's cold hands were clutching his arm, and he could hear her voice, but he couldn't quite gather her words. He watched through the tall thin windows that stood on either side of the old wooden front door as the lights of the detectives' car turned around in their driveway and pulled out toward the road. The sensation on his arm turned to pain and pushed him to attention. "Jack! Should we go? Should we follow? Jack?"

He shook his head, pulled away from her grasp, and rubbed at his arm. "No." He turned from her fully. "No."

"What do they mean that he was in areas of the house that are suspect? What does that mean? Jack? I don't get it. I just don't get it! Things have been so good. He's been doing so well. Jack, what are we going to do? Jack?"

"Would you just shut up?" Annette took in a sharp influx of air. "I mean, please. Just shut up…." Then, of course, his wife was crying, which he felt badly about, but he really just couldn't think with her constant yapping. "I'm going to go call Ash. Let me please just go call Ash."

Asher was a criminal lawyer. He was also Jack's friend. It was a friendship that hadn't always been easy. Asher had walked into the first day of seventh grade as the new kid in a school that was as close-knit and cliquey as a school can get, as if he'd always been there, as if he'd been born in Skaneateles like most of the rest of them. He just came strutting in with his black stringy hair, which was longer than what was generally accepted, even in the late 1960s. He wore a frayed denim jacket to which an array of multi-colored peace signs were sewn on, the threads looping haphazardly from the patches to the denim. He wore a red headband that read: END IT NOW! He had a dark, foreign look that was hard to define, which he carried like a badge. He looked you in the eye with a challenge that was nothing more than: *I challenge you not to be my friend!* And this was off-putting and intriguing and irritating and endearing, starting an immediate competition between Jack's classmates, girls and boys alike. Who could win the spot of Asher's best friend?

But Jack was not without his own swagger, placing himself purely as a spectator. As unbiased as he tried to remain, it was hard to deny the threat this new boy posed. It was not surprising that when Asher, having quickly scrutinized the hierarchy, challenged Jack directly in the school cafeteria, Jack's immediate reaction was that of refusal. Jack was carrying his lunch tray from the cafeteria line, which held a plate of rubbery cheese pizza, chocolate milk, and a tub of french fries. Before he could sit at the table and join his two friends who were already seated, Asher stepped forward and blocked his path. Jack stopped and took in the smirk on the face of this rival. "You want something?" he asked. Ash stared at him a moment, then reached out, picked up the slice of pizza, and took a bite.

"Me and you ought to team up," Ash said through the food in his mouth. "Kick some asses." Ash took one more bite of the pizza and then replaced it on Jack's tray.

"Oh, is *that* what all those peace buttons mean?"

Ash swept his hands over his array of antiwar symbols and said, "Oh, these are just general statements about what's wrong with the world as a whole. This," he waved his hands to indicate the cafeteria, "needs some serious ass-kicking."

"How 'bout I just kick *your* ass?" Jack said. His friends at the table laughed.

Ash shrugged. "Hey, far out, if that's the way you want it." Ash picked up a french fry, started to put it in his mouth, stuck it up his nose instead, wiggled it around a bit, and then replaced it on Jack's tray.

"Why you…." Jack let the tray drop with a clang. His friends jumped up. Jack gave Ash a shove that sent him into the table. Ash quickly recovered, and the next thing Jack knew they were both rolling around on the floor, punching at the air, inflicting little or no damage to one another, with the entire lunchtime student body on their feet and cheering. It was only a brief few moments before Mr. Myers was pulling them apart and dragging their sorry butts to the principal's office.

Ash threw Jack clownish faces while Principal Davis paced behind his desk, his bald head gleaming under the harsh fluorescent lighting, his thick, black horn-rimmed glasses slipping from his nose, his wide, yellow paisley tie swinging as he shook his head. "Boys, boys, boys…. Violence is never the answer. For every conflict there is a possible peaceful resolution." He sat down and faced them glumly. Jack had never been in the principal's office. He'd never been in trouble. His father would kill him if he got suspended. Jack worked very hard not to rile his tumultuous father. Even detention would freak his old man out. "Why were you boys fighting?" the principal asked.

"Well, you see, sir—" Ash began earnestly.

"He stuck my french fry up his nose!" Jack blurted out. And to this day, Jack didn't know what caused him to utter such childish nonsense. He was, after all, nearly fourteen at the time. Principal Davis seemed momentarily taken aback, and Ash burst out laughing.

Ash turned immediately grave. "It's true, sir." Ash nodded. "I did. I did stick his french fry up my nose. I then proceeded with malice to put it back with the others. Perhaps it would not have been so offensive if I'd simply left it up my nose, or if I had eaten it. The altercation was entirely my fault, sir. My apologies to both of you." Ash turned his gleaming brown eyes toward Jack and held out his hand. "Peace," he said. And Jack had no choice other than to shake this new boy's hand. Then Ash stood up and held his hand out to the principal. They shook hands and Ash bowed slightly with sincerity. "Again, my apologies."

Jack jumped up from his seat and followed Ash toward the door, waiting as they reached the threshold for Principal Davis to call them back, for him to dole out some sort of punishment. But he didn't. Before Jack knew it, they were both back in the hallway, and Ash was swaying next to Jack down the hall. Ash grinned Jack's way. "Cool, man. Are we cool?"

Everything appealing about Ash was streaming off of him. He had an energy, a warmth, a neediness, a genuineness, and a hint of danger that was irresistible, and Jack fell in love with it all right then and there.

Ash was frenetic—there was no better word to describe him. And when he wasn't being charmingly frenetic, he was dark and angry—a side that Jack had spent a small but significant section of his life dealing with. It was then, in Ash's darkest moments, that he truly needed Jack; and deny it as he might, Jack needed to be needed. So it was perhaps not so odd that Jack had gathered people around him who depended on his sound, stable presence. But there were times, like now, when the tables were turned. And right now, as he thumbed through his contacts on his cell phone, his surgically stable fingers shaking, Jack really needed his friend.

The phone rang four times and then went to voicemail. Indecisiveness took hold. Should he leave a voice message? Without really making up his mind, he ended the call. "He's not picking up," he told his wife.

"But you didn't leave a message! Jack!"

"I'll try again. I'll just keep trying." She scowled his way, then disappeared into her studio, closing the door harder than what was necessary. He knew she'd call Ash herself and leave a desperate message, which was only likely to delay Ash's return call, but there was absolutely nothing he could do about that.

It was his third call, somewhat over an hour later, when he finally got a hold of Ash. "Hi, Jack," Ash said briskly into the phone, and Jack's heart sank a bit. He'd caught Ash at a dark moment.

"Trey's in trouble, Ash," he said quickly. "Maybe real trouble."

There was a long pause. Jack could feel Ash's contemplation, the gathering of a proper response. Jack was prepared for anything, even the sudden silence of disconnect—the phone gone dead because Ash had decided to end the call. He was about to check to see if they were still connected when suddenly Annette was there talking into his other ear. "Is that Ash? Did you get a hold of him?" she asked.

Then he heard Ash sigh. "So, my friend, what now?" Ash said.

Jack closed his eyes with relief, silenced Annette with a quick wave of his hand, then quickly and precisely told Ash all he knew. Ash was quiet as Jack talked, and when he was done, with nothing left to say, they were both quiet. Jack waited, knowing how his friend's mind worked. A good five seconds went by before Ash cleared his throat and said, "I'll call over there, talk to Sheriff Buckson. Let me see where their head is."

"Okay."

"If they're going to keep him much longer," Annette said, "he's going to need his meds. He usually takes them at ten. He never ate, Jack. Didn't eat dinner. His pills bother him without some food in his stomach. Jack, tell Ash that!"

"Tell her I heard her," Ash said in his other ear. "Tell her to fucking relax. It's only eight-thirty."

It was no secret that Annette annoyed Ash more than she annoyed most people. "He heard you, Annette," Jack told his wife.

"I'll call you back in a few," Ash said, then disconnected the call.

Asher Kadaji, Annette Fisher, and Jack Barkley: an odd threesome right from the beginning. As Jack and Ash's friendship tightened in the first year of junior high, both boys began to recognize the expanding advantages of their female classmates. It was a gradual and mutual thing, without the awkward period of one boy still wanting to blow up frogs and the other longing to explore Michelle Bremen's spanking new tits. They both, without question, wanted to explore this amazing phenomenon. They worked and plotted together. They were two exceptionally smart, talented, and good-looking boys who understood, even at thirteen, the advantages of hunting in packs. And their hunting skills were outstanding, so that by ninth grade, at the very beginning of the sexual revolution, the older high school girls proved quite willing to offer up their bodies for exploration—both boys joining the ones who had "done it" by infiltrating a senior end-of-the-year party on a very warm spring night.

At some moment toward the end of eighth grade, Annette had entered their immediate orbit. She was a skinny, stick-like thing with wispy blonde hair and big green eyes. She was really not the sort of soft that either boy found all that interesting. But there was a certain vigor and need and desire she emanated, which terrified

Jack, and he knew innately to stay away—that she was a sticky sort of girl, not easy to bounce off. And at fifteen and sixteen and seventeen, and even eighteen, it was all about the bouncing. She got to him, and she knew it, so he avoided her through most of ninth, tenth, and eleventh grade. Even as she turned into something other than a stick and Ash started sniffing around, Jack held back. Maybe it was inevitable that Ash would be the one who eased himself into Annette that very first time. Jack knew that this act, this deflowering of sorts, was her revenge, and that it would always be there between them; she had done her own successful plotting and hunting. And it was the memory and the possibility of its reoccurrence that she still, thirty-five years later, served up like a bayonet.

NINETEEN

As Barkley sat down in the interrogation room, Detective Wooley assisted him. The last thing Seth wanted was to be forced to call the paramedics due to Trey falling flat on his face. "Relax," he said again. "We just have to get some stuff straight, that's all. Take a seat." Barkley shrank into the chair as much as one can shrink into a metal folding chair. He hadn't said a word the entire drive from Skaneateles to Syracuse. He'd just sat in the back of the car shivering for a full forty minutes, even though it was a hot summer evening. Seth had turned the air conditioning off in the car, but still the unmistakable sound of the guy's teeth chattering dominated the car. Finally, Zuke had flipped on the radio and turned it up a bit, rolling his eyes Seth's way. Seth had acknowledged the act with a sigh.

They'd had to practically carry him from the car, his legs not appearing to be able to function. They'd both been kind, Zuke on one side, Seth on the other, slowly making their way from the parking lot and into the Onondaga Sheriff's Department building, which was located in downtown Syracuse. It was heartbreaking, really—like dragging a lamb to slaughter. Seth was trying to keep his professional edge, but he was feeling very uncomfortable and doubting himself. He also felt soft, which made him angry. Did they really have enough to bring this guy in? Should they have waited for the forensics to come back from the tube of shampoo and the guy's clothes? If they came up clean, then they didn't have enough to even consider an arrest. A lot depended on what they might be able to get out of him. This crazy dude was on the edge. If he cracked totally, he'd be worthless.

And now, here they were, just the three of them in the closet-sized interrogation room. Barkley sat in a chair in the left-hand corner of the room. The small pull-out table was open in front of him so that he could, if he wanted to, lean in to the table. The one-way viewing window was to his left. The room was so small that Seth had to wait until the door was closed before he could pull a chair away from the wall and sit across from Barkley. His chair actually blocked the closed door of the room. Zuke chose not to sit in the third chair, instead leaning against the right-hand corner of the room, his arms crossed over his chest while staring down at the suspect.

"Would you like some coffee?" Seth asked. Barkley shook his head. "Something else? Water? Maybe some hot tea?"

Zuke laughed. "A pastry? Would you like a pastry to go with that tea?"

Seth shook his head slightly Zuke's way. "Come on. Give him a break. He's cold as hell. Some coffee or something might warm him up."

"All the more reason for him to just answer our questions quickly, so he can get outta here." Zuke pulled the third chair away from the table, the scraping sound reverberating through the tiny room. He turned the chair around as he sat down with his chest against its back and faced Barkley.

"So you knew Florence Loughton pretty well. Is that right?" Barkley continued to stare at his hands, which were folded across his lap, and didn't answer. "Been walking her dog for a couple years now. Is that right?" Zuke waited until it was obvious that he wasn't going to get an answer. "Well, that's what the neighbors say, anyway…."

Zuke drummed his fingers of his right hand slowly, rhythmically, on the table. "So…I guess you don't really need to answer that one," he continued.

Every few moments Zuke would strike the metal surface with the nail of his forefinger, sending a slight ting through the small room. Seth could see a subtle flinch from Barkley each time Zuke's nail hit down.

"In fact, the neighbors had a lot to say about you." Barkley didn't move a muscle other than his steady shivering. Zuke glanced Seth's way and then narrowed his eyes toward Barkley. "Would you say you were friends with Florence Loughton?"

Seth studied Barkley as Zuke paused. A long moment passed before Zuke shifted slightly toward Barkley, his eyebrows rising as he said, "Would you say you were *more* than just friends with Florence Loughton?" Barkley shifted in his chair and moaned slightly. "She's a widow, right?"

Zuke paused again, then hit his right index finger hard against the table. "Was Florence Loughton a *really* lonely widow? Did you help her out there—with that loneliness?"

Barkley's head came up as he shot his first direct look Zuke's way. "Fuck you," Barkley said, then quickly retreated.

Zuke chuckled. Seth sighed.

"Listen, Detective Zukerman, go get Mr. Barkley a cup of coffee, will you? Maybe a pastry."

Zuke rolled his eyes. He studied Barkley for a long uncomfortable beat before saying, "Sure. Whatev."

He stood up, scraping the chair loudly against the floor. Seth had to stand and move his chair away from the door. A quick knock and the door was opened from the outside by one of the officers.

Seth waited until Zuke left before he sat back down. He frowned slightly before he smiled sadly and said, "You know, I love dogs. My mom's a dog lover too. We had a ton of dogs while I was growing up. She still has a ton of dogs. So many dogs have come and gone in my life."

Seth shrugged. "Me? Do I have a dog? Nope. You see, I've got this tiny little apartment. Can't really have a dog. Wouldn't be fair to the dog, you know?"

He waited, tapped his pen softly against the table, and watched Barkley shake for a moment.

"Hey," Seth said. "Something just occurred to me." He waited until Barkley lifted his eyes ever so slightly his way. "Barkley. Do you think your last name had anything to do with your career choice?"

That's when Barkley looked at him fully. Seth had to fight the impulse to reach for his gun—the look was that intense.

"Detective Wooley," he said in a cold, clear voice, "my total SAT score was twenty-two hundred. Do you even know what that means? I studied organic chemistry at Brown; my GPA was four point O. Four point O. Although *you* may find it interesting that there is a similarity between my last name and the rather inaccurate noun that represents the sound a dog makes, this has nothing, *whatsoever*, to do with why I have chosen to walk dogs to occupy my time."

Seth sat back and crossed his arms across his chest. *You little fucker*, he thought. That's when he noticed that Barkley had ceased shaking. "Tell me why you were in Florence Loughton's bedroom the day she was killed," he asked. Barkley shot him a look, brought his legs onto the chair, wrapped his arms around his legs, turned toward the wall, and flatly refused to utter another word.

There was a sharp knock, then Zuke's head was suddenly there. "Stymied by counsel. We're done for now."

TWENTY

Trey was angry. And he was tired. It was getting to the point that he was so angry and so tired that he'd pretty much forgotten to be frightened. He was also hungry, but there was no way that he was going to eat the nasty-looking, cellophane-wrapped, vending machine chicken sandwich or touch that coffee they'd plopped down in front of him just before they'd both disappeared, leaving him in this miniature cold room for what seemed like hours now. He had to pee, but he wouldn't give them the satisfaction of banging on the door and asking to use the john. The door opened while he was seriously considering peeing in the corner. Much to Trey's relief, it was Asher who walked in.

"I really have to piss."

Asher nodded and waved Trey toward the door. "My client needs to use the facilities," Asher said as Trey reached the door.

Client? Trey stopped short and stared at Asher. "Client? Did you just say *client?*"

Asher waved away the word and the question as an officer stepped forward. "This way," the cop said and indicated for them to follow. Once in the bathroom, both Asher and the cop stood off to the side, just left of the urinal. *Seriously?* Trey stood there a moment, unsure. He stared at his shoes. *Fuck.* And the next thing he knew, he was crying—standing in the middle of a filthy public toilet in the Onondaga Sheriff's Department, his bladder about to explode, with two guys looking on.

"Use the stall," Asher said gently, stepping up to Trey and easing him into the stall. "We're going to wait outside. Aren't we officer?" The cop grunted a *no.* Asher sighed. "We'll be waiting right out here." He shoved Trey into the stall and pulled the stall door closed.

It still took a while for Trey to stop crying enough before he could relax enough to actually pee. When he was done, he slipped down to the floor next to the toilet, unable to move, unable to zip up his jeans, and unable to get a new flood of tears back under control. He didn't know how much time had passed before Asher was there helping him off the floor, helping him wash his hands and rinsing off his face with cool water, rubbing the wetness away with rough paper towels, and pulling Trey's body into his, the cop looking on. Asher gave Trey a quick hug and said into his ear, "It's going to be okay, pal." He pulled away from Trey and gave him a little shake. "Do you hear me? It's going to be okay." Trey nodded for no other reason than he didn't want to be shaken again.

They made their way back to the interrogation room, where Asher sat him down, then pulled up a chair close. It was just the two of them now, and Asher pulled open his briefcase, removing a small bottle of Fiji water—the only kind that Trey trusted. He then removed a bottle of Trey's meds and a spinach veggie wrap. "From your mom," he said. "Extra mayo." Asher slid the wrap across the metal table. When Trey made no move to unwrap the sandwich, Asher reached over and unwound the Saran Wrap, spreading the clear sheets open as a makeshift plate and pushing it a little closer. "Eat, dammit," he said.

Trey sighed and picked up the wrap. Asher opened the bottle

of water and set it back down. He shook out one white pill and set it on the Saran Wrap. Then he was still and quiet. When Trey had eaten half his food, he took a quick intake of water, then wiped at his mouth with the side of his arm. He picked up the pill, swallowed it with another swig of water, and said, "I want to go home."

Asher was quiet for a long time. Then he said, "Eat the whole sandwich. You want your mom to rip me a new one?"

Trey shrugged.

"Eat, and then we'll talk."

"I'm scared."

"I know you are."

They were both quiet. Trey finally sighed. Then he picked up the remainder of the wrap and ate it in three quick bites.

"I'm feeling really shaky."

Asher nodded. "As soon as we're done here, you're going to be seen by the nurse practitioner. Do you think you need another one of your meds?"

Trey shook his head. "I don't want to see anyone. I just want to go home."

"Well, you can't right now." Ash frowned. "Do you want another pill? Your mom said you could have two if you thought you needed more."

Trey once again began to cry. "Why can't I just go home?"

"Not possible. Work with me here, will you? I'll get you out of here just as quick as I can." Asher handed Trey a crumpled paper napkin, which Trey used to mop at his face.

"You want to tell me?" Asher asked. "You want to tell me what happened yesterday at Mrs. Loughton's?"

Trey shook his head.

"Ever? Or just not now?"

Trey shrugged. "I can't right now," he finally said.

"Fair enough. Did you say anything to them?"

He shook his head again.

"Good. Good. Let me tell you what they're telling me. Mrs. Loughton appears to have been murdered. You know that, right?" Trey managed a nod before Asher went on. "They've found your fingerprints in the kitchen, in the bathrooms, in the bedrooms, on various items.... They found Mrs. Loughton's shampoo in your possession—in your bedroom. There's blood on your shirt. The neighbors saw you sneaking around the house, hiding in the bushes." Asher stopped for a moment. "That's all they're telling me. But they seem to think it's enough." He sighed. "Trey, they're talking to the district attorney right now. I'm going to do my damnedest to get you out of here tonight, but, pal, there's a very good chance they're going to arrest you for this. You have to talk to me, just as soon as you can. Okay?"

"I want to go home. I want to know where Hector is."

"Hector?"

Again Trey found himself crying. Then his brain got all jumbled. The next thing he knew he couldn't breathe. His chest was all tight, and he felt cold and hot. His heart began to beat like mad. His vision got all funny, and he just knew—he just knew that this time it was going to kill him. As he bent down in his chair, panting and clutching his chest, he was mostly feeling bad about his mom. How sad that her youngest son died in an interrogation room at the age of only twenty-six; but at least she would not have to live through the agony of her son's conviction for murder.

TWENTY-ONE

"So this is what we have," said Maddy, poking her gloved finger into the laceration in Florence Loughton's forehead. "This was caused by a blunt impact. I'd say you're right; she hit her head on the edge of the night stand, which explains the blood there. It's deep. Deep enough to cause her to lose a lot of blood, and hard enough to cause this." Seth nodded his head. That fact had been pretty obvious at the scene. Maddy lifted a piece of the skull off the victim and revealed a large mass of blood clinging to the brain. "That's what killed her." She then moved over to the victim's right arm. "You see these bruises? These were caused by someone grabbing her upper arm. And then there's bruising on both her shoulders, but more significant on her right. See?" Maddy pointed to the oval bruise on the left shoulder and then on the right. "That's from the thumbs." She lifted the right side of the body slightly. "And here…on the back of the shoulder…. In the shape of four fingers? The same thing's on the left shoulder, only really faint."

"A man?" Seth asked.

"Maybe. Hard to say from the bruising. Women don't usually grab one another."

"Sad, but true." Maddy didn't crack a smile, and he regretted his poor attempt at humor. "So he might have grabbed her hard by the shoulders and shoved her into the bedside table."

"Maybe. She hit the table pretty hard."

"Or they might have been struggling—the blow to her head an accident. Then we're talking manslaughter."

Maddy shrugged and brought her finger to the victim's neck. "But these very faint bruises on her neck, and the petechiae…they aren't caused by someone's hands. They're too uniform. Ligature marks. Caused by some sort of strap. Maybe a belt? "

"So she was choked?"

"Well, they're too faint for me to want to use the word *choked*. But they are undeniably there. Something was tightened around her neck."

Seth looked at the faint bruising on the neck. "A dog leash?" he asked.

Maddy shrugged. "Maybe."

"If we brought the leash in, could you tell?"

She shrugged again. "Maybe."

Seth rolled his eyes.

"What?" she asked.

"Nothing. I'll get the dog's leash to you. What else?"

Maddy moved over to the victim's left arm. "There's some more bruising on the wrist here." She showed Seth the marks right above the hand. "Again, most likely from someone's fingers." She bent slightly over the body and peered up at Seth, her wet lips parting slightly, her blue eyes smoldering with what she was about to show him; and in spite of the smell that permeated the room, and the fact that there was a cut-up dead body between them, Seth felt a distinct stirring and fought the urge to bend down, pull Maddy's face to his, and stick his tongue in her mouth. "And here, if you look closely," Maddy used her right index finger to point to Florence Loughton's grey mouth, "is very slight bruising and mild skin abrasion. Around the mouth…."

"Someone hit her?"

"Nope. I'd say a very…." Maddy looked up at him. "A *very* intense kiss."

Seth had to blow out air and shift his weight, pulling his left leg forward. Did this woman have any idea what she did to him? He blew out another puff of air. "Signs of sex?"

"Nope."

"Any saliva? DNA found around the mouth?"

"Too soon to get the reports back." Maddy scrunched up her face and shook her head slightly. "But I don't think so. The victim appears to have just taken a shower before she died."

"So this guy kissed her. She took a shower, and then he killed her?"

Maddy shrugged. "The timeframe isn't exact."

"Hair fibers on the body?"

"Nope. Well, just dog. We're looking at several different samples of human hair picked up in the kitchen area."

"Skin under her fingernails?"

"Trace. We're looking at it. Nothing of significance."

Seth sighed. "So, no real sign of struggle on her part."

Maddy shrugged. Then Seth had a vivid scenario run through his mind. He'd step around the table, grab Maddy roughly by her right upper arm, grab her left wrist with his other hand, and kiss her—hard. Maybe he'd press her up against the wall of the autopsy room, the tray of instruments being pushed aside. And the kiss would last the perfect amount of time, and then he would break from her. He'd step back, her eyes not leaving his, and then she'd tilt her head and shrug.

TWENTY-TWO

Flo Loughton was none too pleased when she walked into her relatively new coffee shop that Monday morning less than two weeks before her death to find Stanley's hairy face smiling up at her. His laptop was open, his fingers were on the keys, but he was looking up as if he'd just been sitting and waiting. Almost one year after their ill-fated date and here he was as if no time had passed at all. She considered pivoting on the heel of one of her snappy, purple pumps and permanently giving up coffee, but there was a certain amount of stubborn routine that dominated Flo's days. Anything that caused the slightest deviation was a considerable source of irritation. Then there was the standard social protocol that was necessary to uphold. So she planted both of her heels squarely on the floor of the coffee shop and smiled. "Stanley," she said.

He closed his laptop, rested his fingers on its shiny black surface, and grinned, his white mustache curling upward, the stiff hairs of his beard under his lower lip shooting forward. "Flo. So here you are. Come. Sit. I've already ordered your coffee."

That's when she noticed that he had two of the fancy paper cups on his table. "*My* coffee?"

"I remember just how you like it."

And that's when the hairs on Flo's arm stood up just a bit, and a creepy, cool chill caressed her neck. "Well, that's a little odd, don't you think?"

Stanley laughed. "Perhaps some would find that odd. Others might find it endearing."

"I find it odd."

He laughed again. "You always made me laugh."

"Always? Perhaps you might revisit your sense of humor. And our history. It was one dinner. One disastrous dinner."

Stanley pulled on his beard with his right hand, the hair of his eyebrows coming together to form a single white unit. There was a flicker of doubt that slipped across his face, which Flo noted with satisfaction, but then it was gone. He stood, her coffee in his hand, and came to her. "Here you go, Floie." And the way the word came out of his mouth was the way the word had come out of Frank's mouth all the years of their marriage. *Floie.* It was an unacceptable word coming out of anyone's mouth other than Frank's.

The sudden memory of Frank came to her—how he'd turned to her in their bed, his hand coming out and sliding down her arm. She remembered how her body had recoiled just enough for him to know that tonight was not a night that she wanted his body as part of hers, his hand moving back to her shoulder. Then there was the soft kiss he'd placed on her dry, cracked lips. "Goodnight, Floie." "Goodnight, Frank." Then, as she'd tucked in her body and shut her eyes, she'd considered, just for a second, telling Frank that she loved him. But the words never left her mouth. She'd simply fallen asleep. And it was that—those words that were never spoken—that was the last to pass between them.

Flo stepped back from the coffee offering and stood up a little taller on her pumps. "No, thank you, Stanley."

the chocolate debacle

Then there, like the flicker of doubt, darkness—maybe even hatred—moved in around Stanley's eyes, and Flo knew, just knew, that she'd gone too far and thrown social protocol too much to the wind. This man somehow blamed her for some sort of need she could not fill—maybe even blamed her for what surely must be his scarred scrotum. So she smiled, more out of the fear of a social scene than any real need to spare this man's feelings, and said, "Stanley, look, I'm sorry." She reached for the coffee. "Thank you. It was very nice of you. I'm just not my best in the mornings."

He smiled. "Then tonight, perhaps."

Flo closed her eyes. A mile—he'd stepped a mile for having received an inch. "No." She looked him squarely in the eye before she turned around and removed herself from his presence. "No."

When Flo arrived inside her building, she threw the coffee, untouched, into the large, shiny metal trashcan near the elevator. As she waited for the elevator, she began to regret her disposal of the coffee. Caffeine notwithstanding, she longed for something soothing and warm against her tongue and resented the fact that the smooth routine of her morning had been so rudely derailed.

The day had started off normal enough. Flo had shifted in her bed at precisely 6:45, as she did every morning. This shifting had sprung Hector into action, as it did every morning. He'd bounced from his little bed on the floor and onto her bed, planted his tiny feet near her head, and sent his pink little tongue her way. And Flo, as she did every morning, had shifted away and moaned, which caused Hector to moan. Then she'd softened, gathered his soft whiteness in her hands, and taken in the gentle dogginess of his odor. She'd pressed Hector against her face and smiled. It wasn't long before she was showering. Even though Hector had already made a quick potty trip in the backyard, he sat as he did every morning with his leash in his mouth, which he'd retrieved from the hook in the mudroom, and watched as she dressed.

Then as Flo made her way downstairs and into the kitchen, Hector flew ahead, the leash trailing behind. By the time Flo reached the kitchen, Hector was there, leash in mouth, his little tail all aquiver. "Breakfast," she told him. "You know that." She glanced at the clock. "At ten. First you must eat." And that morning, like every morning, Hector refused to let go of his leash, only dropping it momentarily to gobble down his special mixture of organic chicken and vegetables. Then as Flo left the house, Hector, like every morning, sat slightly dejected, leash in mouth, on the kitchen floor and watched as she retrieved her car keys from the hook near the side door. "At ten," she said. "Trey will be here in one hour and fifty minutes." Hector cocked his head at the sound of Trey's name, so she said it again. "Trey."

"Do you have a girlfriend?" she had asked him three days ago on Friday evening.

Trey wiped at his mouth. "A girlfriend?"

As Flo nodded, she wondered what had possessed her to ask him such a question.

He shook his head. "Girls are complicated." He smiled sadly then, and Flo had the sudden urge to pull him to her chest. To be so young and so all alone. She pushed the plate of Keebler Cheesecake Middles his way. Trey shrugged slightly and reached for her offering. When the cookie was gone, he looked up and said, "You must miss Mr. Loughton a lot."

The elevator doors of her office building opened, and Flo stepped into the perfect mirrored square. She was alone, and everywhere she looked she looked back.

TWENTY-THREE

Annette Barkley knew about the general unfairness of the justice system when it came to dealing with those with a mental illness. She knew that the largest mental health care facility was the penal system. She knew the police needed to be better trained and that there needed to be a separate court system that dealt with crimes committed by people with a history of mental illness. She knew that in most towns such a thing did not exist. She also knew about the good laws—the ones that tried to help, like the controversial but necessary Kendra's Law, which dealt with forcing people into treatment rather than jail. And there was Timothy's Law, which prevented private insurance companies from refusing treatment to those suffering from mental illness. But she also knew that many state-subsidized insurance programs did not cover mental illness and often did not have parity when it came to treating it. She knew about the American Disabilities Act and its attempt to prevent unfairness in the workplace and school. And she also knew that it often did not work. She knew there was discrimination against those with mental illness—a lot of discrimination. And she knew that most of this discrimination was based on ignorance; people just didn't know any better.

So naturally, discrimination was the first thing that came to her mind when she heard Jack say into the phone, "He's being charged, Ash? For murder?" She bit her lip to keep from crying again and leaned into Jack's chest. "Okay. Okay," Jack said into the phone. He ended the call and said, "Okay," one more time. Then his arm went across her back.

Murder. Perhaps she said the word aloud, because Jack's other arm came out, and he hugged her to his chest. "Oh, Jack," she whispered. Her son could never commit murder.

"What's wrong with that squirrel?" Trey had asked, looking up at her with three-year-old frankness. Annette looked to where Trey's chubby little finger was pointing and saw the dead squirrel, lying near the base of the tree. It was on its back, its legs sticking up from its bloated body as if it'd fallen to the earth mid-climb. She had to look away.

"Cool!" exclaimed four-year-old Samuel, who broke from his mother's other hand and ran from the sidewalk into the neighbor's yard to thoroughly investigate the death.

"It's dead, Trey," she told him gently.

"What?"

"Dead, as in no longer alive." Trey seemed confused by her answer, and Annette wished Jack was there. Jack would know how to explain it so that Trey would understand. "Everything lives a certain amount of time and then dies—becomes dead."

"Why?" he asked.

"Just because."

Trey's face turned fretful. "Why?" he repeated.

Samuel picked up a stick and used it to poke at the bloated body. "Bet it was murdered," Samuel said as he pushed the stick against the body until the tight skin indented and the surrounding tissue puffed out frightfully.

"Samuel, stop that," said Annette.

"Mur-ded?" asked Trey, his voice becoming shaky.

"Yeah! Murdered," said Samuel, who was poking even harder. Annette was horrified, torn between shrinking back and stepping forward to snatch her older son away. "Bet someone bopped it on the head," continued Samuel. "Look at the eyeballs. All popped out." He moved the stick toward the eyes.

Trey began to cry, and Annette all but shrieked, "Samuel! Get away from that thing!'

Samuel looked up from the body—the stick poised directly over the squirrel's open mouth—raised his shoulders, cocked his beautiful head, and said, "When you're dead, you're dead."

"Now!" shrieked Annette. Samuel dropped the stick and returned to her. She grabbed his hand and continued down the sidewalk, with Trey crying on her left and Samuel sulking on her right.

"Let's go get ice cream," she offered.

She had not been an exceptional mother.

And now, even at his very worst—after things had changed regarding her son—Trey was never violent. Sure there was that second-degree assault charge, but that wasn't Trey being violent; that was Trey being sick. Who wouldn't fight back when you were convinced you were going to be killed? Delusions were as much Trey's reality as reality was reality. But this…this reality was just too much to take in.

"Jack, there must be a mistake. How could they arrest him? It's because he's an easy target—a scapegoat. It's just so easy to blame the crazy person." She was suddenly so angry that she pushed against Jack's chest. "Dammit, Jack!" Then the anger from the injustice was overwhelmed by fear. Her son would fall apart. He would slip back into what he had worked so hard to overcome. Even a healthy individual would stagger under such a thing. But Trey…. How would he survive?

Survive. The image of her husband holding up Trey's limp body came to her, the rope tied around Trey's neck. She'd stood stock still as she'd taken in the scene. "A knife, Annette! Get a knife!" She'd almost fallen down the stairs as she raced to the kitchen, her heart beating in her ears, the image of the tiny stream of blood that coursed from Trey's mouth, down his chin, and onto Jack's forehead pressed into her mind. She'd grabbed the largest serrated knife she owned and took the stairs three at a time, the thought of falling and stabbing herself—never run with a knife—pulsing through her mind. "Dear God! Dear God! Dear God!" she chanted as she sawed away at the rope. Jack was crying silently, doing his best to shift Trey higher, attempting to loosen the rope from Trey's neck, which shifted the rope and made her task more difficult. Then finally, it broke free; the sudden free weight of his son brought Jack to his knees. He'd started CPR while Annette had tearfully called 911.

"Dammit, Jack." She banged her hands against his chest. "This is going to kill him. He can't be arrested. This is going to kill him, Jack." She began to cry. Jack caught her hands before she could hit him again. "How's he going to keep it together? How? How, Jack?"

"I don't know, Annette. I just don't know." This was not the answer Annette was looking for.

TWENTY-FOUR

Trey remembered the first time he was hospitalized the way he remembered the night terrors he had as a child—with crippling fear. There were no details, no hard images, no clear facts—just the deep sensation of his impending death. Then the slow, groggy awakening. Then the slow realization that his core was lost. Lost. Lost.

"We believe you have schizophrenia," the woman at the hospital said when he was coherent enough to ask why he was taking so much medication. "You're taking this medication so that you'll continue to improve."

Improve? Improve from what? To what? There was nothing wrong with him other than his core being lost. He just needed to relocate his core. Then he just needed to keep it together. Keep it together. Find his core and keep it together. But everyone—the doctors, the nurses, his caseworker, his parents—insisted that he needed these meds to relocate his core. Only his brother, Samuel, who had come all the way to Providence from Georgetown University to visit him in the hospital, seemed to get it.

Samuel was missing his midterm exams as he sat in the dayroom of the hospital, his long legs bent awkwardly, his knees close to his face, his large frame comically dwarfing the folding metal chair. Trey had the distinct urge to pound on his brother's chest. Trey glanced at the orderly who was playing cards with another patient, reached out, and gave Samuel one quick, soft punch in the middle of his ribcage. "Neanderthal," he whispered.

His brother smiled. "Dork."

It didn't seem all that long ago that Samuel had leaned against the doorframe of Trey's bedroom and watched as Trey packed for his freshman year at college. "So my little shit brother is going off to college?"

Trey grinned up from the folded stack of T-shirts he was carefully placing into his suitcase and said, "That's right." Trey had everything carefully laid out and organized: his pants in one pile, his long sleeve shirts in another. He had exactly fourteen pairs of underwear so that he'd only have to do wash once every two weeks, and fifteen pairs of white socks—the extra pair was in case of a rain emergency. His toiletries, books, laptop, cell phone, camera, room fan, laundry bag, towels, sheets, and Mets desk lamp were each carefully labeled with tiny block lettering: PROPERTY OF TREY MATTHEW BARKLEY; he didn't want anyone in the dorm messing with his stuff. Trey began to recount his underwear, just to be sure.

Sam lumbered in and cuffed Trey gently on the side of his head. "Maybe you'll finally get laid."

Trey responded to the cuff by letting go of the underwear he was holding, wrapping his left arm around Sam's back, and socking his brother hard and repeatedly in the chest with his right fist. "Maybe," Trey said. "But not before I kick your ass." With one quick movement, Sam had Trey's head in a grip lock under his right arm. Undeterred, Trey continued his assault, only now with less effect. Samuel laughed, and in a flash Trey went from fun to fury. He twisted unsuccessfully, unable to extract himself from his brother's hold.

"Are you mad? Huh? Are you?" his brother taunted. Then, as suddenly as he'd found himself trapped, Trey was now in his brother's embrace. "You take care of your skinny little ass. You understand?" Trey wrapped his arms behind Samuel's back and returned the hug. "Don't let anyone give you any shit. You hear?"

They pulled apart. Trey smiled. "Oh, I'll be just fine, as long as your dumb ass stays at Georgetown. How'd you ever get in there anyway? Jack off the dean?"

"Ha! Not even close." His brother cuffed him again. "He shook my hand, jacked *me* off, then gave me a scholarship."

Now, a year and a half later, his brother reached out and cuffed him gently on the side of his head. "What are you doing, man? You don't belong in here. Stop being such a little freak."

Trey shrugged and struggled not to cry. "You gotta get me outta here," he mumbled.

"I will. This is crazy."

But by Trey's fourth hospitalization, Sam had stopped visiting. He rarely answered Trey's texts, and he'd almost stopped calling. He even stopped coming home during the summers, insisting that he needed to stay in Washington for internships. Once he'd gotten into med school, he became even less visible in Trey's life.

Trey had spent a lot of time during his last few hospitalizations working out critical mathematical formulations. Samuel's formula went something like this: S = Samuel, T = Trey, SS = Societal Success, EFS = Embarrassing Family Skeletons. If $S = SS$ and $T = EFS$ and $EFS \neq SS$ then $S + T \neq SS$. It was pretty basic stuff.

So it was ultimately his parents who'd stuck with him. Trey continued taking the meds simply because it was just easier to keep them off his back, and it really seemed to give his mom some sort of joy every time he took a pill. As annoying as she could be, it was still awfully nice to bring her a little joy. He had, after all, brought her so much pain.

It had never been his intention to hurt her. It had never been his intention to hurt anyone.

So when they came to get him from the interrogation room and move him to the Justice Center for booking, it was his mother he was thinking of. He was specifically remembering the horror on her face—the first thing he saw when his father had forced him back to consciousness. He hadn't planned it well, that was for sure. The number one rule for a successful suicide is to do it when no one else is around. Duh! He blamed his scattered thinking for that one, because at the time he was quite certain that he'd wanted to die; his poor planning had nothing to do with any deep desire to actually survive. It was not a plea for help. And what he got, what came of it, was his third hospitalization. That one he remembered like a nightmare, all of its horror fully intact.

And then, with time, he found his core. It was in a slightly different place, and it was more fluid and squishy now, but found nonetheless. He seriously doubted that the medication had anything to do with his improvement. What resulted in his improvement was the readjust, the acceptance, the realization that he was fucked up and would probably always be fucked up, and the knowing that it was really nobody's fault. He relearned. He learned. He figured out his triggers. He took care of himself. He took his meds. He'd even come to believe that he might actually need the medication. The last thing he wanted was another hospitalization.

But the memories of the horror of that third hospitalization—of all five of his hospitalizations for that matter—were nothing, *nothing*, compared to the sensations that were slicing through him now. These were not people trying to make him better; these people—these cops—were trying to shred him apart.

They'd walked him through the long underground tunnels.

They'd yanked off the handcuffs to do the fingerprints. They'd shoved him unnecessarily roughly against the wall and snapped his photo—front, side, other side. They'd taken his washed-out Kenneth Cole jeans, his classic Snoopy T-shirt, his Wayfarer sunglasses, his green All Star Double Tongue Converses, and even his navy blue and white Express boxers and forced him to put on an ugly green shirt, a nasty pair of white canvas sneakers, and tan drawstring pants. He'd been adamant in his refusal of the random underwear that was offered; just the drawstrings pants would have to do. They recuffed his hands behind his back and shuttled him from this place to that. Everything was too bright, his head throbbed, and the shoes rubbed against his big toes. His balls were too free and too vulnerable, his voices were a steady chorus in his head, and the rough shirt made him want to scratch, which he couldn't do with his hands secured behind his back. His mouth was dry, but all they would offer him was pale, cold coffee and water from the tap, which he refused with a shake of his head. Tap water was nothing more than repeatedly recycled sewer sludge, and public coffee was once-removed tap water. He was interviewed by one person, only to be asked the same questions by another and then another. He found nearly all the questions too insulting and trivial to entertain. What is your name? Where do you live? What do you do? What's your medical history? Your education? Have you been arrested before? Skipped bail? He'd refused to answer all but his name and his address, knowing that these were facts they already had. Finally someone gave him a can of Coke, which he drank down eagerly, only to find himself thirstier than ever less than an hour later, all the while continuing to be shoved from this place to that place and asked a never ending stream of questions.

The next thing he knew he was back in the detectives' car and heading back to Skaneateles. Even though he felt with every fiber of his being that he was going home, Asher's earlier words were the bigger reality: "They're going to go ahead and book you now. Okay? Once that's done, you have to go back to Skaneateles to see the judge there. I'll be there with you. I'll follow along. There you'll be arraigned, you see? They'll arraign you and bring you back." The words that were coming out of Asher's mouth just moments after Trey had begun to recover from his latest freak out—his heart returning to its normal rhythm, the clammy feeling almost gone, his breathing deep and slow—made absolutely no logical sense. Yet here he was in the backseat of the car, shivering like hell and heading to his hometown at 11:40 at night, only to be forced to stand in front of the old guy who always seemed to be walking down Fennel Street every morning at the exact time Trey always walked down Fennel Street. "How you doing?" "Good. And you?" "Good. Duke looks happy today." "Yup," Trey would answer, patting the large setter on his head as the town judge walked by. The arraignment was all pretty much a nightmare of a blur; the only words that stuck with him were: "Held over. No bail."

Then he was brought back to the Justice Center, where even the ugly green shirt and tan pants were taken away and replaced with a nasty green smock and a crude blanket with a pillow sewn right in. The skin of his naked body scraped against the rough green fabric as he was brought to a simple cell, the front of which was glass. There he was left alone. It was almost a relief to be taken to a cell and left alone. Alone. Other than the cop who sat right on the other side of the glass, he was ALONE. If he shut his eyes and pulled the blanket over his face, he could block out most of the light, and the cop, and the dingy white walls, and the view of the cell block, and almost…he could almost…stop the constant humming of complaints from the voices that swirled throughout his head.

TWENTY-FIVE

Seth slipped the leash off the hook with a gloved hand Monday morning. He carefully deposited it into a plastic bag and tucked it under his arm. Then he stepped into the kitchen. He'd wanted to come back here himself to take another look around without the distractions of other people and try to get to know Florence Loughton just a bit better. He tried to put all thoughts of the reports he'd read out of his head and look with fresh eyes—with eyes that had the picture of Trey Barkley, murderer, pasted nearby.

What was Florence Loughton likely to have been doing the hour before she was killed? The night before? The week before? Did she have friends over? Had she sat at her kitchen table and had tea with the ladies? Was there a man in her life? And crazy Barkley? What was her relationship with him? So far, Seth had been able to piece together a picture of a bitter older woman, married to her job, and pretty much a pain in the ass. But why? Why would Barkley want to kill her? Seth had a lot of good, solid, physical evidence, but it was all a little sketchy—all perhaps easily explained, though, especially if Barkley had been more than just the dog walker. But if Barkley had been more than just a dog walker, then perhaps there was a motive somewhere in that *more*. Or perhaps that *more* had turned into some tryst turned tragic, some kinky accident of sorts, as Maddy had obliquely suggested. Then there was the possibility that Barkley had just gone nuts— lost it—and Florence Loughton was just the unlucky victim of his madness.

Seth walked slowly around the large, round oak kitchen table and noted the slight sprinkling of sugar or salt toward the middle. He licked the tip of his gloved pinky finger, dipped it into the sprinkling, then brought it to his mouth. Salt. He stepped into the main kitchen area. On the counter was a pan of brownies, its contents half gone, the edges of the remnants uneven as if some-one had ripped a piece free with their fingers. He turned toward the sink, where he found a single white mug in the basin, its bottom coated with a thin dried film of creamy coffee. There were no other dishes; the kitchen was otherwise as neat as a pin. There was a hint of lipstick on the rim of the mug. Interesting. Florence Loughton was either a woman who put her lipstick on before she drank her morning coffee or a woman who drank coffee before she went to bed.

He lifted up the lid of the tall metal trash can and inspect-ed its contents. Sitting right on top were the remains of dinners from Doug's Fish Fry: two greasy paper bags, two paper plates, several plastic containers that had held coleslaw and tartar sauce, a few uneaten french fries, and a chunk of mangled fried fish. Hmmm…. Either Florence Loughton seriously loved to eat or there'd been two for dinner. He was annoyed that the ETs hadn't noted this in their files. He carefully pulled the plastic bag from the waste can, pulled the plastic drawstrings together, and set it aside. He'd take this down to forensics along with the leash.

He stepped over to the fridge and took a look inside. It con-tained a small smattering of the normal assortment of edibles: a half gallon of 1% milk, jars and bottles of ancient-looking condiments, a carton of eggs, a half-empty container of orange juice, two wrinkled apples, a bag of wilting romaine lettuce, a half a pint of cream, a tin of organic Kona coffee, one sad-looking lemon, and a new-looking bottle of ketchup. That was about it. He pulled out the carton of milk and gave it a little sniff—still just fine. He put it back and shut the door.

He checked the freezer. Other than a half gallon of fudge marble swirl ice cream, numerous tiny Ziploc packages of what looked to be a mixture of vegetables and chicken, one frosty-looking unidentifiable package of meat, and ice cubes, the freezer was empty. He checked the pantry, which was also sparsely furnished: one box of wheat pasta, a hodgepodge of dusty seasoning containers, a nearly empty five-pound bag of sugar, a can of black beans, two cans of Campbell's Chicken Noodle Soup, three cans of tuna, one bag of organic dog kibble, five bags of various types of Keebler cookies, two boxes of Hostess Ho Hos, one box of Hostess Zingers, and a box of Little Debbie Zebra Cakes. Florence Loughton was obviously not a woman who did a lot of cooking or eating at home, but she did, apparently, have a sweet tooth and a love for store-bought bakery goods. He was about to close the pantry cabinet door when his eyes caught something hiding behind the boxes of Ho Hos. He slid one of the boxes to one side and there, lying on its side, was a half pint of Jack Daniels. The cap was slightly askew, allowing some of its contents to have escaped. A tiny dried puddle of the fine golden liquid stained the red checkers of the shelf paper. He cocked his head, licked his lips, and considered for a moment.

His father's drink of choice—his mother's too, for that matter. Jack Fucking Daniels. It was that smell—that smell he loved and hated—that had permeated his seven-year-old senses the night his father was killed. And it was that smell—that wonderful taste—

that still brought his father back to him and still conjured up a plethora of emotions toward his mother.

Baggage. Fucking baggage. Now his mother, aged and broken into so many pieces, sat in her little Jack Daniels-soaked house, surrounded by her odd assortment of misfit mongrels. And here he was, a thirty-five-year-old, never-married man who still carried his growing-up baggage around like an infant, throwing its contents at whomever might get in his way. Nice to have a gun and be able to use it now and then.

He laughed…and then the image of the last man he'd sent a bullet toward, who was really nothing but a child, came to him.

Had it really been necessary to shoot him? Would he himself be dead if he hadn't?

It was just last year when he'd walked into a robbery in progress in the Red Apple Kwik Fill on exit 10 off 81. His only intention was to grab a coffee, and maybe a donut. He never intended to kill anybody. But having your perfectly acceptable evening disrupted by some guy screaming at you and then pointing a gun at your face tended to bring out the worst in Seth; he'd pulled his gun and shot out of instinct. What sort of person does that out of instinct?

Well…*a cop* is what he'd been told by the Department, by the psychologist he'd been forced to see, and by Zuke. But still, there must have been some better way to respond, especially when that guy behind the gun turned out to be only a fourteen-year-old boy. Sure the gun was real, and sure it was loaded, but the kid didn't fire; he hadn't said he was going to fire. He'd just turned quickly, yelled, "Stop right there, motherfucker!" crouched, and pointed the gun Seth's way. Seth was dressed in plain clothes; the boy had no idea that he was a detective. No do-overs where bullets were involved—none whatsoever.

Another fucking tragedy. After over ten years on the force there were so many others that he was on the periphery of…that he had knowledge of. Was it this—the knowledge of so many other tragedies—that made his childhood story just a little more run-of-the-mill tragic, making it all just a little bit easier to swallow?

He sighed, turned away from the Jack Daniels, and shut the pantry door.

Seth left the kitchen and walked down the short hall that led to the living room, formal dining room, and stairway to the upstairs. He took the steps two at a time, pausing as he reached the top to glance at the family photos. His eyes came to rest on an old shot of Florence Loughton; she was hanging from the trapeze line of a sailboat. The creamy tops of her breasts were only overshadowed by the look on her face, which was one of pure, unabashed joy. It was the sort of look that could make you fall in love, the sort of look that even now, even knowing that this woman no longer existed, nearly aroused Seth in a way he wasn't expecting. *Damn!* Had he ever brought that kind of joy to a woman? To any human being? He blew out a sigh and turned his attention to the master bedroom.

The crap from the dog had yet to be cleaned, the crime scene still intact, so he treaded carefully through the piles as he entered the bedroom. Everything was as he remembered it: the bed barely disturbed, unmade on the left side, the room neat, no signs of multiple occupancy.

Maddy had put the time of death at some point between late Wednesday night and early Thursday morning. She was typical Maddy in her refusal to be more specific. "There are just too many variables to be more exact," she'd shrugged without emotion. But the coffee in the sink, the unmade bed, and the evidence that Loughton had taken a shower right before she'd died caused Seth to lean toward an early morning death rather than late night. Every indication was that the victim had spent the night before her death alone—that she had not shared her bed with her killer. Yet at some point she'd been with someone. The *someone* who was most likely responsible for her death. He stepped to the side of the bed where Florence Loughton had lain dead. He stared at the spot where she'd been—the spot where someone had left her, maybe while she was still alive, naked and dying. He studied the pool of dried blood before he looked away. But how? How had it played out?

Seth brought his hand to the three-day-old stubble on his face and scratched at the right side of his chin as he stared out the window of the bedroom that looked out over the backyard. He noticed it was open just a crack, which he found odd considering the air conditioner was running. Maybe she liked a little fresh air more than she liked efficiency. Or maybe it was just an oversight on her part. He turned away from the bed and stepped into the bathroom. He narrowed his eyes as he took in the room. Perhaps Florence Loughton had woken up Thursday morning and padded into the bathroom to pee. Maybe she'd washed her face and used her special facial moisturizer that sat near the left-hand sink. Then perhaps she'd smeared a little of the pink-red lipstick, which sat next to the face cream, across her lips. Seth picked up the tube of lipstick off the bathroom vanity and checked the color. It appeared to be a match to what was on the coffee cup. But why the lipstick? Maddy was pretty certain she'd taken a shower right before her death. No lipstick was found on her lips during the autopsy, but it was clearly on the coffee mug. Was she expecting someone? Was he still there, but slept like a neat little mouse? Seth didn't think so. Maybe the coffee was from the night before, but Seth just didn't like that scenario. It just didn't sit right with him. He took one more look around the bathroom and continued with his replay.

Then, after she'd fixed herself up, she'd padded back through the bedroom to go make herself coffee. Seth did this now, making his way out of the bathroom and through the bedroom. He walked back down the stairs and entered the kitchen. She had most likely let the dog out first thing. Seth checked the backyard. Sure enough, it was fenced in. So she had let the dog out, then made herself coffee—one cup of coffee from the Keurig machine, which sat on the counter next to the full-sized Mr. Coffee stainless steel coffee maker. He checked the Keurig. There was a single used coffee pod left in the machine.

While the dog peed in the backyard, she drank the coffee quickly, simply for the influx of much needed caffeine, then set the cup in the sink. Next she walked across the room, the front of her light green summer robe sliding open as she opened the door to let the dog in. And then, right before she closed the door, he was there, shoving her into the room by her shoulders. Then he grabbed her left wrist, pressed his stubbly face hard against her lips, and dug his fingers deep into her right shoulder. Perhaps at first she'd been startled, but then she'd pressed back.

Seth looked at the oak kitchen table and noted that one of its chairs was shoved aside in an unusual way. So she'd pressed back against the kiss, and the two of them had struggled as one to the table, where he'd shoved her down, her legs naturally falling apart, her lipstick now smudged up under her nose, her hair in wild disarray. And as he'd leaned in, pulling at his pants to free himself, she'd laughed wickedly and said, "Trey, honey, wait. Let me just take a shower first."

Shit. No. That was just wrong. Wrong.

So she'd pressed back against the kiss, and the two of them had struggled as one to the table where he'd shoved her down, her legs naturally falling apart, her lipstick now smudged up under her nose, her hair in wild disarray. And as he'd leaned in, pulling at his pants to free himself, she'd laughed wickedly and said, "Trey, honey, I'm too old for kitchen-table sex. Let's go upstairs."

Seth laughed. *Yeah. Riiight.* But somehow, some way, they'd ended up upstairs. Perhaps they'd taken a playful shower together, then stepped from the shower, one blue towel in hand along with the tube of conditioner meant to be used as some sort of kinky lubricant. They'd wiggled their way to the bedroom doorway, and there, dropping the towel and the conditioner, they'd wrestled one another roughly toward the bed. Once there, next to the bed, something had gone terribly wrong.

But the dog leash...or belt...or whatever had made the marks on her neck.... *When had that come in?* "You like it rough, don't you, bitch?" Trey had said, holding the dog leash so that it was folded over itself. He had moved his hands together and then quickly apart, forcing the pieces of leather together. *Snap!* Trey had grinned. *Snap!* The harsh sound had made Florence quiver with anticipation. She'd nodded, her lower lip between her teeth.

Seth rolled his eyes at his own debauchery and laughed again. But really, you just never know. And why not? It wasn't like he hadn't done some pretty intense things with women in his life. A dog leash.... *Why not?* Could be fun—a lot of fun.

Seth frowned, nodded slightly, and looked around the kitchen one more time. Yeah. Maybe.... Why not?

TWENTY-SIX

Two weeks before Flo Loughton's death she sat in her office, the coffee she'd purchased from yet another new coffee shop steaming before her. Her options were shrinking; Syracuse was not that large a city. But it wasn't Stanley she was thinking of; she was thinking about Trey. Rather than concentrating on the contract that glowed before her on her laptop, she was strangely fretting about those Hostess Zingers. She'd chosen the vanilla cake with raspberry icing and coconut. Maybe the vanilla cake with vanilla icing would have been better. Although she had no issues with coconut, a lot of people did. Was Trey one of those coconut-spurning people? He was very kind—very polite. Would he eat the coconut even if he despised coconut, simply out of politeness? She knew he was easily stressed. Would the conflict cause him stress? The last thing she wanted to do was cause him stress.

Flo had heard a lot of talk regarding Trey Barkley. She remembered when his mother was on the board of the Skaneateles Festival. She was a nice enough woman. Then Trey had suddenly come home from Brown, and Annette had disappeared from Skaneateles society. "Her son's gone nuts!" one of the other women on the board had declared. "I always thought he was strange. He used to play with Michael, you know. Weird. Weird little kid." Then at another meeting a short while later when they were supposed to be reviewing the choices for the next summer's musicians: "Did you hear? Did you hear about Trey Barkley? He was arrested last night. In the P&C. Right in the produce section. He threw tomatoes at the police officers. Tomatoes! Can you imagine?" "Yes. I heard he actually knocked Rob Smiley to the ground." "Poor Annette."

Flo had cleared her throat. "That's very sad," she'd said, "but I really think we should decide between the violinist or the more jazzy pianist."

Flo had never given Trey Barkley much thought. She'd seen him walking dogs and knew who he was, of course, but she could never quite recall his first name. And now here she was, so many years later, wasting her time musing over him and nasty store-bought confections. It was truly a ridiculous thing for her to be thinking about when she should be doing her work. When her secretary came in without knocking, Flo naturally snapped at her. "What? What do you want?"

Connie, only slightly taken aback (she'd worked for Flo a long time), said, "I'm sorry. But Raymond Watson is here. He's insisting that he see you," she continued, not quite hiding the pleasure of her words.

Flo closed her eyes. A little pulse of unpleasantness pushed through her. She had done her best not to dwell on Raymond Watson since she'd seen to his firing less than a month ago. He had deserved to be fired and was lucky that the company hadn't pressed formal charges against him. It had taken her just a day or so to get over the slight trauma of being called a fucking bitch in front of a handful of people who had worked with Raymond. The CEOs of the company had been grateful and paid her well for stepping in and taking over the nasty duty of disclosing to

Raymond that his thievery had been discovered. She'd found out since then that the man not only had a wife and a girlfriend but also three kids, two vacation homes, two dogs, and four vintage Jaguars, which he maintained with a passion. She'd been forced to hear all the sordid details of this man's life while she sat in at the most recent board meeting of the company. He'd been well liked, even respected. He'd played golf every week with many of the board members. He'd gone to the weddings of their children. He'd attended their holiday parties. Some had even vacationed with Raymond and his wife in one or both of their vacation homes. They'd gone to his children's graduation parties, ridden in his vintage cars, shared stories around his dining room table.... The board was more traumatized by his corporate thieving than she'd been.

"He's insisting he sees you," said Connie.

Her immediate reaction was to refuse, but then Florence Loughton sighed with resolve. She would not allow herself to be intimidated. He wasn't the first man, nor likely the last, to call her a fucking bitch. Flo smiled grimly toward Connie and said, "Then by all means, send him in."

It had been less than a month since she'd seen Raymond Watson. He was not quite the man Flo remembered. He was unshaven, his clothing disheveled. His eyes were wide and red-rimmed. She might have felt a measure of sympathy toward him if it weren't for the fact that he was leaning over her desk, spraying his alcohol-laced droplets her way as he screamed almost incoherently. What was Connie thinking? Did Connie hate her that much? The situation obviously called for security; he never should have been allowed in the building, much less into Flo's private office. Flo hit the intercom. "Connie, get security in here! Now!"

It was after they'd dragged Raymond Watson away, after Connie had apologized with a certain smugness, after Flo was left alone in her big office that looked over downtown Syracuse, that Flo sat watching her hands shake, feeling the loss of all that she'd ever lost descending upon her. Feeling more alone than she'd ever felt, she made the uncustomary movement of putting her face in her hands. Fighting off tears, she was quite certain that she'd made a terrible error—she most certainly should have chosen the Zingers with vanilla icing over the ones with raspberry icing and coconut.

TWENTY-SEVEN

Annette Barkley entered the large, crowded courtroom right as the bailiff said, "People against Trey Barkley."

The last time she'd been in court was two years ago after his arrest regarding the tomato incident. That had been a different judge, a smaller room, less people. The judge had looked up from the papers he was holding in his hand and had said, "Now let me get this straight. This is a second-degree assault charge?"

The prosecuting attorney, perhaps already realizing that he was in trouble, had cleared his throat. "Yes, your honor."

The judge frowned and looked down at the papers a moment. "And the assault weapons were…let me see…." He looked up again at the prosecuting attorney. "Tomatoes?"

"You'll see on page two of the arrest report that a banana was also involved."

The judge raised his eyebrows. Annette glanced at Asher, whose mouth was twitching toward amusement. She bit her lower lip just as the judge smiled. "Mr. McLean, are you making a mockery of my court?"

Ash ran his fingers across his mouth. The prosecuting attorney stood a little taller. "No, your honor." He paused a moment and said, "Your honor, in all due respect, the assault was against an officer of the law."

The judge nodded in acquiescence. "Was anyone injured?"

"You'll see on page three of the police report that the stock boy, Robert Smiley, suffered from a sprained wrist when he slid and fell during the incident."

"From the tomato or the banana?" asked the judge.

Ash cleared his throat to mask a laugh and said, "Your honor, may I interject here?"

"By all means, Mr. Kadaji. Please do."

"Your honor, it is well documented by this court that my client, Mr. Barkley, suffers from a long history of mental illness."

Annette looked at her son. He was bent over, his hands visibly shaking. As if he sensed her eyes were on him, and without looking up, he moved his hands to his lap.

"This was clearly a case of medication failure," Ash continued. "My client, being in a delusional state, felt that he was under immediate danger when the police arrived. He was only protecting himself."

"But why were the police called to begin with?" the judge asked.

"My client was causing no harm to anyone. He was simply talking in the produce section of the store in what people felt was an excessive manner. When he failed to leave the store when asked to do so, the store manager called the police. This only intensified the situation. The throwing of the tomatoes," Ash glanced at the prosecuting attorney, "and yes, one banana, notwithstanding, my client's actions were never threatening. I have here documentation from my client's doctor and from his caseworker that he is in treatment, taking medication, working, and contributing to society in a positive way." He held out the papers. The bailiff stepped forward and brought them to the judge. Ash gave the judge a few moments to glance over them before he went on. "My client never intended to harm anyone. Considering the medical origin of this unfortunate incident, I move to dismiss."

The judge looked at the prosecuting attorney. "Mr. McLean, do you have anything to add?"

"Yes. I have here the hospital records from Mr. Smiley stating that his wrist injury was due to his fall." He handed over the documents.

"Your honor," said Ash, "Mr. Smiley's injury occurred while my client was being forcefully removed from the store. Mr. Smiley fell on his own accord simply because he failed to watch where he was walking. Out of goodwill on my client's part, all medical bills associated with this minor sprain have been paid by my client. The charges of second-degree assault are ludicrous. I move to dismiss."

The judge frowned. "Granted. The defendant is released. But, Mr. Barkley," the judge waited until Trey's head came up slightly, "I don't want to see you back here again. Do you understand?" Trey nodded. "Now can we please move along to the next case?"

But this room, this arrest, this judge, and the words "People against Trey Barkley" brought up a whole other kind of fear in Annette Barkley as she made her way into the courtroom. As soon as the words "People against Trey Barkley" were uttered, they immediately brought her son into the room. He was handcuffed like a criminal, his face pale, his hair disheveled. He had a trapped-wild-animal look to his eyes. He looked deranged. He looked totally deranged. She found Asher sitting near the front of the room and caught his eye. *My God!* she mouthed. Asher frowned and turned from her before she could add, *You have to help him!* She just stood there, not sure what she should do. Where was Jack? Jack had promised he'd try to be there. She looked around, then turned back to the door as it opened. It was not Jack but some scurvy-looking character—someone who looked like they belonged there. The entire room was filled with such people. Even most of the attorneys were a scary bunch.

She'd dressed carefully after she'd received the call from Ash that he'd managed to arrange Trey's bail bond hearing for that Monday morning. She wore a simple, straight, off-white mid-calf summer skirt with a teal, silk short-sleeve blouse and a matching paisley silk scarf. It was very much on the conservative side relative to most of her wardrobe. Her shoes were off-white ballerina slippers; she just couldn't tolerate high heels under any circumstances. But even with her dress-down shoes, she looked like a bride relative to the rest of the people who filled the small courtroom.

Asher was one of the few exceptions as he stood up and stepped to the front of the courtroom. He was immaculately dressed in a gray silk suit, light blue shirt, and striped, dark blue tie. His dark hair was cut neatly and combed so that the gentlest of bangs covered half his upper forehead. She watched his profile as he joined Trey. They stood before the judge. To their right stood a short bald man who must have been the prosecuting attorney. He looked hot and slightly flustered, especially relative to Ash's cool, crisp demeanor.

The place was packed and pulsing with stress. Annette could feel the stress down to her core. Even though words were spoken in whispers, the room was noisy with the shuffle of humans, the air hot and stale. She'd been there for less than a minute, but already her head was aching and her chest was constricting. Someone to her right coughed harshly, causing her to jump. Her eyes shifted toward the sound just in time to catch the individual as he hacked up a notable green glob, which he studied with considerable interest as it lay in a wadded-up tissue in his hand. She groaned slightly and shifted her eyes away and back to Ash, who now stood next to Trey and was whispering in his ear.

Where? Where was Jack? Then Ash's dark eyes found her and saw her distress. The way his eyes softened along with the gentle tilt of his head, telling her to come forward, caused her throat to tighten and her eyes to fill with tears. She didn't quite make it to the front before the bailiff was saying something. "We waive the reading," was what she thought she heard Ash say. Then Ash and the district attorney were up at the bench near the judge. Papers were being shifted around. The judge said something that Annette didn't quite catch. Then there was a quick, confusing exchange between the two lawyers and the judge. "Notices." "One-ninety-fifty is being served," the DA said. "Cross one-ninety-fifty," said Ash. The door of the courtroom opened; it wasn't Jack. The door shut with a harsh click. Annette stepped a few feet closer, straining to hear. Then there was a brief barrage from the prosecuting attorney, something about past priors, the seriousness of the crime, proven instability of the accused.

Annette tried to see Trey's face, tried to catch his eye, but he was fixed forward, his face tilted toward his chest, his hands pulled rudely back behind his back—his tan-covered back. No one ever looked good in that shade of tan.

"The prosecution recommends the accused be held without bail."

Without bail? Annette shook her head repeatedly yet didn't brush at the tears that were now running down her face. She took a few steps closer to the judge. Then Ash was talking, but she just couldn't make out his words.

The judge was frowning, and the next thing she knew he looked right at her and said, "Bail is set at five-hundred thousand." Then it was apparently over—over so fast that Annette never did quite make it to the front.

Ash whispered a few quick words in Trey's ear, and then the officer was leading him away—leading her son away before Annette had had a chance to say one word or simply look him in the eye. "Trey," she called. "Trey. I love you! Trey!" And then he was gone. He'd never looked her way.

What? What had just happened? "Ash. Ash?"

Ash turned from the bench, shoved papers back into his briefcase, looked up at her, and smiled grimly. Then he stepped her way, took her elbow gently, and led her from that godforsaken hell hole.

"The bail is doable, right?"

Annette looked at Ash as they stood in the walkway of the courthouse. She leaned in, resting one hand on his arm, trying to catch his words, trying to quell the wave of lightheadedness that threatened her stability. "What? What?"

Ash blew out a puff of air in exasperation. "The five-hundred thousand. You guys can come up with that?"

"Trey didn't kill anyone, Ash."

Asher sighed deeply. "That's a bit beside the point right now, Annette. The first business is to get Trey out of here. Right? Are you with me? Hello? Is anybody home?"

Annette couldn't help it; her eyes overflowed with tears. Why did he always have to be so mean? How was it that he was even her friend when he was first and foremost a total ass? She removed her hand from his arm, teetered slightly, and replied, "Yes. I'll have to talk to Jack, but I'm sure we can get the money."

"Good." He turned away from her. "That's the priority. Get Trey out of here. ASAP."

And as customary as his lack of response was to her tears, Annette still, after all their years of knowing each other, longed for him to soothe her—for him to reach out, pull her to his chest, run his fingers through her hair, and tell her that everything would be okay—longed for him to want her, and for him to remember, like she remembered, that one moment when he'd almost loved her.

TWENTY-EIGHT

Jack Barkley handed over the five-hundred thousand dollars in the form of a cashier's check on Tuesday morning. He'd had to pay a hefty penalty for cashing in some of their stocks; it wasn't like he had half a million in cash stashed under his mattress. Here he was, a fifty-four-year-old thoracic surgeon who'd always done everything he was supposed to do, who'd never stolen as much as a pack of gum or screamed incoherently at his parents, whose biggest lifetime mistakes were wrapping his father's Mercedes around that oak tree at seventeen and jumping into the whole dot-com debacle of the late nineties, who'd married the girl next door, who'd stayed in the area for college, who'd stayed in his hometown, who'd given money every year to the local animal shelter, and who'd always returned his library books on time. So here he was, this decent, law-abiding human being, standing in the Justice Center handing over his hard-earned cash to get his son out of jail—and not even for the first time, and God help him, perhaps not for the last time. Unless, of course, his son was convicted for murder; then this might certainly be the last chance to bail him out of jail.

The bail cashier handed him his receipt, which Jack folded

carefully and put in his wallet. Then Jack passed over the change of clothes he'd brought for his son. He was told to have a seat and wait. He sat in one of the chairs, closed his eyes, and sighed. At twenty-seven he was not so sure he'd been ready to get married, especially with years of surgical residency ahead of him, a thirteen-year-old Chevy Vega as his only source of transportation, living with six other guys in a rat nest of a house near Syracuse University, tons of student loans, and doubts—he'd had tons of doubts. His love for Annette was like tiny tentacles entwined with his healthy cells; it was a part of him that couldn't be destroyed without compromising his health.

"Don't do it," Ash had warned.

"But I love her. It's what she wants."

Ash had rolled his eyes and refilled both their shot glasses with the cheap blended whiskey he'd bought to celebrate Jack's completion of his medical degree. "That chick I fucked last night…." Ash closed his eyes and put on his best dreamy, reminiscent face. "Oh, God, Jack!" He opened his eyes and grinned. "To think I'd never be able to go back there without some fucked-up guilt all over me. That's all I'm saying."

"Yeah, well, I'm not quite the man whore you are." Jack took the shot glass and knocked it down with one quick, unpleasant gulp.

Ash laughed. "Sure you are. You're just a little ill right now."

It was Jack's turn to roll his eyes. "So you're never going to get married?" Jack asked.

Ash scrunched up his face, twisted his lips to one side in thought, picked up his glass, and downed the whiskey. "Nope."

"Not even once?"

Ash laughed. "It's gonna be either zero or seven. And zero's a lot cheaper."

Jack nodded his head. "True."

Ash had stayed true to that declaration. The longest he'd ever been with one woman was three months, and even then Jack had his doubts about Ash's exclusivity. The fact was, the closest thing Ash had to a wife was Annette. The closest thing he had to a family was Jack's family…which is why Annette and Jack both loved and hated Ash. Family: when love and hate become the same thing, and it doesn't even matter what you call it anymore.

"So I did her," Asher declared one month before their high school graduation.

"Did who?"

"Last night." Ash took a long drag from the joint and passed it Jack's way. Once Jack had freed the joint from his friend's hand, Ash used that hand to free his face of his long black strands of hair, pulling them into a ponytail and then releasing the smoke from his lungs in one blue puff. "Annette. Popped her like a balloon."

Then almost before the joint hit the floor, Ash was wiping at the blood coming from his nose, and Jack was on him. "She's like our sister, you fucking moron!" Jack slammed another punch home, this time making connection with Ash's jaw, blood spouting from Ash's lip. Ash started fighting back, and they proceeded to beat the shit right out of each other.

Jack had found Annette in her bedroom at her parents' house. Her eyes were irritated, her face puffy. Jack had never seen her so tragic; she must have spent hours crying over what Ash had done to her. With one look at Jack's torn-up face she started all over again, like a slime-filled faucet. "He did that to you?" she wept.

"He did *that* to *you*," he stated. And then he was there, next to her on her bed, trying to lend some comfort, his hands somehow stumbling across her breasts, her hands somehow pulling at his jeans and tugging at his shirt, her panties slightly blood-stained, all of him somehow free and searching through what Ash had left behind.

"I'll never know," she'd whispered in his ear as he pushed harder than was necessary into her body. "I'll never know who the father is. If I get pregnant, I'll never know."

And even that hadn't knocked him back to reality, because he was in the thick of a battle he would not allow himself to lose—a battle that, in the end, he'd clearly won.

Or had he?

He'd married her, years later, Ash standing at his side as the trails of Annette's white gown swept across the grass of the park, her face aglow with victory, their friends and family looking on, his future father-in-law staring him down in a challenging, friendly sort of way, his mother mopping at her face, his father looking proud. But right before Annette had reached them, Jack had turned to Asher. He had turned his eyes to his best friend. With the slightest tilt of his face, Ash had asked him, "Are you sure? Are you fucking sure?"—a question, even all these years later, he never did quite answer.

And had he known then that twenty-nine years later he would be sitting in the Onondaga County Justice Center waiting for his mentally ill son—the son who had virtually put him through every conceivable level of hell—would he have answered that question right there and then? "Yes! I'm sure! I'm sure that this is *not* what I want!" And then he and Ash would have run like hell away from the wedding, away from Annette, away from a certain future—run right on across the street to Morris's and gotten out-of-their-minds drunk.

"Dad?"

Jack looked up at his child who he loved and hated, pitied and admired. He felt his face turn into something soft. "Hey, Treyman," he said as he stood. He took three steps toward his son. "Are you ready? Are you ready to go home?" Trey nodded his head but seemed unable to take another step. Jack placed one hand on Trey's back with little effect. He then placed his entire right arm across his son's back, gave him a little shove, and guided him firmly out of the building and into the car.

TWENTY-NINE

Annette brought up the last load of her son's laundry and set it on his bed. She looked around the room with satisfaction. She was content with her decision. Regardless of what Jack thought or how he believed Trey might respond, she'd spent the last three days digging out her son's room. She knew, *she just knew*, that Trey still longed for neatness, still preferred order, as he had as a child. She also knew that he now lacked the organizational skills necessary to maintain his fastidiousness. Rather than remain frustrated, he'd chosen the opposite—at least as far as his bedroom was concerned. He'd just let everything go to hell. Jack was wrong; she was not doing this for herself. She truly believed that Trey's stress would be less if he returned to find an ordered room, his clothes clean, the dust and cobwebs gone, and a smell of something other than death.

She opened his closet and hung the remainder of his long-sleeve dress shirts. She placed them first according to brand and then according to color, just as he'd insisted on when he'd been a boy. It wasn't until after his third hospitalization that he started dropping whatever he had been wearing to the floor, where it stayed until he was forced to pick things up, do a little laundry, or otherwise be naked. In spite of the way he now treated his attire, it amused Annette that he insisted on wearing only certain brands of clothes: Express, 7 For All Mankind, Converse, anything officially sanctioned by the Mets, what he considered vintage T-shirts, Jack Wells…. His response to the Armani shirt she'd given him last Christmas should have made her angry, but she'd simply returned the shirt. She could have sworn Armani was one of his brands. She'd been wrong.

She placed his neatly folded boxers into his dresser and laid his socks out in flat rows, again according to color. She opened the next drawer down and carefully added the last of his jeans in a neat pile. She then stepped back and took in the high, narrow windows on either side of his desk. She'd already pulled the blinds open on the one, but the other was still half covered with black construction paper. Should she remove the black paper?

No.

No. She should not.

Annette took one more visual tour of the room. She walked over to the left window and pulled the blind shut—just as she had found it. She nodded her head, then rested her eyes on the photo on Trey's desk. She had put it there after finding it in one of Trey's drawers. She reached over and picked up the old photo of Trey and Samuel. It was the one with the go-cart, snapped right before the race. They'd come in second, which was pretty darn good. Trey had been so excited—you could see it in the photo. He was grinning from ear to ear, but not quite looking at the camera. Instead, his head was turned slightly, his shining eyes on Samuel. She set it back on the desk and shifted it slightly so that it could be easily seen from Trey's bed.

"I really think you should try to come home," she'd said to Samuel on the phone the day prior. "I know. I know you're busy, but Trey could really use your support. He'll be released any day now...." She'd nodded, rubbing at her face with her free hand. "Sure. Sure. I understand. Well, try. Okay? I love you."

Annette sighed. She sat down at Trey's desk, taking in each of the items that she'd left sitting on it after she'd removed the obvious trash and unnecessary clutter. His notebook; his favorite pen; his laptop; the last two issues of *Dog World*; his childhood Mets desk lamp; an organic chemistry textbook; a lopsided, poorly painted ceramic mug he'd made in elementary school, which was filled with pencils and pens; the gold watch that his grandfather—her father—had given him; an old bumper sticker with only the word BROWN in dark brown lettering; an open metal box filled with an assortment of cuff links.... She once again picked up the photo of Trey and Samuel. It seemed to belong on the desk, yet she'd found it in his drawer. Like the black construction paper, there were some things she needed to respect and leave well enough alone. She pulled open his bottom desk drawer where she had originally found the photo, then replaced it on top of a stack of papers. She slid the drawer closed, the photo now safely back in hiding, but something had caught her eye right before the drawer had fully closed. She paused, looked around the room as if to make sure no one was watching her, then reopened the drawer and lifted the pile of papers out of the way.

"What in the world...?" she said. "What is all this stuff?" She carefully placed the pile of papers she was holding on the desk and peered into the drawer. Her hand went out and picked up a small white gift box. She opened the lid. Nestled in a white square of cotton was a set of lovely silver earrings. Odd. She put the lid back on, set it back down, and picked up a longer cream-colored gift box. In it was a silky black scarf with tiny threads of silver running through it. Another box contained a chunky silver necklace. Another held a funky wooden bracelet. Gifts. All gifts for women. She felt a sliver of fear sweep through her. Why? Why were they here? Was there someone in his life whom she didn't know about? Were these things he'd purchased for some covert woman? For Flo Loughton? What sort of secrets did her son have? Did she really even know him—what he was, who he was, what acts he was and was not capable of? Her hands began to shake.

"Oh, God," she said. She put back the box with the bracelet and reached for a white bag with zebra stripes. She pulled the tissue paper aside and found a perfect tiny box. Black. And on the box was a perfect orange rose—her favorite. She held the tiny box.

Her favorite.

"Oh, God."

It was for her. All of it was for her. Each and every item was something she might have picked out for herself. She set the box gently down and rested her head in her hands. It wasn't all that long before she was gently weeping.

She had never been an exceptional mother.

THIRTY

The first thing Trey did Tuesday when he got home was finish taping the black construction paper over his bedroom windows. He wasn't all that surprised when he walked into his room and was struck with order and the smell of lavender Refresh. But even in her delusional state, his mother could see what was necessary; the one thing she'd left untouched in his bedroom was the destruction of the windows. If ever he needed to protect himself, it was now. It was quite evident that security had been breached; facts were bleeding out all over the place. He'd let things get out of control. Shit was going down, and somehow Mrs. Loughton was unwittingly involved. He'd allowed for complacency. Complacency begets Tragedy. Tragedy begets Punishment. Therefore, Punishment is Tragic.

$C \Rightarrow T \Leftrightarrow P$.

Mrs. Loughton had received the ultimate punishment. That was fact. It was reasonable that he react defensively. When he was done with the last window, he dug through his desk drawer until he located his roll of black electric tape. He removed the old tape and carefully re-taped the five layers of black electric tape over the camera lens on his laptop, then cut tiny circles of tape and secured them over the tiny lens on his cell phone. He placed a large black sweatshirt over the TV in his room, but then, not satisfied, he undid the cable connection, unplugged the TV, and put the unit outside his bedroom door. Then he carefully taped over the end of the cable connection, taped over all the unused electrical outlets in the room, and taped over the lighted face of his alarm clock.

Now that his room was somewhat secure—the only light coming from the dull 25-watt bulb in the lamp on his desk—Trey sat on his bed, leaned against the headboard, and wrapped his arms across his chest. His hands brushed against the soft, worn-out cotton of his T-shirt, and he actually managed a smile. His vintage 1977 Han Solo Star Wars T-shirt…. Stephanie had been with him when he'd found it. Three weeks and five days before the end. He remembered because it had been her birthday. They were actually shopping for her in a crowded vintage clothing store near the university. He'd offered to let her have the T-shirt, but luckily she'd refused, opting instead for a silky, flapper-style red dress, which tragically he never got the chance to see her wear.

She held the dress up in front of her. The silky material settled itself into her body. Even though she had her winter coat on, the overall effect was still breathtaking. "You like?" she asked.

"Very nice."

She smiled, then twirled around, the silk of the dress flaring out, her fine dark hair sweeping the air. She stopped, everything settling down except the way he was feeling. He was flying. "I love you," he declared, his voice too squeaky, too loud, causing a general disruption, eyes turning his way. And to say it there, that way, for the very first time, in front of strangers and vintage clothing to which the DNA of so many dead clung…. Stephanie's smile was gone. She turned red. From anger? From embarrassment? From excitement? From what? Then there was nothing but stillness and the smell of moth balls, dust, and his own sweat, which seemed to be seeping from every pore. He said it quieter. "I love you." He couldn't help himself. It was as if the words had a life of their own—a life he had no control over. "I love you."

She turned from him, her eyes sweeping the room, and he knew that every eye in the place was on him, but he didn't look away from her.

"I love you," he said again.

"Stop," she said. Then she was there, brushing his face with her lips. "I love you too, if it'll make you shut up."

Then he knew that every eye in the place was shining with happiness—for him, for Stephanie, for humanity…for LOVE.

"I love you." He whispered it this time, and she slapped him gently.

"Stop," she said.

So he did.

LOVE. Three weeks and five days of LOVE.

He felt again the worn-down softness of the T-shirt. He just knew his mom had thought hard about, maybe even agonized over, which shirt to give his dad to bring to the jail. There was something sadly worth admiring there. He rubbed the thin cotton and closed his eyes. He hadn't truly slept for four nights—ever since the day they took him to jail, which was Friday, and now it was Tuesday evening. He hadn't eaten either, for that matter. He had finally agreed to eat some cellophane-wrapped crackers and drink soda, both from the vending machine, but there was no way he was willing to eat the food or drink the water they'd brought him. Even when Franklin, the case worker who was assigned to him, tasted it all first, and even when Asher came with a signed affidavit stating that the food was not poisoned, Trey knew better than to risk his life.

Despite his best efforts not to do so, he'd fallen asleep a few times over the past four days, wrapped up in the blanket they'd given him, only to wake up from the most awful dreams. Mrs. Loughton sat at her kitchen table, dressed in that same bathing suit she'd worn in the sailboat photo. She laughed as she passed him a plate of blood-raspberry coconut Zingers. His hand was shaking as he extended it forward. Then, almost reaching the closest rectangular cake, he screamed as the slices of the cake parted, jumped off the plate, and sunk teeth into his flesh. Blood-raspberry juices flowed from what was left of his hand, which was now just a useless stump.

Mrs. Loughton laughed. "Have another, dear."

Hector, dead, floated in a sea of chocolate.

Mrs. Loughton's lips parted as she pressed her face against Trey's.

Hector wagged his tail as he held the leash between his teeth.

"I'm going to have to bathe him."

The pool of blood-raspberry liquid slipped across the hardwood floor.

Mrs. Loughton's head was thrown back, her hair frozen in the wind, her ass dangerously close to the water.

"Did you help her out there—with that loneliness?"

Hector bounced and bounced and bounced.

The next thing Trey knew it was morning; he could tell from the tiny beam of light that streamed through the air of his bedroom like a miniature searchlight. It came from one tiny hole in one of the pieces of construction paper; the beam could only exist due to the way the early morning light rose over Skaneateles Lake and hit their house. He crawled out of bed and groaned from the achy stiffness of his joints. He retrieved his electric tape, pulled his chair closer to the window, climbed atop the chair, and destroyed the beam with one well-placed piece of tape.

He recoiled as the light from the hallway slapped his retinas, and as he padded to the bathroom, he considered what he might be able to use as a bedside urinal.

Once in the bathroom, after he'd peed and brushed his teeth, he considered the shower. He hadn't showered in five days. "Ehh," he finally said, then turned on the shower and stripped off the Star Wars T-shirt and shorts. He dropped his boxers to the floor, stepped into the shower, and gasped as the hot water hit his body. He adjusted the temp and reached for his shampoo.

Mrs. Loughton had taken a shower. Five days ago she'd taken a shower—slipped her light green summer robe from around her body, dropped her pink silky panties on the bathroom floor, stepped into her shower, and then, once clean, had stepped onto the bathmat. Her perfectly painted toenails had left just a hint of indentation on the bathmat as she'd stepped away and reached for the light blue towel. The odor of her primping had filled the room. And that odor—that odor of a perfectly cleaned Mrs. Loughton—filled Trey's senses even now, sending through him a jolt of jagged panic and then deep sadness.

"Keep it together. Just keep it together."

When he was done, he stepped from the shower, dried off, and redressed in his boxers, shorts, and Star Wars T-shirt. It was now necessary that he go downstairs and get something to eat. It was also Wednesday. Like it or not, he had to deal with his job. He'd already missed Monday and Tuesday, his mother putting in to place his emergency backup plan. There were two other dog walkers in Skaneateles—hard to believe for a town that size. The three of them had an agreement: each would cover for the others if an illness or other such emergency should arise, and with that agreement was the strict understanding that stealing each other's clients would be just totally messed up.

Trey sighed as he stood in front of the mirror and pushed his fingers through his wet hair. There was no reason not to go to work. Of course, he had one less client now. One less Mrs. Loughton…. One less dog…. Hector. No one seemed to be able to tell him what had happened to Hector.

Trey slunk downstairs, careful of the squeaky stairs, and made his way into the kitchen. He would force himself to eat one of the bagels his mother had left out for him. They were the cinnamon raison bagels he liked so much—the ones that you could only get at Dunkin' Donuts, which meant that someone, probably his father, had made the eight-mile trip to the closest one in Auburn. First he poured a cup of coffee from the pot she'd left warming in the coffee maker. He added a healthy dose of half and half and then two full teaspoons of sugar. He took a sip. Not satisfied, he then added another half teaspoon of sugar. He nodded his head with approval as he retested. Perfect. Trey then removed one of the pre-sliced bagels from the plastic Ziploc bag and spread on cream cheese in one thick layer on both sides of the bagel. He pushed the two pieces together until the white goodness eased down the sides. He took his time, sitting on the kitchen stool, licking the excess away. The house was quiet, his mother gratefully leaving him alone, remaining inside her studio with the door shut. He knew she was in there, and he knew she knew he was there. Was it possible that she'd just leave him alone?

It was after his breakfast was eaten, after he'd rinsed his coffee mug and placed it in the dishwasher, after he'd resealed the bag of bagels and put away the cream cheese and the half and half, while he was adjusting his Mets cap on top of his head, readying for departure, that she suddenly appeared. "Where are you off to?" she asked.

"My job." He gave his cap one more minor tweak.

"I'm sure Rhonda will walk for you again."

Rhonda: she'd like nothing better than to break the rules and steal some of his clients; she was always breaking the rules. He'd once seen her walk away from a pile of shit as if it weren't her responsibility. There was just no excuse for that. None.

"I'm sure you must be really tired," his mother continued.

"Nope." He checked his cell phone, then dropped it in the pocket of his shorts before he turned and looked his mother in the eye for the first time since he'd been arrested. The dark circles beneath her eyes made her raccoon-like; it was necessary that he look away.

"So you're feeling okay?" she continued.

"Yup." He motioned toward the bagels. "Thanks. Thanks for the bagels. Dad get them for me?"

"Yes. He grabbed them before he left for an early surgery."

Trey retrieved the cell phone from his pocket and checked it one more time. "Well," he said. He dropped it back into the pocket.

"There're also muffins. Blueberry. I made them yesterday when Ash told me you'd be home." Her hand came up and pressed against his face lightly. His immediate reaction was to bring his hand up and forcibly remove hers from his face, but when his fingers touched the cool softness of her skin—the powdery clay feeling like childhood—his hand lingered on top of hers. "Cool." He stepped away from her touch as he moved to depart. "Thanks."

"They're in the breadbox."

"Okay."

"Take one with you. I can put one in a bag for you."

He stopped. It was a long moment that he stood there, his back to his mother. Then he said without turning, "Okay."

He turned and watched as she moved quickly to the breadbox, taking out one of the muffins and placing it in a small paper bag.

Her back was to him when she asked, "Are you afraid?"

Trey's mind stopped for a moment. Everything stopped: the voices buzzing in his head, the sound of the refrigerator, the ticking of the clock in the hallway, the crackling of the paper bag as his mother folded over its edges, his breathing, his blinking, any possible movement of his tongue…. And then, just as clear as day, he said, "Terrified. I'm fucking terrified."

She nodded her head without turning. "Me too, baby. Me too." She turned. There was a flicker of something almost dangerous in her eyes. "I don't need to say it, right? How I feel about these ridiculous charges?"

He looked her in the eye. "Nope."

Annette nodded. "Okay, then." She handed him the bag that contained the muffin.

"Thanks," he said.

Once in town, Trey made it as far as Doug's Fish Fry before he noticed that everyone was looking at him. He'd thought he'd picked up a slight vibe as he'd walked along West Genesee, but now that he was on Jordan, it was much more than a vibe—it was a full-blown visual hazing. Every one of them was silently saying the same thing: "You crazy murderer. Who let you out to roam the street?" Then the words were in his head: *Murderer! Murderer!* He shoved up his sunglasses and pulled his baseball cap further down over his face, but that just made his guilt more apparent. They were going to arrest him and take him back there. "Citizen's arrest! You scummy little fucker! Just walking the street after killing Mrs. Loughton. Murderer!" Or worse: "Just kill him!" The sharp pain of a rock. "Let him who is without sin cast the first stone." But where was Jesus? Not there. Not there when he needed him. Another rock. Then a million rocks. A bloody pile of gooey rock.

Oh shit. Oh shit! Keep it together. Just keep it together!

THIRTY-ONE

Annette Barkley was more than a little surprised that Wednesday morning when she found Trey fed, showered, and determined. She was relieved beyond words that he was eating, but when he'd answered her question of "Where are you off to?" she'd felt conflicted.

She was an honest, decent person. She'd always paid her taxes. She'd never belittled her husband or children—at least not publicly. She'd always been a good neighbor, bringing over dinners to those who were battling cancer, offering to water plants of those going off to the Caribbean, volunteering for this committee or that fundraiser, and shuffling other people's children around to soccer practice and little league when her boys were small. She'd contributed financially to this cause or that benevolent activity, helped sponsor the Skaneateles Festival and Dickens's Christmas, and supported the building of the new firehouse—even if it did seem a little unnecessary. All her life, she'd been a contributing and positive addition to The Village. But now that her ill son had been accused of this terrible crime, she suddenly found herself in the same position she'd found herself in six years ago when Trey had come home from his first hospitalization—judged, ostracized, and pitied. Only this time the judgment, the ostracism, and the pity were all tenfold.

"My job."

She'd felt parental joy and pride, worry and admiration. Her son was stepping up to the plate, keeping his life intact despite the unfair situation in which he found himself. And she felt some sort of horror. What would people say? What would they think when they saw her accused son walking the streets a free man, when all over the village, all over the local and even state news her son was being judged a murderer? And how would it affect her? What would they now be saying about Annette Barkley? Artist, benefactor, wife of a doctor, lifetime resident of The Village, mother of a son who was a resident at Johns Hopkins, and mother of another son who was a crazy murderer? What would they say now when they saw that she was letting her murderer child roam free? It didn't matter that everyone who knew her and her son knew that she knew in her heart of hearts that Trey would never be capable of such a thing. Regardless, it just wasn't proper village etiquette to allow the accused to roam the streets. So Annette Barkley's innate reaction to her son's statement—*My job*—had been to argue against the idea. It wasn't strictly for appearance's sake.

Now here it was less than one hour later, and he was back, looking white as a sheet and shaking—her every mental prediction apparently having come true. "I'm so sorry, Trey." He couldn't look her in the eye as he shuffled quickly by on his way back to his room. "I'll call Rhonda. Don't you worry," Annette called, but he was already gone.

THIRTY-TWO

Seth Wooley walked into the house Wednesday evening prepared for the assault. He received exactly what he was expecting. In one mad explosion of tongues, claws, yips, and whines, he was nearly knocked over by canine enthusiasm. "Okay. Okay. Everybody settle down." He pushed his way to the kitchen table and set down the two bags of groceries. "Settle down!" he said with more force. But, as always, it was a good three or more minutes before he got the dogs calmed to some sort of manageable level and was able to search for his mother. He heard the TV and headed in that direction.

"Ma," he called as he passed from the kitchen—a trail of pooches at his heels—down the hallway, and into the den. "Ma?"

Other than the light from the TV, the den was dark. It was only 6:00 p.m., the sun still high, but she had the drapes snuggly closed. "Ma, I wish you wouldn't sit in the dark." There was the slightest sound of acknowledgement, and Seth felt, as he always felt, that odd combination of relief and disappointment: his mother was still alive. He stepped over to the window and pulled the drapes open. The light streamed in, bringing the dingy, dirty reality fully into view. It was worse than normal—much worse.

the chocolate debacle

The odor of dog seemed to increase as he took in the visual insult of the room. The dull tan carpet hadn't been vacuumed since the last time he'd been there. Every surface was layered in dust and fine puffs of dog fur. Dirty dishes littered the coffee table. A fly struggled on its back in a glass of some unknown liquid, moving without effect in hopeless circles around a small island of mold. A white Styrofoam container was chewed to tiny white pieces near the TV. Wet spots—no doubt, dog piss—dotted the carpet. A pile of shit sat near a withered potted plant. Newspapers and magazines layered the floor, some wrinkled with yellow dampness. One of the dogs, a large, brown mangy thing, sat near Seth's feet, wagging its tail, its face turned up toward Seth, thick drool dripping from its mouth and onto the carpet. Seth wanted to pull the drapes together and flee, but he blew out a breath with resolve and turned his eyes to his mother. She was now bathed in full sunlight, her right arm poised over her eyes, the flabby skin dripping like icing. "Ma, hasn't Gloria been here to clean the house?"

"I sent her away. She messes with my things."

Seth sighed. "Ma, there's dog shit on the floor." She looked at him blankly. The sunlight caught the cut glass of her highball, which shimmered on the side table. All that was left of the ice were small opaque balls, the liquid now light and harmless. "How you doing, Ma?"

Then her arm came down, and she smiled. She extended her hands his way, and he took the four steps toward her, grasping her soft, boney hands in his. He leaned in and kissed her feathery cheek. She was definitely in need of a bath.

"Hello, my darling boy," she said, patting his face before he moved away. "Have you had your supper?"

"Nope." His eyes strayed toward the nearly empty glass. "Have you?"

She grinned, almost, but not quite, sheepishly. "Just a tiny appetizer while I waited for you."

He nodded softly and returned her grin. "Well, okay then. Let's go throw something together."

Seth picked up the fly-inhabited glass and as many used dishes as he could carry. All six dogs followed along as he balanced the dishes and helped his mother toward the kitchen. She was slowing down, failing quickly, even though she wasn't yet seventy-five. But a hard life usually equaled a fast and furious descent to decrepitude, and his mother, the house he grew up in, even her present pack of mongrels, all were the definition of decrepitude. He did what he could. He came over at least four times a week, paid for a house cleaner twice a month—which was really all he could afford—drove her to all her various doctors and hair appointments, picked up groceries, and provided the never-ending supply of dog food. Hell, he even bought her the steady supply of Jack Daniels, having decided years ago that her drinking was a not stoppable train. But everything he did was quickly becoming not enough. Already what little social life he had was suffering. His only real social activity was poker once a month with the guys and those early morning donut and coffee stops with Zuke. The last real date he'd been on was early in the spring when snow was still on the ground, the air still quite cold, which pretty much matched the disposition of his date.

Just yesterday he'd gone out of his way to take the Loughton dog leash directly to Dr. Maddy Hatcher, hoping for something that was unrealistic if not borderline delusional, because he couldn't quite get that look she'd given him out of his head as she'd looked up from Florence Loughton's body and said, "I'd say…a very intense kiss." He'd entered the medical examiner's office area and found the door to Maddy's office open. She appeared to be knee-deep in paperwork at her desk, and he had a moment to contemplate the knit of her brow before her eyes drifted up his way. He almost imagined he saw some sort of pleasure pass over her face before she frowned slightly and said, "Hello, Detective Wooley."

He'd been known to have an overactive imagination where women were concerned. He'd been burned plenty of times and had learned a few things, so he naturally chose the frown rather than the possible hint of pleasure. He didn't smile as he said, "Dr. Hatcher," feeling defeated, deflated, and angry. He was tired of the whole dating game. Either she was interested or she wasn't, dammit. He took two long steps into the room and placed the plastic bag with the dog leash firmly on her desk. "The Loughton dog leash," he stated. Then she smiled, and his anger almost spilled right out of him. But he checked his irritation and smiled right back at her. He placed both of his hands on her desk, bent over it until he was within one foot of her face, and said, "Come to the Syracuse Chief's game with me next Tuesday."

She sent her Maddy stare his way, and just before he was almost forced to look away, she shrugged and said, "Sure. Okay."

So his first outing with a woman in a very long time was happening in a week. A baseball game. It was something.

He watched his mother refill her tumbler, and he shook his head to her offer of his own. As he pulled out the box of Hamburger Helper from the grocery bag, his mother leaned forward, standing slightly on her toes, the fluid in her glass tilting dangerously to the rim as she peered into the closest bag of groceries. "Seth, my dear boy, did you remember? Did you remember the dog treats?"

THIRTY-THREE

Flo Loughton laughed. Trey smiled slightly, then laughed along with Flo. How long had it been since Flo had enjoyed a good laugh with another human being? Not since before Frank had died, and even then it was rare. It wasn't as if Frank hadn't laughed—and laughed a lot—it was just that it was rare that Flo had found anything as laughable as Frank had found laughable. But still, she'd liked to hear Frank laugh. But hearing Trey laugh brought a whole different kind of pleasure. Maybe it was the pure rareness of the event or the fact that he seemed rather taken aback by his own laughter, which was how Flo often felt—her laughter out of place with her idea of self. And it seemed that she and Trey were doing a fair amount of laughing together over the last few weeks. He was, in spite of his rather flat façade, a very interesting and extremely bright young man.

When the moment of laughter abated, she tore off a tiny corner of the raspberry-iced Zinger—the white interior cream easing onto the plate—and placed the piece between her lips. "What were you studying at Brown?" she asked.

"Organic chemistry."

Flo made a face. "I hated organic chemistry. It's what turned me toward the law."

"Shame," Trey stated. "Organic chemistry *is* law. The basis of everything." Trey licked at his Zinger, easing a little of the white filling out with his tongue, and all anxiety regarding the raspberry-coconut icing eased from Flo's mind.

"I'm glad to see you like coconut," she stated.

"Uh-huh," he nodded.

"Why organic and not inorganic?" she asked.

"Élan vital, or the possibility of such."

Flo frowned. "Élan vital?"

"Yeah. Henri Bergson talks about élan vital in his book *Creative Evolution*, 1907. Did you ever read it?"

"1907." Flo smiled. "No."

"Well," Trey leaned forward with enthusiasm, "élan vital, or vital force, is...you know, the psyche, the spirit, the soul. But even before Bergson, Jöns Jacob Berzelius wrote about vitalism when talking about what differentiates organic from inorganic." Trey wiped at his mouth, knocking loose a crumb that had stuck to his upper lip. "And in spite of the fact that Friedrich Wöhler synthesized organic from inorganic when he created urea in 1828, life has yet to be created from the lifeless."

"Like Frankenstein?" Flo asked.

Trey shook his head. "No. The Frankenstein monster is theoretically possible, right? I mean, the monster was created from chopped–up, living parts—the élan vital present. But try to make him out of stone. Not happening." Trey held out a piece of Zinger, looked at it, popped it in his mouth, and said, "Nonliving becomes living. But how do we define nonliving? Eat a rock, you shit out a rock. Eat a Zinger, it becomes part of what we are."

Flo laughed.

Trey shrugged. "Vitalism is currently quite out of favor, even though disciplines like reiki, acupuncture, and many other techniques used in alternative medicine depend on it. I think élan vital is a finite, measurable entity that has just yet to be measured. It's just a matter of time before someone figures out how to measure it."

Flo smiled. "Perhaps that someone might be Trey Barkley, 2032."

Trey smiled shyly. "Perhaps."

What Flo wanted to ask, but didn't, was if it were possible. There was so much potential in this young man. Was it possible that Trey could return to school someday? How was he really? Did voices still sing in his head? Was he always just moments away from another break? Was walking dogs all he could really handle? What was it like? How did it feel to be considered The Village Idiot, when in fact there was nothing idiotic about Trey Barkley? Flo knew that Trey's presence was only just tolerated, and that toleration stemmed not from some sort of understanding of mental illness, but from some standing respect for this young man's parents and their position in the community. She had always felt indifferent about Trey Barkley, but now she felt this undeniable urge to feed and protect, to covet and enjoy, to dissect and scrutinize. She wanted to know Trey Barkley—know him in every sense of the word—perhaps more than she'd ever wanted to know anyone. And her feelings were basal and exhilarating and inappropriate…and just plain wrong. So, what Flo really wanted to ask, but didn't, was, "How do you feel about me, Trey Barkley? Do you find me nearly as intriguing as I find you?"

THIRTY-FOUR

Annette considered going directly to the DA, but she remembered the way Detective Wooley had shot her a sympathetic glance as they dragged Trey out of the house the night of the initial inquiry. It had been quite unexpected; he'd seemed like such an ass. But then there it was—a look, ever so brief, but deep in its compassion. There was something quite human in him. So she called the sheriff's department to set up a meeting. Seth got right on the phone and told her he'd meet with her anytime. He even offered to come out to the house, but she told him she'd prefer to go there; she wanted to see the place that they'd taken her son that very first night.

"My son's not doing so well," she told him after she'd refused the coffee he'd offered. They sat at a small table in a room off the main area.

"I'm sorry to hear that," he said out of obligation, still managing to sound sincere.

"What do you know about severe mental illness?" she asked.

"Not a lot, I'm afraid."

"Well, that's a shame, considering probably at least half of the people you arrest are suffering from some sort of mental illness."

"Actually, most are drug addicts."

"Drug abusers who are self-treating an undiagnosed, untreated mental illness. Over fifty percent of them."

He concurred with a tilt of his head. "I'm sure you're correct."

They stared at each other for a moment. "My son is a law-abiding, functioning, contributing citizen," she finally said. "Having a mental illness doesn't make him any more likely to be a murderer. If anything, especially in Trey's case, it makes him less likely. He's fragile, easily stressed, and much more likely to withdraw from a conflict than to elicit it."

"Mrs. Barkley, let me assure you that your son's mental illness has nothing, whatsoever, to do with why he was arrested."

"Then why? Every piece of evidence you have can be easily explained. He's never been violent."

Detective Wooley shuffled through some sheets on his desk. After a few seconds, he pulled one free from the pile. "Arrest for assault, 2012. Disturbing the peace and public indecency, 2013."

Annette waved away his comments. "The park arrest...well, that hardly constitutes a tendency to murder. And the other...that was dismissed, Detective Wooley. Trey was ill at that time. You'd throw tomatoes at people too if you thought they were trying to kill you."

"Actually, I'd probably shoot bullets—right out of my gun."

Annette laughed, in spite of herself, and then everything about Detective Wooley seemed to soften.

He laughed also. "Mrs. Barkley, I don't even want to say this, because it's just so darn cliché, but I'm only doing my job. It's up to the DA to prove the case. Not me."

"It's up to you to keep looking. To keep looking for the real killer." Annette put both her hands on the desk and leaned the detective's way. "I don't even want to say this, because it's just so darn cliché, but my son did not kill Florence Loughton."

Detective Wooley tilted his head and suppressed a smile. "And as long as we're talking cliché, the investigation is ongoing. All leads are being fully explored."

The conversation wasn't getting anywhere near where Annette wanted to go. He might as well have been spewing out written lines for a press conference. What she wanted, what she needed, was to get to the soft underbelly of this man's humanity, to give him something that might keep him up at night with doubts, to make him dig a little deeper, to make him see that he was so terribly wrong about her son. But everything she thought to say seemed as if it would only prejudice him more fully against her son: *He cries every day. He hides in the corner of his bedroom. He paces his room for hours. He's threatened to kill himself. Do you not understand how well he's being doing up until this? Do you know how terribly hard it is for him to keep himself sane? Do you know how hard he works? Can you even imagine what that must be like—to fight constantly for your sanity? This is killing him, Detective Wooley! Killing him! You're killing him! And no matter what, no matter what the final outcome, you have, quite decidedly, and perhaps permanently, derailed his life.*

This was the best she seemed to be able to come up with. So she stood, again placed both her hands on the desk, leaned in so that she was hovering just slightly into the detective's space, and said, "My son *loves*, Detective Wooley. He loves life. He loves his dogs. He loves me. He loved Flo Loughton. He deserves better than this. You have derailed his life without giving it much thought. And no matter what, even if the true murderer is found, his life will never again be that which he's worked so hard to obtain. Think about that tonight when you're lying in your bed, most likely alone. And before you close your eyes, you ask yourself, 'Am I sure? Am I damn well sure?'"

And then she left him sitting there.

THIRTY-FIVE

Trey jumped from the firm knock on his bedroom door. "Are you ready to talk to me, Trey?" Ash asked through the door. "We're getting down to the wire here. You need to talk to me if I'm to build any kind of case." Trey considered crawling back into the space between his dresser and the wall. He'd been pretty much hugging himself in the corner since he'd tried to go back to work that past Wednesday, and now here it was already Tuesday. He'd spent most of the last six days either sleeping or crying. Every time he slept, he dreamed of Mrs. Loughton. And every time he woke up, he found himself crying. He didn't even know anymore if he was crying because he so terribly missed the idea of Mrs. Loughton being alive, or because he'd been so out of it that he'd yet to find out what happened to Hector, or because everybody was so sure that he'd killed them both, causing him to be uncertain where truth ended and untruth began. Does Collective Belief make Truth?

CB⇒T.

Does willing a fact to be true make it fact?

How could he talk to Asher about what happened that morning at Mrs. Loughton's when he wasn't even sure?

There was another knock. "Trey?"

Trey sighed heavily and forced himself up from his bed. He carried his sheet, still wrapped around his body, with him and waded through his newly formed mess. He flicked open the lock on the doorknob, turned it, opened the door slightly, and then shuffled back to his spot on his bed.

"Jesus, Trey," Ash said as he entered. "Do you think we could talk downstairs? It smells like every sort of crap in here."

Trey tucked himself further onto his bed and chose not to answer. Ash took a moment before he sighed and made his way into the room. He pulled the chair away from the desk, sat down, rubbed at his face, and asked, "How are you doing?"

Trey shrugged.

"Before I forget, your mom says if you don't take a shower today, she's calling the health department." Ash smiled grimly. "I think she means it." Ash stared at him for a long moment, and Trey used all his energy to silence the chaos in his head.

"You know that the grand jury has returned an indictment, right?"

Trey nodded, trying to keep his inner panic at bay.

"The DA wants to bring it to trial as soon as possible. I'm going to try to slow it down. I need more time." He paused, then sighed. "Trey, I need you to talk to me. I need you to pull it together. Do you hear?"

Trey tried to ignore the way the nasty voice was chattering away in his head.

Ash equals Condescending Asshole. Condescending Asshole is directly proportional to Social Status. Truth is equal to Fact. Trey is equal to Truth is equal to Killer. SS, CA, A…F, K, T, T…T, T…TT.

It was so damn exhausting. Perhaps he should just give in to it. There was a definite appeal to the safety of Madness.

If M is a representation of Madness, then M must also equal Mur-

der. M, M, M…M, M.

Ash was waiting for some sort of response, but Trey was afraid of what might come out of his mouth.

Ash sighed again. "If I have to have you declared incompetent to stand trial…. If I have to go with an insanity plea…." He paused. "Trey, if that happens, they'll lock you away in a mental health care unit somewhere—for a very, very long time."

That quickly shut up the bastard in Trey's head. He glanced up, looked Ash in the eye for the very first time, and shook his head. "I'll off myself good and gone before that ever happens."

Ash sighed again. "Now that's just the sort of talk that will land you right there, kiddo. Talk to me, dammit!"

Trey shifted on his bed and wrapped the sheet a little tighter around him.

"Did you see Flo Loughton on the day she was killed?"

Trey felt his heart begin to beat harder. A long moment went by.

"Okay. Let's start at the beginning. Flo Loughton's dog is the first dog you walk in the morning, right?"

"Hector. His name is Hector."

Ash rolled his eyes in his typical Ash way that Trey had been watching all his life.

"Where is he?" asked Trey. "What's happened to Hector?"

Ash shook his head. "No idea. Can we please try to concentrate on you and not some dog?"

"His name is *Hector*."

Ash closed his eyes and exhaled. "Okay…Hector. Is *Hector* the first dog you walk in the morning?"

"Can you try to find out what happened to Hector?"

"I'll try. Now, *is Hector the first dog you walk in the morning?*"

Trey shook his head.

Ash raised his eyebrows in expectant impatience. A few moments ticked by. "You know, buddy, I'm charging your parents by the hour here."

A equals CA.

Trey laughed. "That's right," he agreed. Ash stared at him. Another long moment went by before Trey said, "He's the third."

"Okay. So you walked the first two dogs. No problem."

Trey shook his head.

"What?" Ash asked.

"Max's owner was out of town with him. I only walked Emma."

"Okay. So you walked one dog. You got to Mrs. Loughton's early then?"

Trey nodded.

"What time?"

"I was probably twenty minutes early."

"And what time was that?"

"Nine-forty."

"You picked up Hector at nine-forty. Did you go into the house?"

Trey shook his head.

"Did you notice anything amiss? Anything odd?"

"It was a right-hand-turn day. We were both a little stressed."

"Right-hand turn?"

"I turned right onto Fennel rather than left."

Ash raised his hands in a *so what?* sort of way, and Trey almost told him to go fuck himself. Ash must have read his mind, because Ash's face suddenly grew soft, and he nodded. "Okay. So things were a little off. You were a little early. You were both stressed. But you didn't go in the house when you first picked up the dog?"

Trey shook his head.

"So nothing amiss? Did you notice anything else off that morning when you picked up the dog?"

Trey shook his head but then added, "The side door was

locked."

"And that was odd?"

Trey nodded.

"So you unlocked the door and took the dog for its walk without going in. So it was later? You went into the house later?"

Trey nodded.

"Why?"

"Because of the chocolate."

"The chocolate that was found on the dog?"

Trey nodded.

"And…?" They both stared at each other. Ash sighed. "How did the chocolate get on the dog?"

"That fucking little brat Caleb. Right by the P&C. I had to try to clean Hector. Mrs. Loughton likes Hector clean. Liked. She liked Hector clean."

"Caleb…?"

"Rossiter. Caleb Rossiter."

Ash nodded. "By Tops?"

"I prefer P&C."

Ash sighed. "So the kid got chocolate on the dog. I'm guessing Hector ate some, right? That would explain all the dog crap and vomit found at the scene," Ash said more to himself than to Trey.

"Crap and vomit?" Trey asked.

"Sure. It was all over the crime scene. Chocolate's like poison to dogs, especially a dog the size of Hector. Surely you know that."

"Hector was sick?"

"So you went into the house to clean up the dog…."

Trey's heart began to race a bit, his chest tightening as he pictured poor little Hector as sick as a dog. And he was directly responsible for that sickness; he should have never let that kid get anywhere near Hector.

Ash was nodding away, not noticing that Trey was unable to

breathe. "So that would explain the chocolate on your shirt. But what about the blood? The blood on the dog is easily explained; he was all over the crime scene. But what about the blood on your shirt? What do you know about that?"

"Blood?"

"Sure. We talked about that before. The day you were arrested."

Blood? On his shirt? Trey bent over, his hands clutching at his chest, his vision getting all jumbled. Oh God, he didn't want to do this again, especially in front of Ash.

"Trey? Are you okay?"

Trey's face began to burn; his body began to tremble.

You're such a fucking loser.

"Trey, take deep breaths." Trey instinctively shrunk away from the danger of Ash's touch.

M, M, M…M, M.

THIRTY-SIX

"How many people have you killed?"

What? What sort of question was that? He stared at her, waited an uncomfortable moment, and finally decided she hadn't meant to be offensive. She apparently just wanted to know.

"Directly or indirectly?" Seth asked.

There was a loud crack, which drew their attention to the base-ball field. Base hit. Maddy jumped up and encouraged Watterson to go for second. Seth had had no idea she was such a baseball fan. Maybe it was the game and not him that had been her motivation in accepting his invitation. It was the bottom of the fourth with two outs and the Chiefs up by one. The evening was hot. She wore a red Syracuse Chiefs hat, a nicely fitting red T-shirt, and *very* nicely fitting pair of white shorts. Her dark hair was pulled up and through the back of her cap, and her face was covered with an appealing luster of sweat. She sat back down with a small pout when Watterson stuck to first. Maddy was right; he should have gone for it. Seth had always thought Watterson was a wuss. The minors was as far as he was going.

She turned to Seth and made a face. "Watterson's a wuss," she said. Seth grinned faintly and nodded with agreement. They watched as Rivero headed to the plate. A long series of fouls and balls ensued until he finally walked. Two on. Maddy made another face and shook her head. "Kaminski's up next. We're so screwed." And sure enough: two quick, awkward fouls, one swinging strike, and the inning was over. Maddy sighed, reached over to Seth's lap, helped herself to his popcorn—he'd moments ago offered to buy her her own—and said, "Directly."

Seth knitted his brow, peered out toward the field, and answered, "One."

"Really?" She had that gleam in her eye—that same gleam she had as she'd looked up at him from Loughton's dead body. "Only one?"

"You sound disappointed."

She shrugged. "Maybe a little."

"What? You want me to kill them so you can chop them up?"

She smiled her first genuine smile. "I do so like to chop them up."

"Wow. That's a little weird." She shrugged, and suddenly Seth didn't feel so hot. He no longer cared that her ass looked delicious or that her lips were so enticing. "I mean, you're kidding, right?"

And there was that shrug again. Maddy turned her attention back to the field. "That was a strike!" she yelled to the ump. "The guy's an idiot." She took another handful of Seth's popcorn.

The boy's eyes had gone wide right after the bullet had hit him. It was then that his face turned to that of a fourteen-year-old boy, right as the boy let his gun fall to the black and white linoleum, right as the chick behind the Kwik Fill counter screamed, right as the weight of Seth's gun seemed too much to bear—he'd dropped it back into his holster before approaching the boy. "Call 911!" he'd yelled to the girl.

The boy was on the floor now, weeping, grasping his stomach, looking beseechingly Seth's way as his blood seeped across a white tile of linoleum. *You did this. Now fix it.*

Seth cradled the boy's head in his hands. "Hold on, kid. They're coming." But the boy died a few minutes before the paramedics arrived.

Maddy munched on the popcorn and said, "Once someone's dead—"

"They're meat and you might as well dissect them?" he interrupted.

She stared at him. "They're dead and someone needs to figure out why—" She stopped. "Do you have a problem with what I do?" she asked.

His dad hadn't looked dead. Seth had stood slightly on his toes and looked inside the coffin. It was two days after the car accident; the fact that his dad was not coming back was still foreign and remote. He'd looked asleep. But not asleep like Seth had ever seen him sleep. His mouth wasn't gaped open. He didn't smell like cheap whiskey. His hair wasn't matted. His clothes weren't a wrinkled mess. He looked asleep like someone ought to look while they slept. A fairytale sleep. A male Sleeping Beauty sleep with his hands folded neatly across his lower chest. So this is what death looked like—what it looked like in a seven-year-old boy's world. Peaceful. But the fourteen-year-old boy who died with his head between Seth's hands hadn't looked like he was asleep. He'd looked dead. Just like all the other dead people Seth had seen as a cop looked dead. Like twisted-squirrels-on-the-road dead. And that's the way death felt: a twisted-in-the-gut sort of pain. Dress the dead up all you want—chop them up if you'd like—but there's no way of getting around that gut-twisting pain.

"I don't have a problem with what you do," he said. "And you're right. Once they're dead, they're dead, but that doesn't take away the loss—that feeling of loss. Someone's gonna feel loss. It's a very rare individual who nobody loves."

the chocolate debacle

He'd gone to the dead boy's funeral, stood near the back, and taken in all the sorrow. The image of the boy's mom writhing with grief, surrounded by her family members, pulsed through his mind.

"I don't know," Maddy said. "Some of the bodies that come through my door are pretty hard to imagine anyone loving."

This was so not what he wanted to talk about with this girl. He wasn't sure how they'd gotten here, but he sure as hell wanted to go somewhere else. The date was quickly treading near disaster. He didn't like her. He didn't like anything about Dr. Maddy Hatcher right then. She reached for more popcorn, and he almost pulled the bag away. "Are you sure you don't want a bag of your own?"

"No. I'm trying to watch my fat intake. That stuff's loaded with triglycerides. You ever take a good look at the inside of an athero-sclerotic vessel? Nasty, nasty, nasty!"

"Oh, and this popcorn," he shook the bag a bit, "because it's *mine*, is somehow free of triglycerides?"

"Absolutely!" She smiled again, but this time the smile was directed at only him, pulling him back quite suddenly from the brink of disaster. "Someone else's food is always more healthy... and better for you."

He felt every part of his body ease up just a bit. "Well, by all means then, help yourself." Her smile deepened. "I'd like you to remain healthy." She laughed, and the dead boy and Seth's dead father both slipped away. Seth's face eased in to a smile, which made Maddy's eyes take on that gleam that pushed his mind even further from disaster. This just might end up okay after all.

THIRTY-SEVEN

Jack found Annette and Asher deep in discussion Tuesday evening. They were sitting in the far corner of the study, their chairs pulled close. Their heads were bent together, and before his presence was noticed, her hand went out, rested briefly on Ash's knee, and then went to her mouth.

Jack was tired. There was no better way to describe it. Not just physically tired, but deep brain tired—so tired that he wasn't the least bit affected by the way Annette tucked her chin to her chest and peered intensely Ash's way. And even though he knew he should want to know the newest developments and strategies concerning his son, he was very tempted to turn from the room, turn on the TV, and console himself with the evening news. But the very real possibility that his son might be featured on that news caused him to step further into the room.

"Asher," he said, coming forward and grasping his friend by the shoulder. He bent down and pecked his wife on the lips.

"Oh, Jack," Annette said. "I think we may have to do it. We may have to try to get Trey back into the hospital."

Jack closed his eyes. "I don't think that's necessary, Annette." He stepped back a few feet and sat on the couch.

Ash scooted his chair a little away from Annette so that he now faced Jack and said, "He's got to talk to me. He's got to pull himself together."

"He had another panic attack," Annette said. "This one worse than the last. He showered the day before yesterday, but then he put back on the same dirty clothes. He's still wearing them today."

"He's eating," Jack stated.

"Yes."

"So what if he stinks?"

"Jack, it's more than that, and you know it." Annette countered.

Jack shook his head. "There's absolutely nothing they're going to do for him that we can't do here." He said the last sentence with finality. There was no way he was going to let his son go back into the hospital, unless it was to save his life.

Out of Trey's five hospitalizations, only two of them had done him any good. And he'd been in four *different* hospitals. Only twice had he been kept long enough to fully recover. Only twice had there been a proper discharge plan. The other three times he had been treated just long enough to be given a new diagnosis by some new doc who was seeing him for the first time, disrupting his schedule, putting him on new medications, and then quickly discharging him while still unstable. It would then take him months to reestablish what had worked for him in the past.

Too many cooks who didn't know the menu.... Too many cooks who were clueless about the recipe...who didn't even have the time to glance over the past ingredients. Too many kitchens. Minimal continuity of care. Minimal integration of services. The system wasn't broken, because broken implies that it was once whole.

The hospital was not where Trey needed to be; Annette just didn't want to deal with him. Jack understood that. After so many years, he knew she too was tired—deep brain tired. But she chose different battles than he. The lack of showering, the filth of his bedroom…these were secondary to his ability to function. Regardless of how Annette and Ash felt, Jack believed Trey's response to the death of his friend and the subsequent mess he found himself in was not particularly abnormal. Jack was pretty sure he'd be holed up in his room, depressed as hell himself if he'd been accused of killing one of the few people in this God-forsaken town who had ever shown him any true compassion.

"You know, Dad, she came to visit me the last time I was hospitalized," Trey had told him just the other night when Jack had brought him his dinner and insisted he eat. "She brought me Thin Mints."

Jack had smiled at Trey sadly, remembering how he'd sit at the kitchen table with both his sons, a mug of hot, chunky, brown milk in the middle of the table, the three of them in the midst of a fast and furious dunking contest. Trey was so small he could barely reach the mug, but he was determined, as he was always determined. The idea was to dunk your cookie for as long as possible in the hot milk and still be able to get it out and into your mouth in one piece. The rules were simple: each person was in charge of his own counting and was expected to be honest. The winner got to drink the chocolaty milk concoction when they were done. "Twelve! Thirteen! Fourteen!" Trey would shout, and then quickly and deftly transfer the cookie out of the liquid and toward his mouth. Almost always pushing that envelope, the cookie would plop to the table. "Darn!" But then he'd laugh, suck the cookie off the surface with his lips, and reach for another, all of them laughing with glee.

"Oh, for God's sake," Annette would complain as she came into the kitchen for a refill of coffee. "Would you look at yourselves and the mess you're making? And you're wrecking your appetites for dinner." But no one paid her much attention; the games went on undisturbed.

Thin Mint Dunking: an annual event that went on until his oldest boy went off to college and Trey started to turn unrecognizable. And the fact that Florence Loughton chose this cookie to bring to Trey…that she even chose to visit his son in the mental ward…. It was a shame that she was dead and that he'd never known the sort of place she'd had in Trey's life until after that death.

"Let me try to talk to him again, Ash," Jack said. "And Annette, I'll make sure he takes a shower, even if I have to drag him there myself." Then he left them alone—left them to do what they may, as long as they left the immediate fate of his son up to him.

THIRTY—EIGHT

Seth was resting his right hand lightly against the roof of Maddy's VW Bug so that his body naturally fell her way as they talked. She didn't seem opposed to their position. They were discussing the car, which was a perfect chick car: bright red with a black convertible top. Thank God Maddy hadn't attached those ridiculous eyelashes above the headlights or plastered large bright flowers on its sides, or worse yet, made it into a ladybug with black dots. Even though it was a car he wouldn't be caught dead driving, it suited her, and he liked it.

"It's actually a vintage Bug. My brother's passion. He takes old cars and gives them a new life. He found this little guy in a junkyard in Mexico City."

"Little guy?"

"Chester." She smiled. "His name is Chester."

"Your brother?"

She laughed. "No. The car." She removed the baseball cap from her head and shook her hair so that it fell forward onto her shoulders. She ran her hand through the top of her hair, fluffing away any indication of hat-hair.

"I see," he said.

"What? You never name inanimate objects?" Her hand holding the hat came out, and she lightly tapped his chest with its brim in a playful manner.

"Oh. Yeah. Sure. My gun's named Clint."

Maddy's eyebrows rose ever so slightly. "Clint," she said with feigned dreaminess.

"My *gun*. The one I shoot."

She grinned and nodded. "Mmmmm."

He was beginning to like Dr. Maddy Hatcher. "As in inanimate…."

"If I had a gun," she continued, "I'd name her Viola."

"I see. I bet Clint and Viola would get along swimmingly."

"Mmhmm," she nodded. "You just might be right."

She looked at him, her lower lip between her teeth, her eyes edging on wickedness. This was the moment that he should lean in and kiss her. He knew that. He knew it was what she wanted. He knew that the date could end with the pleasure of that kiss and the promise of another date. He wanted to. He really did. He'd lean in and kiss her, and that kiss would be just as sweet as he imagined, and she would lean into him, her slight body pressing against him with hope and lust and longing. Then they'd break apart and make plans to see each other again, both of them feeling giddy with anticipation as they drove their separate ways home.

Love. To connect. To be loved in return. Wasn't that all anyone wanted? Wasn't that what this was all about? And wasn't it possible? Even though she was a beautiful young doctor who was just starting out in her career and he was an okay-looking detective in a mid-sized city in Central New York who would never be more than an okay-looking detective in a mid-sized city. Could this turn into love? Even though she'd moved there from Staten Island and longed to return to her family and aspired to become head medical examiner somewhere closer to NYC. Even though her mother was a plastic surgeon with a large practice in the city and her father was the CEO of a large manufacturing company in New Jersey. Even though she'd spent her summers sailing on Long Island Sound and gone to prep school in New Jersey. Even though she'd spent the summer after graduating with a chemistry degree from NYU backpacking across Europe before starting her medical degree. Even though she'd told him all this with a hint of pretentiousness while they'd sat through nine innings of a rather dull baseball game.

Couldn't she grow to love him, even though he'd never left the state of New York other than that weekend trip to Niagara Falls with his parents when he was six? The three of them—his father, his mother, and his little-boy self—had walked across the bridge, stood on the Canadian side, and peered back at the falls. They'd all held each other's hands—the quintessential American family. His father large and muscular, his mother slim then and rather pretty, her fine blonde hair blowing in the breeze, and the little American boy between them, his hair also blowing but in dark reddish curls, his brown eyes wide with amazement. That was until his father got restless and his mother got bitchy. They'd made it back to the American side detached, his father stomping ahead, his mother trying to keep up while calling, "Johnny! Wait! Don't leave us!" as she dragged Seth's little-boy body by his hand while he cried, "I want to stay in Canada. I want to stay in Canada!"

The trip had ended with a nasty quarrel at a cheap motor lodge, his parents' voices rising from one of the dozen tiny white houses lined up along Route 158, his father drunk from his twelve-pack of Bud, his mother weepy and desperate. His father had finally slammed out of the little one-room house, taking the car and leaving Seth and his mother. They'd shared a stale pack of peanut butter crackers that she'd found in her purse for dinner and drank warm tap water from plastic cups. The next morning of waiting—

the chocolate debacle

"I'm hungry, Ma"—had turned into afternoon. "No money, no stay," said the large German proprietor, Seth's mother digging through her purse for the fourth time, finding three quarters and one crumpled five dollar bill. "No money, no stay."

They'd sat outside the tiny white house on hard, white plastic chairs facing the parking lot. When Seth woke up at some point later, the sun low in the sky, he rubbed his eyes and turned to his mother, who still sat perfectly straight, staring out toward the highway. "Mommy, are we gonna live here now?"

It was a moment later, before his mother had a chance to answer, that his father's beat-up, grey Cutlass appeared from over a slight crest of the highway.

But wasn't *love* bigger than class or upbringing or money or aspiration? Couldn't *love* overcome? Wasn't the possibility of *love* worth the possibility of heartbreak?

As he studied the way the lights of the baseball parking lot glinted off Maddy's lips, he couldn't seem to stop the movie of the next six months from flipping through his mind: The fun. The sex. The rush of a new love. Then the slow, agonizing realization that he could be a bit of a prick and that she was a person who named her car Chester. No matter what, *love* wasn't enough. She'd come to annoy him. She'd come to hate him. She'd come to leave him, or he'd leave her.

He'd tripped as he'd been forced to run after his father on the bridge, his hand slipping from his mother's grasp. She'd hesitated; he'd seen it as she took a few more steps in the direction of his departing father. Then reluctantly, begrudgingly, she'd returned to pick him up off the sidewalk. An abandonment issue is what the department's shrink had called it; giving it a name only solidified its existence.

And why on earth was he thinking about all this now when her lips were right there and the sun was setting over the parking lot of the stadium and she was wrapping her arms across her chest because the coming night had suddenly turned the air cold and he was losing her before he even had her and if he didn't do something right then and there then it would always be lost?

Just kiss her, you dumb fuck!

"Well," she said, her body shifting, his heart sinking. "Thank you. I enjoyed the game, and your popcorn."

"Yeah. Me too." He removed his hand from her car and stepped back. "Maybe we can do it again."

"That would be nice."

He bent over slightly and gave her a quick peck on her lips. "Okay. Well, I better let you get going." He stepped back further. "Probably see you around the department on Monday."

"Yup." She turned and got into her car, closing the door gently. Was it too late? Could he whip the door open and still thrust his tongue into her mouth? The car started smooth like chocolate, rumbling pleasantly; her brother had done a good job. She rolled down the window. "Bye." She waved softly as she backed out, then drove away.

Seth stood there a moment, watching as the taillights moved away. Then he turned toward his car, which was parked on the complete opposite side of the stadium.

"Fuck," he said as he started to walk.

THIRTY-NINE

Zuke placed his large black coffee and apple fritter down, pulled out the chair, and sat at the table in Dunkin' Donuts, his long legs having difficulty finding their space under the small table. Seth lifted up his coffee cup and toasted the air with mock formality. "Zuke," he said.

"Wool."

They drank their coffee in silence for several minutes. Seth played with his iPhone, and Zuke gave his full attention to his fritter.

"So?" Zuke finally asked.

Seth shrugged, realizing immediately and unhappily that his shrug had matched that of Maddy's. "It went okay."

"Just okay?"

"Eh. I don't know."

"Kiss?"

"Nah. Not really."

"Second date?"

"Maybe. We'll see." He shrugged again. Damn. He'd have to stop doing that. "The Chiefs won."

"Yeah. I saw that. One nothing." Zuke tore off a large piece of the fritter, popped it into his mouth, followed it up with a coffee chaser, and said before all was swallowed, "I checked out that new lead in the Loughton case. A dead end. Raymond Watson. Turns out he checked himself into alcohol rehab shortly after that confrontation with Loughton. He was there for a couple of weeks."

"Not surprised. Any luck with that phone call Loughton received the night before she was killed?"

"Nope. No one at the coffee shop seems to know who made the call. And no one seems to remember letting any of their customers use the phone."

"Weird." His cell phone beeped and Seth checked the screen. Just a junk mail on his Gmail account. "The dog leash came up positive for a match. Loughton's skin in the fibers, and the pattern matched the one on her neck." Zuke nodded and finished off the rest of the fritter. "There's still that trace of skin retrieved from under Loughton's fingernail. Not a match for Barkley."

Zuke grunted.

"Could be from some other random encounter, I guess." A few more minutes went by before Seth added, "Mrs. Barkley came to see me late yesterday."

"That so? Let me guess: she wanted you to know her son is no killer."

"Pretty much."

Zuke chuckled. "Everybody's baby is as innocent as a newborn lamb."

Seth nodded in agreement. "So nothing else has come up? No man in our dear Mrs. Loughton's life? Other than Barkley, of course."

"Not that we can unearth."

"She wasn't really a bad-looking woman," Seth remarked.

"You can turn off the light to fuck an ugly woman, but fucking a bitch—even the darkness won't mask that."

Seth laughed, then added, "I mean, she was married. It's not like she was a nun or something. You'd think she might have dated at some point after her husband died."

"Her husband probably died in self-defense."

Seth smiled and shook his head slightly. "If speaking poorly of the dead is some sort of faux pas, you, my friend, are the dope of faux pas."

"I'm just saying, I don't think we're missing anything here."

"We really don't have a motive."

"The kid's a crazy fuck. What more motive do we need?"

Seth shrugged. *A crazy fuck.* Was it enough? He'd done a little research of his own after he'd gotten home from the baseball game, in the darkness of his little apartment, the laptop between his knees as he sat cross-legged, alone on his bed, his back leaning against the wall just lightly enough so as not to pull the bed from the wall. The statistics were clear. The rate of violent crimes committed by the mentally ill was only slightly higher than those reported to have no mental illness. And there were specific things that increased the risk of that violence: drug or alcohol abuse, treatment noncompliance, a past history of violence.... Barkley's tomato incident being the only exception, he had none of the increased risk factors for violence. Surely his defense attorney would grab on to that fact. And if anything, the tomato incident would work against the case; who wouldn't feel kinda sorry for the guy? Now if it had been potatoes or even oranges, then the prosecuting attorney might have something to work with. But tomatoes? Come on.

"Hey," said Zuke. "How's your mom?"

Seth laughed unkindly. "Yeah, speaking of crazy...."

"Not a connection there, dude. Just asking."

"Yeah. Right." Seth finished the last of his coffee. "She's fine. Just took in another fucking dog, though."

Zuke laughed. "And how many now?"

"Lucky number seven. She named him Lucky."

"Fucking hilarious. Isn't there some kind of limit? Some kinda law?"

"Shhh! I have no idea. Are you suggesting I turn in my own ma?"

Zuke laughed. "You want a refill?" He stood up.

"Sure," said Seth, handing him his empty cup. "And hell, get me one of those fritter things."

Seth was twelve years old the first time he heard the word *crazy* associated with his mother. It had come out of his Aunt Margo's mouth. He'd slipped behind the couch, trying to get a better explanation of why his mother had suddenly disappeared. The *she's just gone off to have a little rest* that had been offered up wasn't enough. So when he'd heard his aunt on the phone, he'd snuck into the room and hid behind the couch. "Yes, I'll be here for a little while, I guess. Someone needs to be with the boy." Seth leaned against the back of the couch and breathed as quietly as possible. "I don't know. She's always been crazy. But she went so deep this time that she took too many pills. Suicidal," his aunt whispered. Seth had had no idea his mom was suicidal. He'd known his ma had been sad. She'd been sad for as long as he remembered. But so was he, his dad being dead and all. But suicidal? And crazy? Quackerjack, the insane clown from *Darkwing Duck* was crazy. Mr. Banana Brain, Quackerjack's talking doll, was crazy. And Negaduck—he was *really* crazy. But his mom? His mom wasn't crazy; she was just sad. "Yes, she's in the psych ward. I have no idea how long she'll be there." And all that Seth could picture were straightjackets and crazed killers.

His mom had returned home about a week later, and it was shortly after that that they'd taken in that first stray dog. How many dogs does it take to constitute crazy? More than four. That's what Seth had decided years ago. Four was just a little canine overkill. But five? There was no denying that five crossed right over to some kind of crazy. But there was crazy, and then there was that *other* kind of crazy. And Trey Barkley was that other kind of crazy—the kind of crazy that kills for seemingly no reason. And Florence Loughton was just one more victim of another crazy-ass killer. It was as simple as that.

Seth accepted the second cup of coffee gratefully from Zuke, 'cause, like it or not, he needed it. He really hadn't slept all that well last night.

FORTY

Trey had to admit, as much as he didn't want to leave his room, it was awfully nice to be outside. It was early Thursday morning, the sun still not over the hills of the east side of the lake, the summer air still chilly. His father had brought along coffee and Trey's favorite pastries from Patisserie; his dad must have been up before dawn getting the boat ready and buying the baked goods. Trey had been adamant in his refusal to go fishing that day when his dad had brought it up the previous evening, but with his head in his typical early morning antipsychotic fog, he'd relented to his father's wishes. He'd even taken a shower and put on fresh clothing, which did feel rather nice. Even though all of his circumstances were unchanged, like it or not, he was feeling better. Mrs. Loughton was still dead with or without the sun shining, so it might as well shine—and shine brightly.

It was very nice of his dad to rearrange his office hours and drag them both out there. Fishing was something that both he and his brother had been absolutely bonkers over when they were young, something his father had always done with them. It's why his dad had bought the fishing boat all those many years ago. But it had been a very long time since they'd gone. And nobody was fooling anybody; he knew that this little fishing excursion had nothing to do with father-son bonding, and nothing, whatsoever, to do with fishing for fish. Still, it was hard not to appreciate his dad's efforts to recreate a magical childhood experience.

But what he really appreciated was the fact that his father waited what must have been an agonizingly long time before bringing up why they were both really out there. It wasn't until all the coffee and pastries were gone, the first few bass were caught, the sun was nearing its peak in the sky, and their stomachs were considering the sandwiches his mother had made them that his father finally said, "I told Ash not to worry; I'd get you to tell me exactly what happened the morning Florence Loughton was killed. Are you going to make a liar out of me?"

Trey slowly reeled in his line, then carefully attached the lure to the rod before setting the whole thing gently down in the boat. "You got a recorder somewhere? A bug?"

His dad laughed. "No." He lifted up his shirt. "You want to check for wires?"

Trey narrowed his eyes, checked out his dad's bare chest, which was awfully white for it being summer and all, and then he laughed and said, "Nope."

"Okay." His dad let his shirt drop back into place.

"I don't know, Dad. I wasn't in a good place that day. I never should have turned right."

"But you did. You did turn right."

Trey nodded glumly. "Then everything just went fucking wrong."

"Ash told me about Caleb Rossiter and the chocolate."

"I hate that little shit."

"Yes. I'm not too wild about his father either."

Trey laughed. "Should we eat? I'm kinda hungry."

"Sure." His dad reached behind him and pulled two wrapped

sandwiches from the cooler. He handed one to Trey and set the other on his lap. He returned to the cooler and said, "You want a Coke or root beer?"

"Duh. Root beer."

His dad dug through the chunks of ice until he located the can of root beer and handed it to Trey. He took out a Coke for himself, popped the top, took a sip, and said, "So, you have this dog with chocolate all over it."

"All over *him*. His name is Hector."

His dad took another sip of soda and opened up the sandwich. "Then what?"

Trey unwrapped his own sandwich, studied it carefully, then sniffed it. "What is this? Are you sure Mom made it? You didn't get it from Valentine's Deli, did you? They poisoned me the last time I ate there."

"Tuna salad. Your mom made it. And you were not poisoned by Valentine's. You had the flu. And you were nine. Time to let that one go."

Trey rolled his eyes. "I know when I've been poisoned."

They ate for a few minutes before his dad asked again, "Then what?"

"I had to bathe him," Trey mumbled. "I went into the house. I was going to wash Hector in the kitchen sink, but I needed good shampoo. You know Hector has that pink skin and all…." His father nodded encouragingly, but Trey still felt like he just didn't get it. "Ajax Triple Action would have been too harsh."

"I agree."

Trey nodded with relief. "And that's when it got all fucked up, Dad," Trey whispered.

A long moment went by, and then his dad whispered, "Why was it fucked up?"

Trey closed his eyes. "Because she was there. Because Mrs.

Loughton was there, don't you see?"

"She was in the house? Upstairs in her bedroom?"

Trey nodded. "She was everywhere. In the hall, on the wall, in the bed, the bathroom, the shower.... Hector wanted to get away. He started to squirm, to bark. We could smell her, don't you see? We could feel her. I freaked out, Dad. I had a freak out. And then...and then when I dropped the shampoo— Picked it up and put it in my back pocket— When I saw— I saw her, you see? Just as plain as day. She wanted something—something I couldn't give her. I wanted to, but I just couldn't. And there was blood, her lips all red. She looked right at me from there on the floor. I had to get away." He put his head in his hands. "And I left poor Hector there. And Mrs. Loughton. I left them there. Now they're both dead," he whispered. "And it's all my fault."

"Did you really see her?" His dad grasped his shoulder and gave him a little shake. "*Really* see her alive? Or was it a hallucination?"

"I don't know, Dad." Trey raised his face and looked his father in the eye. "I. Just. Don't. Know."

His dad slid his hands slightly down Trey's arms, then let them drop away fully. He rested his arms on his knees and studied the bottom of the boat. "You might have seen the body," said his dad. "She might have been dead, and you just saw the body."

Trey saw, quite clearly, in his mind, Mrs. Loughton's red-raspberry-iced lips. He saw, quite clearly, how they moved as if they had something quite important to say. As if all he'd needed to do was to step over there, bring his lips close to hers, and give her what she so clearly wanted.

His dad raised his head and said again, "She could have already been dead."

The boat rocked gently, the waves of a passing boat slapping at its side. Trey's root beer slipped from his fingers, the can hitting the floor of the boat, the brown liquid fizzing out. The nasty voice in his head laughed. Trey met his dad's gaze and said as quietly as he could to still be heard over the noise of the waves, "Sometimes things just seem so real."

FORTY-ONE

Seth leaned over the desk where Zuke was typing away on the computer late Thursday morning and feigned great interest in whatever he might be working on. Zuke shaded the screen with his body. "Go away, fucker. My investigation into Internet porn is personal and private." Seth laughed and sat down in a chair. He leaned back and placed his feet on the desk. Zuke looked up in mock irritation. Seth tilted his chin toward his chest and pretended to nap. Zuke went back to his computer.

The week had been pretty quiet, and although Seth had lots of little things he should be doing, at that moment he just felt like harassing Zuke. There was just not a lot going on anywhere in his life. So far, his one big, non-work-related excitement for the week would be taking his ma to get her hair done that evening, providing him an opportunity to flirt with the hairdresser. Yup, it had come down to that. Things seemed to be deteriorating pretty quickly with his ma, as if adding dog number seven had truly pushed that insanity envelope. Her behavior was becoming more erratic, and she was drinking more than ever. When he'd refused to bring her more whiskey, she'd enlisted the help from one of the neighbors who just didn't seem to see the harm in keeping an old lady smashed—especially considering how neatly it fit into the guy's almost daily trip to the liquor store. Talking to the neighbor had proven fruitless. "Hey, man, last I checked, your mom's an adult." The neighbor had laughed. "Ain't really your call how much she likes her Jack Daniels, now is it?"

Seth had prickled immediately. "You know, Jared, I just bet if I set up a little surveillance right here in front of your house, it would take me about forty-five minutes to figure out what those random guys stopping by are really doing. And even less time to turn the whole thing over to the narc unit." Well that idle threat had worked, but his ma had seen him talking to the neighbor and gotten pissed as hell; it turned into a real bad scene. Then she had just recruited someone else to go buy her booze. The key was to squeeze her financially so that she didn't have the funds to pay the neighbors to run her errands or pay for the stuff. But that would involve declaring her incompetent and gaining power of attorney; she would never sign over that power willingly.

He was really over it. What fucking difference did it make if his ma drank herself to death? And yet...and yet...it made a difference. She was fucking up his life.

Then there were the dogs to consider. They were all looking a little ragged. Then there was the dog shit all over the yard. He did his best to keep up with it, but damn, seven dogs could shit a lot. It was only a matter of time before someone called the health department. Like it or not, he'd have to deal with his ma, her dogs, her drinking, her aging, and her deteriorating mental health, but he didn't have a clue on how or where to start.

He didn't bother to open his eyes or lift his head from his chest as he said to Zuke, "You know what I can't seem to shake?"

"Haven't a clue," Zuke mumbled.

Seth opened his eyes. "That look that Barkley guy gave me. That sudden look of perfect clarity. Remember how he was all shaky and demented, like he was just going to melt right down into fucking crazy? And then you left to get him that coffee…. I asked him about his name: Barkley. Asked him if that was why he'd become a dog walker."

Zuke looked up and laughed. "Good one."

"Yeah. But then he looked up at me with total sanity. Stopped shaking and basically told me that I was a fucking idiot. And at that moment I hated that little prick; I was so glad that we'd snagged him for this murder. I asked him why he was in Loughton's bedroom. It was right then, right there, right before he turned away and shut down completely, something passed across his face, and I felt, without a doubt, that we were wrong. That we had the wrong guy."

Zuke sat back from his computer and sighed. "You gotta let that one go, dude. It's no longer our concern."

"I guess." Seth sighed. A long moment passed. "It's gotta be hard, you know, to go crazy."

Zuke nodded. "I can't imagine it's a yellow submarine ride."

"And his family. It's gotta suck to have a crazy kid. You know his mom called me this morning. Haven't called her back yet. My guess is she's gonna get all over me again about the arrest, insisting on his innocence and all."

"Hmm." Zuke shrugged. "You just gotta let it go, Wool. Seriously." Another long moment passed. Seth knew he should just get up and leave Zuke to his work, but he felt absolutely planted. "So what are you up to tonight?" Zuke finally asked.

Seth checked his cell phone before answering. An hour or so ago he'd sent a quick *Hey, how ya doin?* text to Maddy. No response. "Nothing, I guess." He slipped the cell phone back into his front pocket. "Other than taking my ma to the hairdresser." Zuke cut him a look. "Yeah. Tell me about it." Seth sighed. "She's driving me nuts, Zuke. Not the hairdresser duty, 'cause the chick who does her hair is so hot. But all the rest. It's driving me fucking nuts!"

Zuke shook his head. "Sorry, man."

"She's not doing so well. Maybe that's what's really eating at me. I think she's losing it. You know, she's not that old. I think she's actually losing her mind. And I haven't one clue on what to do about it."

Zuke frowned. "I don't know, man. Take her to her doctor?"

Seth shrugged. "I guess."

Zuke watched him for a moment, then hit a few buttons on the keyboard. "Time to shut this baby down and grab some lunch." He looked up from the keys and pointed a finger Seth's way. "Strip club. Tonight. It's been too long, man."

Seth laughed. "Yeah. Your girl, Angie, would just love that."

Zuke waved away Seth's concern. "What Angie doesn't know keeps her sweet." Zuke pushed his chair away from the desk and added, "I'll drive. That way you can get as drunk as you like. I'll go home, have a little bite to eat, maybe a quick preemptive Angie fuck, and then I'll pick you up at nine."

Seth laughed. "Preemptive Angie fuck? Nice." It had been too long. He and Zuke used to go out pretty regularly, to bars, clubs, occasional ballgames.... They still had the monthly poker game, but ever since Zuke had started seeing Angie about a year prior, all the rest had pretty much come to an end. They'd tried a couple of double dates, Angie fixing Seth up with her friends, but the truth was that Seth didn't like Angie all that much, and he was damn sure Angie didn't like him, which pretty much automatically prejudiced any possible positive outcome for either party. The double dates were a disaster. And even though he saw Zuke almost daily, he missed their predatory nights, their mutual desire for occasional strip club debauchery, and their drunken fan appreciation as they watched SU lose at football or kick ass at basketball. So, yeah. Why not hang with Zuke tonight? Maybe he would get just as drunk as he liked. And why not pay someone to dance against his pants? So, yeah. He was suddenly feeling a little better.

FORTY-TWO

Annette was considering watching the noon news as she ate her lunch. It had been weeks now since the murder—her son was seldom the top story these days. Never a fan of watching tragic news, she was finding that being the news was even worse. She reached for the remote just as the house phone rang sharply. She jumped, then sighed, counting the rings: one, two, three, four. "Hello. You've reached the Barkley residence. Please leave a message." A pause, then the beep. "Hello. This is Fredrick Spealman from KC105. I was hoping to chat with you. We'd love to have Mrs. or Dr. Barkley come into our studio for an interview. It would give you a chance to tell your side of the story. Perhaps Mr. Barkley would like to join us. Please give me a call at 315-555-9010. I look forward to your call." Annette reached over and hit the erase button.

The Dog Walker. That was actually on the subject line in an email someone had sent her just yesterday. Why she'd opened it, she'd never know. Morbid curiosity, she guessed.

Dear Mrs. Barkley,
My name is Kerry Matheson. You may know me as the author of

the chocolate debacle

Secret Longings. (Annette didn't.) *I would love to write your son's story. I'd write it with delicacy and empathy. My brother suffers from schizoaffective disorder. Please call....*

Annette had deleted the message without reading further and changed her email address that same day. She never answered the door these days, or her house phone. Her cell phone number, so far, had not been compromised. Everybody wanted a statement—wanted something. Ash had given strict orders not to talk to any of them about Trey's case, as if Annette would—as if she'd be that dumb.

Well, there was that one time when she'd slipped. She'd been assailed by a reporter and a cameraman just as she'd stepped out of Mirbeau, right after her aerobics class. She hadn't bothered to shower since she was going home to garden. She was sweaty, still in her workout clothes, her hair in wet slimy strands. The woman seemed to come out of nowhere, smiling sweetly and almost apologetically. Then she pulled a mic up to her mouth, grew grim, never lost eye contact with Annette, and said, "How do you feel about your son's arraignment on murder charges? Given his history of mental illness, do you think he's being treated fairly?"

Suddenly the mic was near Annette's face and, dammit, she just had to give her opinion. "Is he being treated fairly? Do I think he was indicted so quickly, with almost no evidence, because of his history with mental illness?" She pushed a slick strand of hair out of her eyes. "Absolutely! My son is not a murderer. He's not a crazed murderer. But this sort of stuff sells papers, now doesn't it? No one wants to hear about the success stories of mental illness. They'd rather read sensationalized stories about crazed killers." Her eyes welled up with tears. "My son is kind and withdrawn. Vulnerable. He was Flo Loughton's friend...."

Then she'd suddenly realized that she'd said too much, that

she shouldn't have said anything at all—Ash was going to kill her. She'd put her hand up, shook her wet hair, and said, "I've got nothing else to say." Then she'd walked away, the camera following her retreat.

It had made all the local news channels. Her sweaty face and plastered-down hair was picked up and seen all over the state. It was on the Internet along with pictures of Trey, their home, The Village, and Flo Loughton's home. There was even a photo of Trey dressed up as the Ghost of Christmas Present, smiling like a goof and looking a little crazed as he shook his glowing torch over a little girl on a snowy day. Ash had been furious about the Mirbeau slip. He'd screamed at her, even though nothing she'd said would cause Trey harm.

"Don't talk to anyone, about anything!" he'd yelled. "I don't give a rat's ass about your advocacy crap, Annette! Just shut up and let me do my job!" She would have cried, but he was just such a dick about it that she'd told him to go fuck himself and walked away. But she was more careful now, more prepared. She had to trust that Ash knew what he was doing; she didn't wish to make his job any harder.

Annette looked at the clock. It was now noon, the news just starting. She sighed and decided to risk it. She sat down at the kitchen counter, her tuna salad sandwich before her, and clicked on the TV. "Good afternoon, Central New York." The newscaster looked so grave as she looked into the TV camera that Annette almost turned it off. "Our top story, just in, another tragic school shooting."

"Oh, dear God," Annette moaned.

"Four people reported dead and three injured when a lone gunman opened fire on the campus quad of Temple University in Philadelphia. The shooter has been identified as twenty-year-old Mathew Shaver of Frackville, Pennsylvania." They switched to a school photo, probably his high school senior photo, of a nice-looking boy with blonde hair and bright blue eyes. "Shaver has been taken into custody. It's been reported that he has a history of mental instability and was diagnosed with schizophrenia." They switched to a shot of Temple University, at which point Annette turned the TV off before they had the chance to show an interview with a survivor or make the connection with the local schizophrenic murderer—namely her son.

This would set off a whole other round of media hysteria. It would bring them circling heavier than ever. And this would not help Trey's case—at all.

Annette stared miserably at her tuna salad sandwich. She sure hoped Jack could get some answers out of her son. If there were answers to be gotten, Jack could get them; Trey had always shared things with Jack that he would never share with her—even when he was a tiny boy. Ash was chomping at the bit, eager to get some sort of defense underway. The private detective that Ash hired had yet to be able to come up with anything new. No new leads or suspects. The easiest way to save her son was to find out who really killed Florence Loughton. Somehow, someway, there must be something that was being missed.

Annette took a bite from her sandwich, then wondered where she'd left her cell. She looked around the kitchen and found it on the counter by the fridge. And even though she knew the ringer was on, she stood up, retrieved the phone, and checked for missed calls. None. She was expecting a call back from Detective Wooley. Although she couldn't seem to clear her son of murder charges, she could at least give Trey what he seemed to want most: an answer about the dog. What had happened to that little dog?

FORTY-THREE

Flo Loughton felt school-girl giddy, which should have irritated her, but the fact was that it felt rather nice. Hector was
excited; he knew something unusual was about to occur. She'd
left her office early that Wednesday afternoon, stopped by Tops
and picked up what she needed, and ran into Doug's Fish Fry
and placed her order. "Two dinners. One scallop, one fish, please.
Both with fries, one with extra coleslaw." Had it been her imagination, or had the young lady who took the order—Maryanne
Flowers's daughter—tilted her head with mild interest when she'd
ordered two dinners rather than one? Well, it was of no concern.
Let the girl think what she wanted. Then she'd come home to find
Hector already back from his second walk with Trey, almost as
thrilled by the prospect of company as she. They both went to the
garden, where they chose the most perfect of her heirloom tomatoes. "What do you think, Hector? The Cherokee Purple or Bran-
dywine?" Hector jumped up and down twice. "Both? Both, you
think?" Flo considered, then nodded her head and gently pulled
the fruit from the vine.

Once back in her kitchen, she carefully read the directions
on the box of the Duncan Hines Chewy Fudge Brownie mix. It

seemed simple enough. She turned on her oven to three hundred fifty degrees and set about mixing the water, vegetable oil, and egg into the chocolaty powder. Once she had mixed the ingredients with exactly fifty strokes, she immediately poured the batter into the nine-by-nine-inch glass casserole dish she'd oiled, then placed it in the oven. She set the timer for thirty-six minutes. Then she turned from the oven, brushed her hands together, and said to Hector, "Okay. Now let's just go and put something else on, shall we?" Hector cocked his head, lifted up one paw, then flew toward the stairs.

It was after she'd taken off her work clothes, carefully considered her wardrobe, picked out then rejected a teal Polo crew, finally decided on a light purple summer shell that made her shoulders look nice, complemented it with a nice-fitting pair of tan capri shorts, freshened up her makeup, and fluffed up her hair that her house phone rang. Her immediate thought was that he'd changed his mind and wasn't coming. But when she checked the caller ID, it wasn't Trey. Willow Wind Coffee Shop. Now that was odd. She let it ring one more time as she considered, then made up her mind and answered the call.

"Hello," she said briskly into the phone.

"Hello! Floie! Is that you?"

Flo's heart took a little leap. "Who is this?" she demanded.

"Well, Floie. It's me, of course. Thought I'd give you one more chance."

She narrowed her eyes. "Stanley? Is this Stanley?"

"At your service, madam." He laughed.

"Oh, for God's sake. Why would you possibly be calling?"

"Floie, don't be that way. Come on. Let's start over. One more dinner. What do you say?"

Flo closed her eyes and drew in one long deep breath. "Why is it that you persist when it would be quite evident to an imbecile that I will never, as long as I live, subject myself to another dinner with you?"

Other than the hum of human activity in the background, there was silence on the phone. Flo was just about to pull the receiver from her ear and set it back, when she heard the slightest of chuckles. "Because, my dear woman, I am, quite obviously, *not* an imbecile."

"Oh, God." And then Flo laughed. She really didn't have a choice. Like it or not, there was something disturbingly endearing about this man. She shook her head and hung up the phone. She checked the time; the brownies would be about done.

At the exact moment the timer went off, Flo was there, pot-holders in hand. She opened the oven, the warm, chocolaty odor permeating her senses, and pulled what appeared to be the perfect batch of brownies from the stove. This baking thing wasn't so hard after all. She set them to cool, then checked the time: 5:55 p.m. He'd be there any minute. She pulled out one of her metal baking sheets and carefully laid out the fish, scallops, and fries. She put them in the oven to warm, removed the foil-paper seal from the extra-large bottle of ketchup she'd purchased, double-checked to make sure the root beer she had bought was in the fridge, washed and sliced the tomatoes, and pulled out two plates, flatware, and napkins. She looked around the kitchen. What else? Hector barked at the soft knock on the side door. Flo ran her hand though her hair and went to open it.

Trey was wearing his Mets baseball cap and a light blue T-shirt with three colored, interlocking circles and the words *Passion Pit* penned across them. He was freshly shaven, his face still red from the razor. The bangs that hung out from the front of his cap appeared to still be damp from a shower. He looked like a child. "I, um, brought you these." He pulled out two small pieces of raw-hide from the pocket of his jeans. One was shaped like a shoe, the other like some sort of small animal, perhaps a squirrel. He held them toward her, his palm flattened out. Flo looked at his offering in mild confusion. "Well…for Hector," Trey added.

Flo took the rawhide shapes from Trey's hand, stepped back from the door, and motioned for him to come in. "I'm so glad you cleared that up."

Trey nodded solemnly and stepped through the door. "Smells interesting." He cocked his head, the brim of his cap shading his eyes. "Chocolate and fish."

What was she doing? With this child? What in God's name had possessed her to suggest this little dinner?

Trey picked up Hector, gave him a quick hug, then returned him to the floor. He pulled off his baseball cap and ran his fingers through his hair. "Chocolate fish—my all-time favorite."

Flo laughed. Trey's eyes turned to her, and he smiled for the first time since she'd opened the door. Then she remembered exactly why she'd invited this quiet young man to dinner.

FORTY-FOUR

Jack sat down at the bar in Sherwood Inn Thursday afternoon and ordered a beer. He was on call, but one beer wasn't a whole lot different than water these days. It was scotch, which he'd suddenly found worthwhile, that could pack a pleasant punch. The bar was nearly empty as it was only a little after 4:00 in the afternoon. There was a small group of fellow country club members he knew at the other end of the bar, but when he glanced their way ready to bid hello, they looked away and failed to acknowledge his presence. As Jack rubbed his hand across his forehead, the bartender brought him his beer. "Thanks, Les," Jack said. Jack thought he might cry when Les smiled, tilted his head slightly toward the group at the other end of the bar, and mouthed, *They're assholes.* Jack laughed rather than cried and sipped the foam from the top of the glass. He looked toward the door as Ash walked in. He nodded his greeting, and in a matter of moments, Ash was sitting next to him. Ash ordered a beer and nodded to the men at the other side of the bar, who were now suddenly watching them with great interest. Jack frowned slightly and turned away from the small group. *That's right, I'm meeting with my son's lawyer. Get over it!*

"So, how'd the fishing trip go?" Ash asked after Les had brought the beer and Ash had taken his first few sips. He listened without comment as Jack related what Trey had told him. When Jack was done, Ash turned away and drank his beer in silence.

Finally Jack said, "So it will help Trey's case, right? Every bit of evidence they have can be explained."

Ash shrugged in a noncommittal way. "One of the neighbors just came forward. They suddenly remember seeing Trey arriving at Flo Loughton's house Wednesday evening. Right before the county examiner's window for the time of death. Flo opened the door and let him in. Not only does it place Trey there very close to the proposed time of death, it also establishes a relationship that goes beyond dog walker-client. And due to evidence at the scene, Detective Wooley has narrowed the presumed time of death to Thursday morning. No one remembers seeing Trey leave."

"So what? He went to see her. There could have been a lot of reasons. The time could just be bad luck on Trey's part. The morning scenario is helpful to Trey. He came home that night. I'm sure."

"Really? Are you certain? You distinctly remember seeing him?"

"We would have noticed if he had been gone."

Ash shook his head. "Not good enough. And even if you claimed he was there sleeping tight in his bed—" He shook his head again. "You are his parents; it holds little credibility." He took a long swallow from his beer. "There's more. Jessica Flowers remembers Florence Loughton ordering two dinners from Doug's that night. With extra coleslaw."

"So?"

"One fish, one scallop."

Jack rolled his eyes. "So?" he repeated.

"Trey ate at Doug's at least once per week. He always ordered scallops. Always with extra coleslaw."

"Oh for Christ's sake! So they had dinner together. It hardly proves he killed her."

Ash sighed. "It's just one more thing I gotta deal with, that's all. And my PI can't seem to unearth anything that we can use." Ash took a long drink from his beer and turned his eyes toward the golf match that was on the TV above the bar.

Jack suddenly felt defeated. Was it possible his son had been having an affair with Florence Loughton? A woman over thirty years Trey's senior? But then again, what girl Trey's age had ever shown him any interest? The last girl Jack knew about was way before Trey had had his first real psychotic break, back during Trey's first semester as a sophomore at Brown. Jack had always wondered if the breakup with that girl had been part of what had led to Trey's mental demise. She'd really been his first and only girlfriend he and Annette had known about—Trey being a rather nerdy, awkward boy when he was in high school, quietly doing his schoolwork, talking to almost no one, coming home to play video games by himself or with his brother, and never going to parties or out for sports like Sam did.

Always a decent enough student, Sam had gone to undergrad on a partial lacrosse scholarship and really didn't flourish until college. But Trey was quietly brilliant in high school. People had been quite surprised when it was announced that Trey was the valedictorian of his graduating class. He'd flatly refused to give the valedictory address. He wouldn't even attend the graduation ceremony, claiming at the time that commencement ceremonies were nothing more than "assemblies for the glorification of triviality."

Past and present, Trey didn't seem to have any friends. Loneliness had to be unavoidable. But even if it were true—even if Trey had spent the night in Florence Loughton's embrace the evening before she was apparently killed....

Oh, fuck. His son was fucked. He turned to his friend. "Ash, come on. There must be something we can do."

"Play the insanity card."

"But you said he'd have to be committed then."

Ash shook his head. "Better than jail. At least he'd get better treatment."

"Ash, my son did not kill Florence Loughton."

"Really? Are you *absolutely* certain?"

Had his friend of over forty years really just asked that? He narrowed his eyes and tried to check the anger that was suddenly coursing through him. "How can you even ask that? You know him. Since the day he was born."

Ash shrugged. "Sometimes shit happens."

"Sometimes shit *happens*?" Jack hissed, not wishing the men at the other end of the bar to overhear. "Ash, you need to stand by my son. He had nothing to do with that woman's murder. You know that." They stared at each other, and Jack realized his hands were in tight, jumpy fists. He forcibly relaxed them and grabbed onto his knees. "Ash…."

"Jack, I can't tell you what I don't believe."

"So what you're telling me—" Jack lowered his voice further until it was almost a whisper. "Because I want to make sure I've got this right. What you're telling me is that you believe my son murdered Florence Loughton."

"Doesn't matter what I believe. I'll defend him as if he were my own son."

A long moment went by, both men not dropping their gaze. "It matters to me."

"Jack, don't get all fucking pissy with me. There's not a person on this earth who's not at least capable of manslaughter. How many people have you killed? Huh? A little slip of the scalpel at the wrong time. Sure it was an accident, but come on. Shit happens."

Then Jack's hands were back in fists. As much as he wanted to take Ash out, to beat the shit right out of him, to spray his blood all over the Sherwood Inn, he wasn't seventeen anymore. They were both now men, sitting in a public bar, in a town that Jack had spent his entire life in, with country club members looking on. And he was a surgeon with a reputation for *not killing* his patients, who had hands to protect. So instead of beating the shit right out of his best friend, he let his anger melt over to despair. "My God, Ash. What are we going to do?"

Ash just shook his head sadly and went back to his beer.

FORTY-FIVE

Trey sunk a french fry in the mound of ketchup he had on his plate, swirled it around so that it was fully coated, and then brought it to his mouth. He took a sip from his glass and asked, "How'd you know I like root beer?"

"Everyone likes root beer," Flo answered.

Trey nodded. "True."

Then they both continued eating. "Scallop?" Trey offered.

"Thank you." With her fingers, Flo picked the golden-brown morsel off of the fork Trey had extended her way and placed it in her mouth. The meat was tender and sweet. "Oh, it's lovely. I must say, I had never tried the scallops."

"Well, you definitely need to get your own order next time. The scallops are awesome at Doug's."

Flo smiled. "Yes." They continued eating in a comfortable silence, the radio playing in the background. She had tuned in to a jazz station. She wasn't sure if Trey liked jazz, but unlike something like country or heavy metal, she'd decided that no one could be offended or bothered by it. Miles Davis's "Summertime" was playing, and no one could be offended by that.

The song changed to "Flamenco Sketches." A good five minutes went by before Trey looked up from the forkful of slaw he was about to put in his mouth and said, "Um, I'm…um, sorry."

Flo looked at him in confusion.

"I'm not, you know, very good at this sort of thing." He shrugged slightly. "People find me…I don't know…boring."

Flo put down her fork. "Boring? That can hardly be true."

"It's hard for me, you know." He closed his eyes for a moment. "Conversations. They're hard."

"Well, then, this is ideal. I'm not much of a conversationalist either."

Trey nodded and went back to his food. Flo put a piece of fish in her mouth and closed her eyes to the notes of Davis's trumpet. Another five minutes went by. The last of Trey's dinner was gone. The song had changed yet again—still Davis, but now "My Funny Valentine." Flo felt some sort of sensation run through her that she hadn't felt in a very long time, and it had nothing to do with fish or the sweet taste of scallops, but everything to do with Trey and the notes that were surging through the room. She was beginning to question her music choice and what Trey must think. How was she to have known that the jazz station would be honoring Miles Davis that night and would be playing one sexy song after another?

"Thanks," he said. "This is nice." He took a sip of root beer. "The music is nice."

She smiled. "I've baked brownies. And I have marble-fudge ice cream to put on top."

"Baked? Like in the oven?"

She nodded.

"Impressive." He smiled. "Thank you."

FORTY-SIX

By Thursday afternoon Seth was slammed. He and Zuke had just returned from a crime scene. A late morning drug deal gone bad had led to two new homicides in Syracuse, and he'd been assigned to both of them. And on top of that, he'd allowed a bunch of little, pain-in-the-ass petty thefts and domestic violence cases to pile up, and now suddenly they were critical; the DA had just let him know that she wanted to meet with him the next day about several of the cases. And then to top it all off, two second-shift detectives and the department secretary had called in sick, so he was fielding more incoming calls than he normally would have. When he saw amongst his other notes on his desk the note from that morning to call Mrs. Barkley, he was naturally disinclined to jump right on that one.

Trey Barkley was a done deal. He'd been all around it and over it, and no matter how he looked at it, it looked the same: just one more lonely woman who got herself mixed up with some crazy fuck. Sure, maybe Trey hadn't meant to kill her, but the result was the same: Florence Loughton was dead, and Trey was responsible. There was no other explanation.

Seth picked up his cell phone and checked the screen. No

texts. No IMs. Nothing from Maddy. He took a quick peek at his inbox, and finding nothing of interest, he set the phone down and picked up the nearest file. He worked steadily for several hours, clearing up most of the backlog of paperwork, before he finally picked up the note from Barkley's mother late that Thursday afternoon and read it fully. So it was about the dog. Here the kid was still worried about the dog. Well, you had to admire that… sorta….

Mrs. Barkley picked up before the end of the first ring. After the obligatory salutations and mild pleasantries were out of the way, Seth said, "So, about the dog…. Last I heard it was being held at the SPCA in Auburn until the estate gets through probate. Guess there was some sort of arrangement made for the dog in—"

"So the dog's alive?" Mrs. Barkley asked in surprise.

"Well, sure. I thought you knew that."

"No! How could I possibly— Oh, thank God! Thank you, detective. Thank you!" Then she disconnected the call.

Seth looked at the receiver. *Huh. Well, that was easy.* He placed the receiver back in the cradle.

FORTY-SEVEN

Trey slipped out of his bedroom late Thursday afternoon and quietly made his way down the stairs on his way to the kitchen. He really just wanted a little something to drink—maybe there was some root beer left from the morning's fishing trip. He stepped carefully on the old stairs. "Fuck," he muttered as one of the oak boards complained loudly under his bare foot. The stairs were totally sneak-proof, something his mother had had installed—he was quite sure of that. If she'd installed something as obvious as security cameras, the jig would be up. So she'd gone with the subtle and innocent-appearing squeaky stair approach. Cunning—his mother was cunning; he had to give her that. He stood stock still, listening for any movement from the front of the house. Satisfied that his approach was still undetected, he made the amazing and slightly dangerous maneuver of shifting his left foot against the wall and using it along with his left hand to push himself to the right, bringing his right leg up quickly so that it made it over the open railing. There was a moment when his body was undecided and considered toppling right over the railing and onto the floor below, but then everything fell into place, and he slid on his ass silently down the wobbly wooden railing.

Now his task was a little easier, for although the downstairs floorboards were still made to squeak, his mother had failed to make all of them squeak, and he'd learned, over time, the exact necessary placement of each foot. Trey made his way soundlessly into the kitchen. He was feeling confidently undiscovered, so he dawdled as he perused the contents of the fridge, the cool air streaming around his body. Should he go ahead and just eat some food too? Have an early dinner? He was contemplating the left-over chicken carcass when he nearly jumped out of his skin.

"Trey! There you are!"

Once the initial adrenaline pulse had dissipated and he'd recovered enough to be irritated, he stepped back, shut the refrigerator door, and gave his mother a look that could put her right to cold chicken carcass status if he actually possessed such powers. "What? What do you want?"

All the excitement melted from his mother's face, and Trey saw the wound he'd inflicted just as clearly as if there were blood pouring from her eyes instead of the moisture that was now taking up residence. How and why did he hurt her so? He opened his mouth to say something—do something that would put that look of young-girl animation back on her face—but then she, with a wave of her hand, waved away his look, his anger, and his rudeness, and smiled.

"Trey, Hector is alive!"

It took just a moment for his brain to realign. *Hector? Alive?* Not dead, but alive somewhere with his little white puff of a tail curling over his back, his tiny pink tongue poised for its next human encounter. Trey's entire body was suddenly too much to deal with. He needed to sit—to sit on this new piece of information, to contemplate, to understand, to weep. His mother, as if sensing this, brought her hand to his arm, the full pressure of her presence suddenly a comfort. "He's being housed, for now, at the Auburn

SPCA. Maybe we could go visit him. If you want. When you're ready." Then she gave his arm one more comforting squeeze and left him alone to sit—to sit on this new piece of information, to contemplate, to understand, to weep.

FORTY-EIGHT

Florence had switched to a nice tawny port. Trey had passed on the wine, but he said yes to decaf with lots of sugar and cream. The brownies were rich and moist. The ice cream, the port, and the chocolate…a meandering symphony on her tongue. She'd taken off her shoes and stretched her bare feet Trey's way, her body easing into the smoothness of the wine, making her want to stretch out fully. She wiggled her toes. "I think people find me snobbish," she stated. When Trey didn't say anything, she went on. "I don't feel like a snob." She sat up a bit, marveling at how just half a glass of wine could make her feel so warmly cozy. "Do snobs know that they are snobs, do you think? Or is that part of the whole persona—the inability to see one's own arrogance?"

"Maybe." He was sitting directly to the left of her at the round oak table, the table being just too big for her to have made his place setting across from her. Frank had picked the table out, insisting that it made the kitchen eating area welcoming. She'd always hated it. And here it was, years after his death, and she'd yet to replace the large, awkward thing. She leaned a little toward Trey.

"I don't think I'm a snob," she persisted. "I think…." Trey

looked her way and bent his head to the side while she thought. "I think," she finally said, "that I lack, somehow, what is necessary to connect." She sat back. "Do you know what I mean?"

Trey nodded. "The inability to connect defines me."

And there it was: she was finally skating around where she wanted to go.

"You were married," Trey stated. "To Mr. Loughton."

Flo nodded her head sadly. "Yes. That is so. But he left me now, didn't he?" She looked at her glass for a moment, then said, "Friendships, relationships...they're hard."

"If not impossible," Trey replied. He took a sip of his coffee and scraped the last bit of brownie from his plate.

"Do you want more brownies?"

"God, no! I mean, it was, um, great, but, I'm totally stuffed." He licked clean his fork, placed it back on the plate, and pushed the whole thing away. He patted his stomach. "Yup, stuffed." Then he rested his right hand against his lips and chin as he put his elbow on the table, naturally falling a bit her way.

Flo took another drink from her glass. "Do you think," she asked, "that a person can lead a fulfilling life without that one deep human connection?" She swirled her wine around and then turned her eyes to him, waiting for, if not demanding, an answer. *Are you lonely, Trey Barkley? Are you as lonely as you've made me become?*

"I hope so," he finally answered. "I'm not very old."

She tilted her head. "So...what? Are you saying you're never going to have that one deep human connection, so you better learn to live the rest of your long life alone, but fulfilled?"

Trey stared at her. She suddenly faltered. She'd gone too far. She'd let the wine mellow her tongue into nonsense and to a level of intimacy that was dangerously treading on offensive.

Then he spoke. "I had a girlfriend. In college. I thought...I don't know…that we were, like, cosmically connected or really more connected on a chemical level. A carbon-carbon triple bond. Acetylene of human connection. Triple bonded. C2H2. But…."

The radio was now off, the room virtually silent, the ticking of the clock in the hallway the only thing that filled the moment until Flo finally whispered, "But…?"

He shrugged. "But pressurized acetylene is super unstable. And exothermic—no oxygen necessary. Just a little bit of agitation," he pulled his hand away from his face in one quick movement, "and KABOOM!"

Flo jumped slightly.

"Then you're making like Humpty Dumpty all over the place."

The hall clock ticked for a long moment. "So you were really hurt," Flo said.

He sat back. "I was devastated." He looked down at the table, pushed the brownie plate further away, and said, "Yeah."

He looked so young, so vulnerable, and she wondered, just briefly, if she was putting him in harm's way. Was he vulnerable to her? Certainly she'd spent most of her life avoiding vulnerability, never allowing *herself* to be put in the position to be devastated. There was safety in disconnect. But looking at Trey Barkley at that moment, his childlike face mixed with the creases of a history of the unimaginable debasement of sanity, knowing that shortly after that devastation his whole world had changed to something she could never quite comprehend, and knowing that he'd gotten so sick that he'd had to leave school and rebuild an entire reality for himself, she felt that deep human connection and felt her own vulnerability. For the first time in her long life, she suddenly found herself in the position to experience her own devastation. She couldn't bear the thought of him in pain.

"Trey—" And then she stopped.

He looked up. "What?" he asked softly.

the chocolate debacle

She hesitated. *What's it like? Are you okay? What's it like to be you?*

She opened her mouth. She closed it. Trey cocked his head—that same tilt, that same inquisitive look that Hector so often gave her. "I…I was just wondering…." His head moved just a fraction of an inch further to the right, and Flo thought she might just burst out in tears. "Are you…are you absolutely certain you don't want any more brownies?"

He narrowed his eyes. "Well. Okay. Sure. But just a tiny piece. And absolutely no more ice cream."

FORTY-NINE

Seth glanced at his cell phone, picked it up, and checked the screen. Still nothing. It was getting late and was almost time to pack it in and go pick up his mother for her hair appointment. He considered sending off a quick email to Maddy about one of this morning's murders since he knew she'd been assigned one of the deaths. It wouldn't seem odd that he'd follow up with her. He brought up his departmental email account on his laptop but then thought better of it. If she had something to report, she'd contact him. They'd had minimum contact since the baseball game—a few *Thanks, Let's do it again, I had a good time* bullshit texts back and forth, and that was about it. He'd meant to ask her out again, but she hadn't really seemed all that interested by his attempts to reach out. And now she was totally ignoring him.

Well, fuck her. He just didn't need this. He just didn't.

He turned from his laptop and picked up one of the domestic violence files that he needed to talk to the DA about the next day. There was nothing more he needed to do there; it was nothing out of the ordinary—just a case where the wife had walloped her husband with his own belt buckle after she caught him with another woman. She got him right in the eye, and now he was doing the whole pirate thing. Damn, people sure knew how to fuck each other up. Life would be so much easier if everyone just lived alone in their own deep hole—like crabs on a seashore. Maybe every once in a while you'd leave your hole, fuck your nearest neighbor fast and hard, and then just crawl right on back down where you came from. No pressures. No expectations. No loneliness. No love. No stupid jealous rages. Just fucking and sitting in your own hole. He chuckled to himself, then sighed.

Hell, he was pretty much already there, although he'd sure like the *fuck your nearest neighbor* part to happen a little more often.

He powered down his laptop and watched as it did its thing. Once the screen had turned black, he shut it and then locked it in the side drawer of his desk. As he stood up, sliding his cell phone into the front pocket of his pants, it made its familiar whistle, tingling gently against his hip and popping Maddy right back into his head. He removed the phone without looking at it and sat back in his chair, then set the phone on his desk. He flipped through more notes that he had to deal with in the morning, straightened out a bunch of paper files, and fiddled with his pens. He sat back a long moment, the springs on his chair complaining, and stared at the little metal contraption. Damn. He snapped back upright and picked up his cell.

Relief and some sort of pleasure pulsed through his body; the text was from Maddy. Here she'd gone and finally answered him back. He smiled as he read, *My imaginary gun, Viola, is lonely.* He set the phone down.

He leaned back again in his chair, brought his hands up behind his head, and thought. A couple of hours of payback-waiting is what she deserved. He'd sent her that first text nearly seven hours ago. Sure she was at work, but had she not taken a lunch? He narrowed his eyes and leaned back further. Just when gravity was about to knock him on his ass, he popped back up, picked up his cell phone, and tapped in, *How about Clint and Viola go see a movie or something tomorrow night? 'Course we'd have to chaperone the two of them….*

Her answer was immediate: *Imaginary Viola would love that.*

Hmmm. Maybe the whole living-in-a-hole thing was as ridiculous as it sounded—a cop out and utter nonsense.

FIFTY

When he entered the house early Thursday evening, Jack was still feeling the effects of the two quick beers and the aftershocks of his conversation with Ash. He knew Annette wouldn't expect him home at such an early hour. He considered creeping past her studio, trying to avoid the squeak of the old wooden floors and the impossibly loud staircase, to make his way to his second-floor office where he had a nice, quiet bottle of scotch awaiting him. If he were called in for a surgery consult, he could claim food poisoning without even lying; he couldn't imagine how else one might categorize scotch—surely it was within the food category. Then, if he were very lucky, it might be hours before Annette came in search of him. He was actually bending over in a creeping sort of way, bringing his right foot forward with care, when he had the sudden image of himself go through his head: a slightly over-weight middle-aged man; his hair more grey than brown; his face constricted with stealthy concentration, exaggerating the lines on his face; his right leg posed for his escape. Was he really creeping around his own house? Was he really coveting the companionship of a nice, quiet bottle of scotch rather than his wife? He put his right foot down and straightened up a bit.

Sure, his wife's jabbering was at times equivalent to aural diarrhea, but it was also endearing, one of the things he'd loved about her most. He recalled those nights of their early marriage, after they'd rolled away from each other's sweaty bodies, as a variety of Annette's moisture lingered pleasantly on his skin, as their bed began to cool, as his mind drifted toward blissful sleep, how the sensation of her soft voice would gently fill the darkness. How it had calmed him then. It had softened the harsh stress of his professional life and had brought him back to the simplicity of life. She'd told him everything in those early months: her dreams regarding their future, her imagined children, what moved her, what she loved most about art, what lingered in the dark caves of her soul, what she most loved about him, what she loved most about them. It was often hours of her pleasant prattle, along with occasional input from him, which dominated their nights.

"You like to hear me talk," she'd stated into the darkness.

"Uh-huh," he'd said sleepily.

She pushed up on her elbow and leaned over him, her hair—long back then—falling across his chest and almost bringing up the sensation of wanting her again. "Someday, before we know it, you'll want to cram your fist down my throat, if only just to stop the next word from leaving my mouth." She'd laughed then.

"What?" Her words had suddenly thrust him into wakefulness. "No. Are you nuts?" She'd traced her fingers across his chest and not so gently bit his left nipple. "Ow!" he'd exclaimed.

"There're parts of you that hate me even now," she'd whispered as her teeth moved down his chest with the constant threat of further pain. He'd shaken his head in mild protest, although if truth be told, he'd sort of wanted to punch her even then. "Sure, there are parts of me that you may grow to love even more…but it's the parts of me that you *think* you love, and *absolutely* the parts that you hate now, that will become so, so large that there'll be moments when our love will seem so very, very small."

He'd brought his hands to her face, holding her teeth a safe distance from his skin, and stated, "You're wrong." He'd smiled and said, "But I guess now I know how you really feel about me."

She'd laughed again and settled back down next to him on the bed. She'd grown quiet. He'd closed his eyes. He wouldn't allow her words to dominate the moment—to concern him. His body blended into the bed, his mind drifting away from her existence. Then, right before her words might have only been a dream, she'd said, "Someday you'll recall this conversation. Someday you'll think, 'I don't want to hear the next word that's about to leave her mouth. I want to cram my fist down her fucking throat.' But you know what? It'll be okay, because with every bit of pain, with every fist I swallow, with every bite I inflict until you bleed, there will lie beneath the pain and hate the steadfastness of eternal joy—of eternal love."

And he stood there, his right foot resting lightly on the floor, recalling this conversation of twenty-eight years ago, but not for the first time. He was recalling it for the umpteenth time, as he recalled it every time he felt his fingers itch with the desire to form a fist, every time he wished she'd go away—to just go ahead and run off with Ash or maybe some fellow artist—or every time he yearned to turn back time to that point where he might have caught Ash's eye and made some sort of declaration instead of never quite answering Ash's question: "Are you sure? Are you fucking sure?" Wishing that he'd not turned his eyes away and then just gone ahead and married her, but rather that he'd smiled with confidence toward Ash and answered, "Yes! I'm sure!" Wishing that he'd spent the last thirty-five years believing, as Annette believed, in the steadfastness of eternal joy—of eternal love. Wishing that he could indeed shove his fist into her mouth and find something worthy of his anger, something worthy of his love. Wishing that their son hadn't become this endless source of frustration and disappointment. Wishing that he could put his foot down firmly on the old floorboards and go to his wife. Wishing that he didn't believe, as Ash believed, that shit happens. And finally, wishing more than anything else, that he believed, as Annette believed, in the total innocence of their son. He felt—as heavy as a stone—his doubt. It lay between his wife and him—bigger than anything that had ever lain between them—and it was insurmountable. He set his right foot against the old floorboards more firmly and then silently eased his way away from his wife and toward his nice, quiet, uncomplicated bottle of scotch.

FIFTY-ONE

Trey heard what must have been his father coming up the stairs. If it had been his mother, the stairs would have sung the song of her approach, but the sounds were subdued and barely audible. He held his breath as he waited for the sounds to dictate the final destination of his father's approach. He was both relieved and bitterly disappointed when the sounds disappeared into his father's study. Trey longed for someone to talk to. He longed to not feel so alone.

He'd spent most of the past hour researching the Auburn SPCA online. It appeared to be a decent place. Even though their website claimed to be a "No Kill" SPCA—that they no longer euthanized for space—Trey was worried. The sooner he got Hector out of there the better. He'd already downloaded the adoption application. It was a complicated document filled with every sort of trickery, trying to filter out the crazies who thought they wanted a dog. He got that, even respected the process, but the document was tricky as hell. He might have to ask his dad for help filling it out, but that would clue his dad to the fact that he was determined to bring Hector home. His dad had a low tolerance for dogs. When his boyhood dog, Jessie, a wonderful black lab, had died at the age of fourteen shortly after Trey had returned home from Brown, his dad had flatly refused to get another dog. Sure, Trey was a little nuts at the time, and sure, maybe his dad thought a puppy would just add to the general state of nuttiness, but Trey's longing for Jessie had been almost unbearable.

Trey placed the pen he'd been grasping in his hand between his teeth and chewed nervously as he read over the application one more time. He sighed with determination, removed the pen from his mouth, and carefully wrote the word *Hector* in the space that asked: *The name of the pet you are applying for*. Adding his name to the application was no problem, nor was his address, but when he got to the part that requested his employer, he faltered. Self-employed was the obvious answer, but was that even true anymore? Then there was the question: *Will you call us if you have behavioral issues with adopted pet?* What did they want the answer to be? Then they wanted his veterinarian's name. Should he lie and state that he had one, even though the previous question asked about his present number of pets, which was zero? If he stated he had a vet, wouldn't that look suspect? Yet shouldn't he have a vet ready and in the wings?

The application was two pages long, each question more cryptic than the last. *Do you live with your parents?* Unfortunately, yes. *How many adults live in the household?* How many indeed? *Have all members of the household visited with the animal as requested?* Of course his mother would go to the SPCA, but would his dad? *Why do you want to adopt this animal?* The space to write the answer to this particular question was so small. Trey was more than capable of writing a thousand-word essay on why he wanted Hector. Should he include a separate sheet? *May we conduct a home visit?* Would they insist on seeing his bedroom? *Are you moving in the near future?* Was he? *Was he?*

Trey's heart began to beat a little faster. He took deep breaths.

He dropped the pen and held tightly to the edge of his desk. Would his mom love Hector the way that he loved Hector? Would she take care of Hector if he was forced to leave? If he were to spend years of his life in prison for being convicted of killing Mrs. Loughton, would his mom bring Hector for a visit? Do they allow dog visitations? Would it be fair to bring Hector home only to end up deserting him for what would likely become the rest of Hector's life? Maybe the rest of his own life?

Twenty-six. Twenty-six, soon to be twenty-seven, and where was he? Holed up in his boyhood bedroom, pretty much a giant failure all the way around. What was it he'd wanted for himself, before just getting out of bed had become a big fucking deal, before his head had been infiltrated by all the fucking chaos, before the climax of his day had become big ol' Rex squatting down to finally take his morning shit? There was a time when his own vast intelligence was almost intimidating, when it was almost impossible to contain all that his brain was capable of accomplishing, and when his mind jumped with the anticipation of all it was going to contribute to the world: the research he was going to do, the places organic chemistry would bring him, or more accurately, the places he would bring organic chemistry. First an undergraduate degree in organic chemistry, then a doctorate in biochemistry, specifically studying the chemistry of the brain.

He might have married Stephanie. They might have had children. They might have even had a dog of their own. He might have had his own personal dog shit to pick up in his backyard.

It really wasn't such a shock; it's not like he hadn't seen it coming. "Trey, you're so weird!" was becoming standard stuff out of Stephanie's mouth. He'd tried to make her understand, but that only seemed to complicate the issues.

Trey had been making his way across the quad after a long night of trying to get her to understand the things that had become so urgent to get her to understand. She'd left his dorm room only hours ago. A brisk winter wind was cutting through his houndstooth jacket and red hunting cap, which he wore just for kicks; no one ever seemed to get the obvious Salinger reference. He was feeling strangely better that day. He'd just cancelled his appointment with Dr. Tondej, had just aced an organic chemistry quiz, and was busy whistling Massive Attack's "Safe from Harm" when he spotted her coming out of the student union. Only she wasn't alone. She decidedly was not alone.

He took a few quick strides until their intersection was imminent and stopped. She might have seen him sooner if it hadn't been for the fact that she was so totally absorbed in whatever the damn guy she was walking with was saying. As it was, she nearly ran into Trey.

He nodded his head. "What's up?"

"Trey!"

"Stephanie."

She turned bright red, and although thirteen minus nine had been four for all of time, Trey had yet to, after all these years, figure out its derivation.

So there was no more Stephanie, no organic chemistry degree, no house, and no backyard dog shit. There was nothing.

The things he might have done if not for the fact that his life had been assailed, his brain permeated by his own fucked-up organic chemistry—fucked by the very thing he'd hoped to manipulate into worldly good. The mystery of what made it all happen, how the brain chemistry was all laid down…he'd hoped to delve into and solve the very mystery of what now made it impossible. The irony that he'd been fucked by what he'd hope to fuck was almost laughable.

When he'd placed that rope around his neck and kicked that chair from beneath him, it wasn't because he'd wanted to die—especially not in front of his own father—but because he'd wanted so much more. Because that *so much more* had been so firmly taken away and no one had offered—even now—more than a lifetime of: *the things he might have done.* Perhaps *the things he might have done* would reassemble in his next life—reconvene in a more appropriate individual. A second chance to get it right. But that had all been part of his own fucked-up brain chemistry, because he now understood, he now got it, that this was it—all he had. He couldn't jar his neurons back into a reassembled order by tying a rope around his neck. Even in his next life the fucked-up would follow.

What he needed was to unfuck the fucked-up. And somehow, what he had, what he did: the dogs; The Village; his family; the part he played as the Ghost of Christmas Present; the scant few friendships he'd managed, including Mrs. Loughton; the dogs that loved him; the fact that he was able to leave his room, manage his own money, not make his parents totally miserable, and maintain a fragile, but still pretty good, relationship with his brother; that he'd learned, for the most part, to manage his meds, manage his freak-outs, and accept the fact that even when he failed there was always that reassemble that brought him back to where he was, for he was indeed surviving schizophrenia or schizoaffective disorder or whatever the fuck the diagnosis de jour happened to be—all of it had somehow unfucked the fucked-up.

He had been happy. It had been enough—until now. Until he'd been directly responsible for the loss of Mrs. Loughton and the loss of Hector. And, oh fuck, how that rope was now once again such a seductive bitch.

FIFTY-TWO

Annette heard the garage door open and the soft rumble of Jack's car as he pulled in. She heard the silence when he turned the car off, then the muffled racket of the descent of the garage door. She waited for him to come to her as he so clearly should have come to her, to share with her what had happened during the fishing trip with their son and let her know how the meeting went with Ash. Was there news? Had something been revealed that Ash could use to free their son of this asinine murder charge? She heard him pause right outside her door. Then she unquestionably heard him squeak his way upstairs.

She wanted to be angry, to be hurt, but it was hard to cultivate anger when the sound of the garage door had made her annoyed. It was hard to cultivate hurt when she'd held her breath and listened to the silence of his hesitation outside her door. "Move on. Move on," she'd whispered, then sighed with relief when he had indeed moved on.

Although, if truth be told, she longed to feel anger, to feel hurt, to feel anything close to an emotion with regard to her husband. Or perhaps more accurately, she longed for him to feel some sort of emotion with regard to her. If only he weren't so removed and then removed again. It was so easy to blame her son. It was so easy to imagine idealism if only Trey were indeed the man they'd both assumed he'd be when he'd been such a bright and pleasant child. So easy, and so wrong. She knew this removal had very little or nothing to do with their troubled son and everything to do with the fact that Jack had never really loved her as she deserved to be loved.

And it was this—this knowledge of not getting what she deserved—that had always left her desperate. And it was this desperation that had always kept him from loving her the way that she deserved. She longed to feel anger, to feel hurt, but all she presently felt was the desperate irony of their screwed-up love.

FIFTY-THREE

Flo Loughton lingered by the gate with Trey. She let the hot summer night's breeze blow through her hair without concern. She closed her eyes and listened to the constant trill of crickets, only broken by the distant rumble of a bullfrog that presided in the neighbor's garden pond and the occasional noise of a passing car. She could smell the sweet night scent of the primrose that grew near her garage and the faint smell of chocolate, which still lingered on her or perhaps was simply drifting through the open side door. Hector sat at her feet; she could feel the soft tickle of his fur on the tops of her bare feet and ankles. The dog sighed softly and leaned his head against the bottom of her calf. She could feel the weight of Trey's existence, his warmth almost heating the night up further. It felt so good to be alive.

"Thanks, Mrs. Loughton, for dinner and the great brownies," he said.

It felt odd to hear him call her that, and she almost said, *Oh for heaven's sake, call me Flo*. But then she checked herself, afraid of what his response might be. So she remained silent, both of them standing near the gate, face to face, only a few feet away from each other, taking in the night sounds and the hot night's breeze and the sweet odors, neither one seemingly in any hurry to press time forward.

The breeze stopped for a moment as the slow guttural call of the bullfrog dominated the night with an urgent, basal intensity; she felt its reverberation pulse through her body. Oh how lonely he seemed in his need. She turned her eyes to Trey and smiled with the soft contentment of being human and sharing this moment of the perfect harmony of sounds and smells and human sensations with another human being. Trey looked away from her gaze and looked down at the ground. He shifted his hands into the back pockets of his jeans and shuffled his feet, making her suddenly alert to the fact that it was now her turn to talk, that his statement demanded a reply, that perhaps one of them, in fact, *was* in a hurry to press time forward. She, too, shifted on her feet, her body suddenly feeling heavy and cumbersome. "It was no bother at all," she said formally. "I am so glad that you could come."

Trey nodded without his eyes leaving the ground, and then, with an awkward movement of uncertainty, he hugged her briefly, the sides of his arm pressing slightly into her shoulders, his hands held straight away from her back, his face never coming near hers. And then he was gone, through the gate, down the driveway, down the sidewalk—gone into the harmony of the night.

FIFTY-FOUR

Trey thought a lot about death and what it meant to be dead. He still dreamt of Mrs. Loughton. Months after her death, her lingering presence still filled his nights and days. It was not horribly unpleasant most of the time. But what did that mean with regard to death? Chemistry being chemistry meant that by now most of what made Mrs. Loughton was now transposed. At least the solid part of Mrs. Loughton was surely unrecognizable. But the ethereal part—the part that had breezed through the air as they stood by the gate, had wiggled from her fingertips, and that lingered with him now—that part was something that couldn't die as long as it was with him.

It was good, and it was bad: to never be alone.

Hector, like Trey, spent his days in limbo. Even though the provisions in Mrs. Loughton's will clearly stated that Trey was to have the dog upon her death, a lot of people, including the Auburn SPCA, seemed to take issue with giving the dog to her accused murderer. So Hector remained in Auburn. He'd become the belle of the SPCA, having gained full freedom to run about the place; the staff of the SPCA had clearly fallen in love. Trey and his mom had been there to visit Hector, but other than the pure joy that Hector had emitted upon Trey's arrival, Trey had found the rest of the event unbearable.

He hated the smell, which was chemical and infused Hector's fluffy white fur. He hated the barking of orphan dogs and the painful mewing of homeless cats. He hated the suspicion of the staff; they never left him alone with Hector, even for a moment.

His mother had offered to take him again, but he had not chosen to return.

Hector, like Mrs. Loughton, filled his nights and filled his days. The ethereal Hector bounced through his bedroom with boundless joy. Was the ethereal part of Hector less real simply because his body still functioned? This was the sort of thing he wanted to measure, to define, to fully identify—

"Trey, are you with me?"

Trey blinked.

"Do you understand what I'm saying?" Ash asked.

Trey had no idea what Ash had been saying, nor was he particularly eager to find out, so he just nodded his head.

"Hang in there for me, okay? Just two more weeks and then this thing will begin. I doubt the trial will go for more than a week or so."

"Did you file the suit against the Auburn SPCA like I asked you?"

Ash rolled his eyes. "One court case at a time. Okay, buddy?"

Trey looked at the floor of his bedroom and caught the strap of his backpack with his left foot. He lifted his leg, the backpack rising from the floor. It dangled a moment before he let it drop off the edge of his toe. "It seems to me that if you're my lawyer and I'm paying you and if I ask you to do something…."

"Technically your parents are paying me—paying me to defend you against a murder charge. They are not paying me to sue the local SPCA."

Hector's little pink tongue tasted like fish. Trey had not meant to laugh, but when he did, Hector was there, lapping away at his open mouth.

Ash sighed loudly. Trey looked up as Hector bounced away.

"I guess I'll have to file a civil suit," Trey said. "I can do that, right?"

Ash sighed again. "Listen, Trey. I need you to try to put all your energies into preparing yourself for this trial. What good are you going to be to Hector if you're in jail?"

Hector bounded back across the room, and Mrs. Loughton called from somewhere outside the window. Hector stopped mid-stride and cocked his head.

"Trey? Did you hear me?"

"What?"

"I said I've decided not to put you on the stand."

"Yeah. Okay." Trey's eyes fell back to Hector, which he knew, of course, wasn't really Hector, but the ethereal Hector.

"Do you have a proper suit?" Ash asked.

"It says in her will that Hector should go to me. I think it's very proper."

"A proper suit to wear. To wear to the trial. You'll want to wear something other than a T-shirt, shorts, and Mets cap."

Trey was alarmed. "My hat brings me luck!"

Ash blew out another sigh.

"I'm getting tired of your sighs," Trey stated. "I might just find it necessary to instruct my parents to withhold your payment."

Trey watched as Ash struggled with this newest development. Perhaps now Ash would become more reasonable. Ash finally dipped his head in acquiesce and said, "You can bring your hat. But best to leave it in your lap in order to show respect to the court. Besides, I'm pretty sure Judge Frankel is a Yankees fan."

It was Trey's turn to sigh. "Well, then I am truly fucked."

FIFTY-FIVE

Annette chose to meet Asher in his large apartment, which made up the second and third floor of the building he owned on Genesee Street. He rented out the very bottom of the building to an upscale gift shop, which carried a variety of unique, if not slightly overpriced, items. His law office consisted of a few rooms on the second floor, its windows facing Genesee Street. The back of the second floor and the entire third floor was his home. All of its windows faced the lake, which was breathtaking on this clear late summer day, the leaves on the trees of the surrounding hills just taking on the color of fall, the sky turning pink with the lateness of the day, and the waters looking the same sort of pink as the sky.

He indicated for her to sit in the large black leather chair that she knew was his chair, which faced the lake and sky and the ending beauty of the day. She sat. She mentally forced herself to stop wringing her hands. She placed them in her lap, one resting on each thigh, her fingers tightening against her muscles until the sensation was just shy of pain.

"Drink?" he asked. She hesitated just long enough for him to smile as he made his way to the bar. "Vodka cranberry, right?"

She nodded.

She sat in silence as she watched him drop three ice cubes into each of two short tumblers. The ting of the ice hitting the glass was pleasant, as was the crackling when the vodka hit the ice. Ash added a generous amount of cranberry juice to hers and left his unmolested by the influx of sweetness. He gave hers a quick mix with the tip of his finger, slipped a dark green cocktail napkin under the bottom of each glass, picked up both glasses, and stepped back across the room. As he handed hers down to her—as she reached for the drink, their hands coming together in the space of the perfect room—he said, "Shall we just get drunk and fuck?"

And just like that, all the horrible things that were going on in her head, all the despair and frustration, all her worry, and her anger evaporated. She laughed. "And that is why I will always love you," she said. "You always know just the right inappropriate thing to say at that perfect inappropriate time. Thank you."

He let go of her drink as she took control. "No problem." He stepped back and sat down in a chair that faced away from the window and toward her. He pressed his glass against his bottom lip and tilted it until the ice fell forward, letting the clear liquid disappear into his mouth. Annette closed her eyes to her own cold infusion and then sat back hoping that the alcohol and Ash's rare fine mood and the glow of the setting sun and the sudden calmness she felt would all settle in, and that she might keep this newfound relief for a least another moment or two. With her eyes still closed, she briefly entertained a fucking-Ash scenario, which initially added a sliver of pleasure to the moment, but then that sliver was quickly replaced with something much closer to reality—something sharp and painful.

She opened her eyes and beseeched him. "Ash, the trial's next week!"

"I'm fully aware of that, Annette."

His words hit her like a slap. The desperation of her words, the belittlement of his words, and her overwhelming fear polluted the lovely room, polluted Ash's rare fine mood, polluted the pleasure of the moment. Any further possibility of sexual jokes or banter was gone. She was brought back to the horrible reality that her son would most likely be convicted of murder in the second degree. Maybe he'd be found not responsible by reason of mental disease, and would then very likely spend all of his youth, if not the rest of his life, in some sort of mental health care facility, which is exactly why Ash had decided to avoid the mental illness defense, explaining that it was possible that Trey could easily wind up a captive of the mental health care system far longer than a possible jail sentence if found guilty of murder in the second degree.

But this made absolutely no sense. Ash was going strictly for a not guilty verdict, but the thought that Trey, if found guilty, might spend at least twenty years in prison for a crime he did not commit…it just wasn't fair.

"Don't be that way," she begged.

"Then stop making ridiculous statements."

"I don't even know why I'm here."

"I don't either."

She stared at him. He stared back. She looked away as she placed her glass on the table. She returned to staring at him. He made no move to speak.

"So you'd like me to leave," she finally said.

"If you'd like."

"Ash…."

"Annette."

"Fuck you." She felt even angrier when her eyes filled with tears.

He shrugged.

She closed her eyes and rubbed her face with her hands. She

willed her body to get up, to turn away from the lovely room, to walk out, to slam the door, but she kept her head within her hands and didn't move. "Ash, you know why I'm here. You know."

"I can't give you what you want," he said almost, but not quite, kindly. "Do you think I like this? Do you think I want to go into court with literally no defense? Do you think I don't love him too?"

She looked up. "So you have nothing for me? Nothing for Trey?"

He shook his head. "As I've said before, I'm going to try to damage their case, point out the weakness of their evidence, build empathy for Trey, introduce other possible scenarios.... It's going to just come down to what the jury believes, how Trey comes off. I've experts who'll testify regarding the misconceived correlation between violence and mental illness. Experts on schizophrenia who'll talk about the unlikelihood of a sexual relationship between Florence Loughton and Trey. That will damage their most likely scenario—that her death was caused by some sort of kinky sexual tryst turned ugly. I don't plan to put Trey on the stand. We'll have your testimony. Jack's. Other character witnesses." He shook his head. "It's just going to have to be enough. We just have to pick the right jury. I have some control over that. Trey will be fine in court. The worst case scenario: he cries or something. That might not be a bad thing. It's not like he's likely to get angry and start screaming."

Annette lifted up her face and wiped at her nose with the back of her hand.

"Really, Annette," Ash continued, his voice softer now, "their case is rather weak."

She nodded, picked up her glass, and removed the dark green cocktail napkin from around its bottom. There was an awkward moment as she held the glass in one hand, the napkin in the other.

the chocolate debacle

Finally, deciding not risk to Ash's disapproval by placing the glass directly back on the wood of his cherry coffee table, she kept hold of it as she blew her nose in the napkin with her other hand. "Well, that's something. You've given me something."

FIFTY-SIX

Seth walked into the coffee shop Wednesday morning two months after Florence Loughton had been found murdered in her home and one week before Trey Barkley's trial for second-degree murder was set to begin. It was the coffee shop that Florence had just so happened to buy coffee every day of the workweek for the past year—that is until two weeks before her death, when she just stopped showing up each morning at 8:40, a fact that Seth found intriguing.

It was the seventh time he'd stopped in during the past couple of weeks. It was a nice place—a far cry better than Dunkin' Donuts—but the coffee and pastries were not why he was there. If he had an extra thirty dollars a week, which was approximately the difference in price between the two places, he might have put up with Zuke's bitching and insisted that they switch their morning ritual from Dunkin' Donuts to there. But it had nothing to do with his culinary cravings; coffee was coffee as long as it gave you what you needed. His cravings to go there came from somewhere other than his stomach—some stupid part of him that he couldn't leave well enough alone.

No matter how hard he tried, no matter how many times Zuke

had told him to let it go, he just couldn't seem to get that phone call that was made from this coffee shop out of his mind. Who does that in this day and age? Who wouldn't use their cell phone? The way he figured, it was either a person who was some leftover-hippy-who-refuses-to-get-a-cell-phone sort, a very elderly person, or someone who hoped the call would be untraceable.

Weeks earlier, Seth had talked to each employee himself, even though he knew that other officers had already done so. He'd asked repeatedly about the regular customers, who Florence Loughton might have talked to those last few weeks of her life, what time she had come each day, what she had ordered, how long she'd been frequenting the place, if she ever sat down and drank her coffee in the shop or if she always took it to go…. The answers to his questions got him no closer to the phone call. No one seemed to be able to tell him who might have made the call; they claimed it wasn't all that unusual for some patron to have lost their cell phone or to have had it die and ask to use the phone.

He'd looked carefully at each of the employees the first few times he'd been in the shop. He'd asked careful questions and done his homework. No one had been fired or left who'd been working that evening of the phone call. None of the employees had acted as if they had anything to hide. No one had seemed the least bit concerned to see him back repeatedly. They called him Detective Wooley and filled his second cup of coffee for free. The darling little blonde college-age girl had actually slipped him a free raspberry scone the last time he was here. He was pretty sure the phone call hadn't been made by an employee, nor were they covering for anyone.

He'd looked carefully at each of the individuals who came in regularly. He'd talked to the ones who were in no way suspicious, hoping they might remember something, but he had gotten nowhere. He'd only watched the other regulars who were men and who fit his personal criteria as possible murderers. When he felt, by observation, that they were unlikely suspects, he would talk to them about the Loughton case, checking them off his list one by one. He'd managed to narrow it down to three random men who just rubbed him the wrong way. Even though he knew it was extremely unlikely that he'd link the phone call to any of these three guys and then in turn link that phone call to a possible murder suspect, he still wanted to know who'd made that damn thirty-eight-second phone call at 5:39 on the last evening that Florence Loughton was seen alive. It bugged the hell out of him.

He ordered his coffee black and sat down at the table he'd come to call his own. Today he was going to get down to serious business. He was going to move this thing forward and get this all behind him. He'd come armed with a photo of Florence Loughton and determination; if nothing happened today, he was done. He glanced at the other patrons. Most people at this early hour just grabbed their coffee to go, but there was a smattering of individuals who were already there, hunkered down in front of their laptops as if they were permanent fixtures.

One was a woman he saw almost every time he'd been there. He'd already talked to her, as had other officers; she lived in her own little computer world and knew nothing about Florence Loughton.

There was a young guy Seth had seen several times. He was a graduate student, aware of the murder case, but could not remember ever seeing Florence Loughton.

Today there were a few people he'd never seen before. There was a middle-aged black man typing away at his computer, and an older man with a shaggy white beard and bushy eyebrows who was staring at his monitor, his hands fixed and poised unproductively above the keyboard. There was a sexy thirty-something-year-old woman who had her laptop open but was tapping away on her cell phone. Her legs were naked and crossed, and her sandal had slipped from her left foot. Seth enjoyed a moment of watching her toes bounce in the air. No matter what, he intended to ask this woman some questions.

Other than that it was just a slow, steady flow of people grabbing something to eat or drink before heading out for their day.

He checked his watch. It was 8:25 a.m. He sat back, spread the morning newspaper out in front of him, and waited.

His iPhone whistled quietly, and he glanced down at the screen. He laughed as he read the text: *Just found a curling iron up this dead guy's arse!*

Dr. Maddy Hatcher. He was becoming quite fond of Dr. Maddy Hatcher. They'd been seeing each other pretty steadily over the past few weeks. They were taking it slow—hadn't had "the talk" yet—which was just fine by him. But they were thoroughly enjoying each other. Shrugging aside, it appeared to be mutual; she seemed to be quite fond of Detective Seth Wooley. That coming Saturday they had plans to go to a movie with Zuke and Angie, then out to Dinosaur Bar-B-Que. A first meeting for the women. Now *that* ought to be an interesting excursion. Seth wasn't exactly dreading it—not in the way he was dreading the day Maddy would meet his mother—but he wasn't holding out much hope for the evening.

He tapped into his phone, *Curling iron? What color? I'm missing mine.* Just as he hit send, the first of his three men entered the coffee shop. Seth put his phone on silent and studied the man. He was in his early forties, tall, but small in frame. He was dressed today much as he had dressed every time Seth had seen him: in simple khakis and a plain T-shirt. He did exactly what he'd done every time Seth had seen him: he headed right for the counter without so much as a glance at any of the other patrons and fidgeted impatiently. His left leg twitched, his hands moved endlessly, and his eyes, as restless as his hands, blinked rhythmically. Seth didn't find any of this behavior all that interesting or disconcerting, but what set this individual apart from the other patrons who came in daily for coffee was the way that, once his large coffee had been secured, once he'd added sugar, cream, and a shake of cinnamon, this man stood stock still in the middle of the shop—his coffee held out in front of him, his body now perfectly still—and stared down each of the other patrons, one by one, until they either acknowledged his existence or moved on. He did this for about a half hour, slowly sipping his coffee, nodding a greeting once eye contact had been established. When his coffee was gone, he'd leave.

"What's up with that guy?" Seth had asked the darling little blonde college-age girl.

She'd shrugged. "Don't know. He's harmless. Nobody complains." The whole daily ritual kind of freaked Seth out, but he also found it intriguing, slightly suspicious, and…maybe useful.

Seth didn't wait for the man's eyes to land on him; rather, he went directly to him as the man continued to stand stock still in the middle of the shop. "Hello, sir," Seth said. "I'm Detective Wooley." He flashed him his badge from his wallet and handed him his card, which the man took readily and studied with great interest. Seth gave him a moment with the card and then went on. "I can't help but notice that you, like me, come here pretty often. And you look like the kind of guy who's super observant—like there's not a whole lot that passes you by." The man narrowed his eyes with don't-bullshit-me suspicion, but Seth continued with his chosen tack. "I was hoping that maybe you could help me." Seth pulled the photo out of the breast pocket of his shirt and handed it to the man. "Do you know this woman?"

The man nodded and stared without emotion at Florence Loughton's professional corporate photo—the one that had been in all the newspapers. "Sure. She was murdered a while back."

"Right. But did you know she used to get her coffee here? Did you ever see her here?"

"The guy who did it is going to trial soon."

"That's right."

"But you're still investigating," he stated, handing the photo back.

"Loose ends. Hate to leave them untied."

The man stared at him until Seth felt uncomfortable, and then the man said, "Loose ends tend to flap around, tangle into a big mess."

Seth laughed. "That's right. I hate that."

There was another long, unnerving stare-down before the man finally said, "I'd seen her here."

Seth nodded. "You ever talk to her?"

This time the stare-down didn't faze Seth. "No. Not me."

Seth waited. He'd won many a staring contest in his day, but this one he lost. He blinked and asked, "But you saw someone else talk to her?" The man indicated the other side of the room with a quick tilt of his head. Seth turned to follow his gaze. "Him? The guy with the beard? The old guy?" Seth had never seen him before today; he was not one of his three, not anyone Seth would have looked at twice.

Seth studied the man a moment. His hands were still resting lightly on the keyboard, his fingers not moving, his eyes never leaving the screen. The only thing that came to Seth's mind was a hippie-fied Santa Clause. He turned back to the other man and waited.

"Just once," the man finally said, staring at Santa Claus. "He gave her coffee. She didn't seem too pleased." Then a thought seemed to pass across the man's face. He turned his eyes back to Seth and stared.

This time Seth didn't lose. When the man blinked, Seth said, "Anything else?"

"Just that that was the last time I ever saw her. The last time she was in here."

Seth didn't bother with his badge or preliminaries; he just walked right up to ol' hippie Santa, pushed the photo of Florence Loughton in front of the guy's computer screen, and said, "Do you know this woman?"

Santa startled with surprise. The word *Floie* left his mouth. His hand reached out for the photo.

Seth smiled. "I was also wondering," he said as he let him hold the photo. "Do you own a cell phone?"

FIFTY–SEVEN

Annette walked around the tall, womanlike structure. It was late in the day; the sun's setting rays were slanting through the high window, the particles of clay floating, the light casting long shadows of the sculpture across her studio floor. If only she could capture that—the lovely shadows of a long day past. Her eyes returned to the structure. She studied her critically. She stepped onto the ladder and looked into what should have been her eyes. They were hopeless in their absence. It was just the look she'd hoped to imprison within the clay, but would it transfer to the permanency of bronze? Sometimes you lost something in the process of making it less vulnerable. She stepped off the ladder and patted her hands together. She decided she was done. Now she would begin the long process of bronzing. She stepped around her one more time. First she must slice the sculpture into smaller, more manageable pieces. She picked up the largest of her wire clay cutters, held the handles—one in each hand—and pulled the wire tight. Where to begin? She eyed the figure's head. She took three steps back up onto the ladder and showed her the wire. "Are you ready?" she asked.

There was a small knock on her studio door. She hesitated. She was reluctant to turn away from the wire poised near her creation's neck.

"Mom." There was a panic to his voice.

With one quick movement she sliced the head clear of its body, moving her hands at just the right moment to capture it as it fell free. She cradled it gently as she stepped off the ladder.

"Mom!"

She turned as he opened the door. Not since Trey was a little child had he opened her door without her telling him that it was okay to enter. She held the head carefully between her hands and stared at him. He held his cell phone out her way.

"I don't understand," he said. "I don't understand what he's trying to tell me!"

He looked like a child. So young. So vulnerable. She drew in a quick breath, the clay head suddenly feeling impossibly heavy. Then Jack was there behind her son, his briefcase still in his hand. Her eyes went from Trey to Jack, the head slipping slightly from her grasp so that she was forced to turn and place it gently on her work table, sitting it upright on the neck, the head's absent eyes turned toward the scene.

What now? What had gone wrong now in her son's short and tragic life? Twenty-six, almost twenty-seven. So young and yet not so young. A short barrage of possibilities flipped through her mind. "Jack," Annette begged.

Trey turned at the sound of his father's approach. "I don't understand," he said to Jack. "I don't understand what he's trying to tell me." He pushed the phone toward Jack.

"Hello?" a voice said from the phone. "God dammit, Trey! Are you there?" It was Ash who cussed into her studio, disturbing the light and the clay particles. "Trey?"

Jack took the phone from their son's hand and put it up to his ear. "Ash?" There was a long moment where Jack listened intently. He looked at Trey, who stood still and stunned. He looked at Annette. He smiled. Then she knew—like she knew that she loved her husband, like she knew he loved her, like she knew that the particles of clay would come to rest only to get kicked up again—that Trey was going to be okay, that the charges had been dropped, that something had happened, that something had occurred to clear her son of such ridiculous charges. It didn't even matter what it was. All that mattered was that something that was terribly off had just now shifted back into place.

FIFTY—EIGHT

As Trey Barkley walked down the street that late fall morning, he was seriously considering updating his Ghost of Christmas Present garb. It had been years since he'd made any significant changes, and the outfit was getting shabby. Sure he was a ghost and all, but he was the Ghost of Christmas *Present*. It was time for a revise. Of course, present was a relative term—present theoretically being 1843, the year *A Christmas Carol* was published. But still. Maybe he'd throw something funky in his mix of the long fur-lined robe, fake brown beard, fat leather belt with a silver buckle, and crown of holly—something funky and modern. Maybe he could replace the plastic holly berries with red M&M'S. Now *that* would be contemporary. Would anyone notice? But the weather was always a little sketchy in late November and December. What if it got a little warm and rained? Would he then look like Christ? Trey laughed loudly, and both the dogs he was walking paused and looked up at him with concerned curiosity.

"It's all good," he told them. The day was sharply colder than earlier in the week, the threat of the upcoming winter in the air, the wind blowing the few remaining leaves to the ground, cutting through Trey's ocher houndstooth coat and his long orange-and-brown-striped scarf. The chocolate lab Trey was walking looked energized by the wind, ready to bound off after every leaf, not the least bit fazed by the cold. Even though Trey had put a bright yellow and green plaid sweater on the other dog, he noticed the little guy was shivering. "Come here, baby," he said, bending over and sweeping the little bundle of white into his arms. Hector wiggled with delight, then settled quickly against Trey's chest. Trey wrapped his scarf around the dog, even though it clashed horribly with the yellow and green plaid. If Trey had thought ahead, he might have chosen Hector's Syracuse University sweater—the match would have been perfect. Hector's shivering stopped immediately, and Trey tightened his grip around the little dog more out of desire than need. He didn't mind carrying the dog. He knew walking all day was too much for the little guy. He didn't really mind that the yellow-green-orange-brown mix was a visual affront. He didn't even mind when people in The Village saw him pressing the white puff of a dog to his face as he and the dog expressed their mutual adoration for each other. He didn't care that it looked ridiculous; he was over all of that. He loved Hector and wasn't ashamed to show it.

There had been a slow resurgence of his dog-walking business. A few of his old clientele had remained loyal once the charges had been dropped; however, most had not rehired him. But he was slowly building his business back up. It helped that Rhonda had gone back to school for cosmetology and had to cut her number of dogs in half. He was making enough to treat himself to Doug's Fish Fry again. He had enough to afford to update his Ghost of Christmas Present outfit and buy Hector his special organic kibble, and he hoped his holiday bonuses would be enough to buy Hector that neat new Mets dog sweater that Aristocats & Dogs had just gotten in. He moved Hector slightly away from his chest and looked him in the eye. "You'd love a Mets sweater, wouldn't you, boy?" Hector licked his approval, and Trey pressed him briefly against his face before returning him to his chest.

There had yet to be a moment when Trey pressed his face against Hector and took in his gentle doggie odor that Mrs. Loughton hadn't come to mind. Perhaps Hector would always link him to her, and he guessed that was all right. He hoped Mrs. Loughton could forgive him for having broken so many of her rules: the ban on demoralizing baby talk, the avoidance of all avoidable dirt, the fact he encouraged Hector to jump into his arms, the fact that he'd allowed him to chase after a squirrel in the park, and especially the fact that he'd never chastised Hector for licking his "privates" in public or otherwise. The biting sadness had softened—that biting sadness that hit him every time he thought of her, every time he thought of her penning out his weekly check or shoving a plate of store-bought cookies his way, or the memory of the way her lips had pressed into a perfect, straight line as she thought some thought, or the way her eyes had sparkled with an excitement he'd never seen before that evening he'd spent with her, before her eyes were never to sparkle again. It was not unlike the way her eyes had sparkled in that photo that had been snapped at that perfect moment of pure joy: her hands holding on to the trapeze line of the sailboat, the wind blowing her hair away from her face, her ass floating dangerously close to the waters of Skaneateles Lake. That biting sadness at each thought of her was now replaced by a gentle, almost pleasant ache.

Because as sad as it was that she was now dead, he'd been given a rare glimpse of Florence Loughton when she was most alive, and it was something he would always own—something, even more than that photo, that would somehow always keep her alive.

Without giving it much thought, Trey turned right onto Fennel Street rather than left, and as he passed the P&C (he would never, as long as he lived, call the grocery store anything other than P&C), little Caleb Rossiter stepped calmly out of the store with his mom, his small hand lost within his mother's. But when he looked up from the puddle on the sidewalk that he was about to jump in and saw Hector, he leapt over the puddle toward the dog, dragging his startled mother along. "A dog in a scarf!" he exclaimed. Caleb's mother recovered quickly, saving the bag of groceries from almost slipping out of her other arm. She shot one quick, fearful glance Trey's way and reeled her son to safety. Once Caleb was tightly to her side, she hissed audibly, "Stay away from that man!"

Trey didn't bother to send her a soft fuck-you look or a fake smile. He didn't even allow the fact that he'd heard her words to pass across his face; he neither shrugged nor closed his eyes in pain. He just held Hector a little tighter, took in a deep breath of Hector, and kept walking. He was over it. The people of The Village, for the most part, treated him now as they had always treated him. A few were nicer. A few were more hostile. But he was over caring. He was actually over a lot of things. It's not as if he didn't have his moments or was freak-out-free or anything, but he was over caring what others might think of him.

He knew his parents loved and supported him as he loved and supported them. His mother almost never got on his nerves anymore, and his father continued to surprise him with the occasional pastry from Patisserie. Trey, too, was trying. He'd brought his mom a pumpkin just the other day. And even though she'd cried in an annoying way, he was glad he'd finally given her the black box with the orange rose. He'd also picked up a book from Creekside for his dad that he knew he'd wanted to read. And although the thought terrified him, he was even considering looking into renting a little room above one of the shops in The Village as his parents had suggested several years ago. It might be cool to live on his own with Hector. The two of them might just be okay.

The wind blew, whipping the ends of orange and brown scarf free from Hector's body. Trey unbuttoned the houndstooth coat and deposited Hector between it and his sweater. "There," he said to the dog. "We're just gonna keep doing the best we can. And you know what, Hector? The best we can is just gonna have to be good enough."

FIFTY-NINE

Flo Loughton lingered by the gate after Trey had disappeared down the street. She listened until his footsteps faded into the other evening sounds. She lingered until the sensations that his arms had left against her arms were gone. She touched the side of her face where his hair had briefly brushed against her cheek. She looked down at Hector, who peered up at her in the gloom of an early moon. "What a silly old woman I am," she said. She laughed as the dog yipped back in agreement.

It didn't take long for Flo to tidy up the kitchen. She hummed "Summertime" as she threw the remainder of the fish dinners into the trash. She picked up the plate from the kitchen table on which one brownie remained and set the plate on the kitchen counter next to the brownie pan, which still sat near the oven. She pulled the plastic wrap away from what was left of the brownies, intending to add the remaining brownie back to the baking pan, but when her fingers sunk into its sides, she brought it instead to her mouth, placed the piece between her lips, closed her eyes, and chewed. Chocolate: what simple pleasure. And truly everything seemed to have an air of simple pleasure. She picked up her glass of remaining tawny port and studied the dark liquid. What was

Trey Barkley doing at this very moment? Was he still making his way through The Village, or was he already home, wrapped in the sheets of his bed? Or was he perhaps thinking about her as he ate that brownie she'd given him to take home? She brought the glass of port to her lips and savored every possible sensation as the bitter pleasure made its way across her tongue, mixing with the chocolate. She brought her hand to her throat, where it lingered, feeling the skin, which was still amazingly in good shape, then she brought her fingers down slowly, where they momentarily rested against her chest above her breasts. She sighed.

She carefully tightened the plastic wrap back down in place over the brownies. She put away the ketchup, then rinsed and placed all the dishes in the dishwasher. Hector watched intensely as she carefully wiped clean the kitchen counters and kitchen table. To his delight, a small piece of breading from the fish found its way onto the floor and into his mouth.

Flo Loughton then sent Hector out the back door. "Do your business," she told him.

While Hector set about his nightly business in the backyard, Flo went upstairs and prepared herself for bed. She took off her clothes and carefully folded her shirt and her capri pants, placing them back in their proper places. She removed her bra and threw it in the hamper to be washed. She slipped her light purple summer gown over her head, enjoying the way the material settled around her body. Miles Davis's "Summertime" was still playing in her head while she washed her face and brushed her teeth. After she'd used the toilet, she stepped back into her bedroom, pulled her summer robe over her nightgown, and made her way back downstairs.

Back in the kitchen, she opened the back door. "Hector," she called. She waited. He didn't come. She stepped slightly into the night and called again. There was a moment of mild concern.

the chocolate debacle

Had she left the gate open after Trey had left? She looked into the dark yard but saw no signs of movement. "Hector?" She took one step further into the yard, ready to call again, but then there was a white blur as Hector came bounding across the yard and scampered between her feet.

It was after she'd shut the back door and turned to head back up the stairs that she heard the smallest of sounds. Hector barked and looked at her with concern. They both paused to listen. Hector exploded into noisy action, and Flo jumped at the sound of a timid knock on her side door. It took a moment for her to recover. Who could be here so late in the evening? "Hush, Hector," she said as she pulled the sides of her summer robe together and tightened the ends of the sash.

It must be Trey. She took a step toward the door. Surely it was Trey.

So it was with the anticipation of pleasure that Florence Loughton opened the door on that evening before of her death, hoping to see Trey with that soft smile on his face and armed perhaps with some excuse. "I think I may have left my cell phone here…" or "Have you seen my baseball cap? The Mets cap? Did I leave it here?" But when Florence Loughton opened the door that warm summer night, she was not met by the sight of Trey Barkley shyly smiling her way, but instead by the smirking, hairy face of Stanley.

She took a step back away from the door. "Stanley!"

Before she had the chance to recover from her shock and close the door in his face, he was there, shoving her into the room, shutting the door, and grabbing her by her left wrist. He then took her by the shoulders and pressed his hairy face hard against her lips, digging his fingers deep into her shoulder blades. She dug her fingers into his arms in protest, then brought her hands to his chest and attempted to shove him away. They struggled as one to the table, where he shoved her down, the salt shaker tumbling over, her body pushing the chair away, her legs naturally falling apart, the edges of her robe sliding open. Hector barked feverishly from somewhere near her feet. She could see the wetness from their lips shimmering against the white of Stanley's mustache as he momentarily pulled away. "Dear God!" she said.

He brought his hand to her hair, grabbed a fistful, and pulled her head back. "You are so sexy when you call to God," he said, then pressed his face against hers once again. She twisted. He grimaced in pain as she slipped away. "You little shit!" he yelled.

It was as Flo moved away that she noticed Hector had attached himself quite neatly to Stanley's middle calf, the white of Hector's body almost matching the white hairiness of Stanley's leg. Stanley shook his leg multiple times, yet Hector still remained attached, his little body hanging in a rather laughable fashion. He growled with each shake. Stanley reached down and dislodged the dog with one quick slap. Hector rolled across the floor as Flo stepped back further. Before she could consider her next move, Hector was back on his feet and quickly reattached himself to Stanley's other leg. "Shit!" Stanley cried.

Flo crouched defensively. "Get out," she hissed. Hector growled through his teeth.

Stanley pulled Hector from his leg by the scruff of his neck and held both his hands up in surrender, Hector dangling from the one on his right. "Floie…. Come on. I didn't mean to upset you. I thought a woman like you would like it rough."

"Get out," she repeated. "Drop my dog and get out."

Stanley looked at Hector as he wiggled and growled in his hand. "If I drop it, it will bite me again." He implored Flo with his eyes. "I really thought we had something, Floie. I just don't get it." He shrugged. "I can be gentle too." He took a step her way.

"I will call the police."

"Floie…."

"Get out!" She yelled the words this time. "Get out of my house!"

"Okay! Okay!" Stanley retreated, stepping backward until he'd reached the side door. He used his free hand to open the door, then stepped out through the doorway until all that was showing was his right hand and poor little Hector. With a flick of Stanley's wrist, Hector was launched into the room. The side door slammed shut. In three steps, Flo was there. Hector recovered quickly from his flight and launched himself at the door, his sharp barking piercing the air. She locked the door quickly, then ran to the front door and locked that one too. Hector continued to bark in frenzied circles, running back and forth between the kitchen and the front entrance way. With her back pressed against the front door, Flo slid to the floor and forced herself not to cry. Hector took one more barking expedition throughout the house. Then he was there licking at her face, and all she could think of were the awful Stanley germs the little dog was ingesting.

She knew she ought to call the police—ought to press some sort of charges. But all she really felt capable of doing at that moment was to sit there with her back against the door. She stayed this way for a very long time. Hector finally lay down near her and fell asleep. Another long period of time passed before Flo got up, made her way up the stairs, and prepared herself for bed.

SIXTY

Flo Loughton woke exactly thirty seconds before her alarm went off on the Thursday morning of her death. She spent those thirty seconds of bestowed consciousness staring at the ceiling. Then, at 6:45 a.m., her alarm beeped into life. Before she could shift to turn it off, Hector was there. His white fluffy face pushed into hers, his tongue lolling out the side of his mouth, his lips curled up in joy. This did not please Florence Loughton. She shut the alarm off and pushed Hector gently from the bed. And rather than getting right up as she normally would have, the awful events of the previous evening mixing with the pleasant events of the previous evening seemed insurmountable.

She'd only planned to close her eyes for another few minutes, but it was some point later when Hector's gentle moans brought her to a more alert state of consciousness that Flo looked at the clock. 8:59! She jumped out of bed, staggered from the sudden movement, and then had to steady herself before she could proceed to the bathroom. After she used the toilet, she glanced at herself in the mirror. She looked every day of her fifty-eight years. Her hair was sticking up in every conceivable direction; she pushed her fingers through the mess with little success. She washed her face with aggression, then smeared her face cream into her skin. Still, she looked like a wrinkled, puffy mess. She gave her teeth a quick going over with her toothbrush. Her lips were red and raw from Stanley's assault, the evidence of his stiff mustache dotting the soft skin around her lips. She spread a little of her Clinique salmon pink lipstick over her lips, easing their discomfort, before she slipped on her light green summer robe.

Hector ran ahead as Flo made her way downstairs. He stopped at the bottom of the stairs to wait for her, peering up her way, his little tail a white blur of movement, his face infused with the anticipation of joy. She paused on the steps and looked down at the dog.

Then all the harshness of her sudden thrust into wakefulness, the disturbing memories of her moments with Stanley, the stress of being late for work, and the unhappy image of her aged face all eased away from Florence Loughton. For Hector it was just another day, like any other day. He held on to no anxiety, no anger, no sorrow, no bitterness. He had no fear of aging or dying. She doubted he worried about loneliness or the difficulties that friendship entailed. For Hector, each and every moment was ripe with the slice of pleasant possibilities. It was as simple as that.

As Florence Loughton took her next step down the stairs, she smiled down at her little dog. The anticipation of pleasure. She would try to hold on to that. She considered the way her coffee might taste, or how the sparkling of dew might lie across her backyard, or the way she might feel the next time she saw Trey, or the very real probability that that large corporation would hire her firm. She entertained the possibility of a long overdue vacation. Perhaps she might take that trip back to her hometown in New England to see her brother.

As Flo reached the kitchen and let Hector out the back door that led to the fenced-in yard, the image of the little dog running through the waves of Cape Cod as she and her brother strolled across the sand pushed through her mind. She made her way to the kitchen counter and turned on the Keurig machine. She stood perfectly still and stared out the window.

She would pick blueberries this weekend. Would Trey enjoy a nice blueberry cobbler? Surely she could concoct a cobbler.

The coffee machine stopped making its preliminary noise, so she placed a new coffee pod in the unit and hit brew. Within moments, perfect, dark liquid was pouring into her cup. She added a splash of cream. She took a large sip and pushed the wrapper off from the brownies and pulled free a piece. She'd have no time for a proper breakfast or to stop for coffee.

Hector scratched at the door to come in. She set her coffee down at the kitchen table, along with the brownie, and made her way to the door. She opened it only wide enough for Hector to come bounding through, then quickly relocked the door. Hector ran immediately to the mudroom as he did every morning, tugging free the leash from the hook. Flo glanced at the clock.

9:17.

"It's not close to the time when Trey will come." The sound of Trey's name as it slipped from her tongue felt nice, so she said it again. "Trey." Hector cocked his head. She sighed as she re-righted the knocked-over salt shaker and sat down heavily at the kitchen table. She ran her hands through the tangles of her hair.

Had she somehow given Stanley the wrong idea? Was it because she'd laughed just before she'd hung up from that ridiculous phone call? She took in more coffee. Was she really sitting there blaming herself for his messed-up delusions? How silly the human mind could be. She quickly took a bite of the brownie and glanced at the clock above the stove.

9:19.

She chased the brownie with a quick influx of coffee, pushed away any thoughts of Stanley, and finished the brownie in one more bite. Hector looked on, the leash still between his teeth, his tail still wagging. Flo again glanced at the clock.

9:20.

Hector jumped to attention as she pushed back from the kitchen table. Flo placed her empty cup in the sink and made her way quickly up the stairs. Hector bounded up behind her, passing her halfway up. The end of the leash slapped around her ankle as he dragged it with him, nearly causing her to fall. "Oh, Hector!" She grabbed onto the railing as the leash pulled free from her foot, its metal end banging against each step as Hector went on ahead.

Once in her bedroom, Flo Loughton removed her light green robe and threw it on the bed. She went into the bathroom, took off her gown, and placed it on the lower hook next to the tub. Hector watched—the leash still in his mouth—as she slipped off her panties and let them drop onto the bathmat. She turned on the shower and washed quickly but efficiently. Then she shut off the faucet, stepped from the shower, and dried herself with her light blue towel.

It was as she stepped from the bathroom toward her dresser where she kept her supply of fresh panties and bras that Hector began to yap, running around in circles, the leash spinning as he spun. "Hector! Stop it! I've had just about enough of this," she said. Again the leash slapped her in the shin. "Dammit, Hector!" She reached down and grabbed the end of the leash. "Give me that damn thing." She had to pull with effort, but once out of Hector's mouth, she placed the leash over her shoulders, well out of the dog's reach.

Then they both heard the distinctive squeak of someone opening the gate to her backyard. Hector took one small bounce. Flo's mind went immediately to Stanley. Hector barked once, then flew toward the bedroom doorway. Flo's heart took a little leap as she distinctly heard someone try the side door. She took three quick steps toward the window by the side of the bed, which looked out over the backyard. Hector changed direction and bounced her way.

Then Hector was suddenly underfoot, interfering with her fourth step. He leapt onto the bed. Her wet foot slipped from beneath her on the polished hardwood floor. The leash flew in front of her face as she fell, one end wrapping around the other. The side of her head hit the corner of the bedside table with a quick hard thud, and then again as she slammed against the floor.

Florence Loughton lay there a moment, stunned, but when she tried to rise, she couldn't. And the next thing she heard was the side door opening and Trey calling from below in what was clearly a patronizing baby voice. "Hector! Where's my little Hector? Are you ready for your walk?"

And then the next thing she saw was the dark red puddle that was forming near her head, and little Hector in front of her face as he pulled with all he had, finally yanking free the leash, which had been wrapped around her neck. He sprang away, the leather leash trailing along from his mouth as he scurried off with such great joy for his morning walk with Trey.

ACKNOWLEDGMENTS

So much has changed recently with our perception of a "book." My daughters used to unevenly tape pieces of their artwork together, add scribbles of text here and there, and call it a book. I still have every one of their books, but they are only fully appreciated through my eyes. Nowadays people pound out a rough draft, send it off to Amazon, and call it a book. And while we certainly can't forget the ability of the writer, I think what transforms a manuscript into a book are the many people who contribute their expertise, their love of the art, their technical abilities, and their emotional support to the writer.

You wouldn't be reading this if it weren't for the people at Goodman Beck Publishing. They have stood by me for years now. An enormous shout-out and deep gratitude goes to David Michael Gettis, my publisher, editor, and friend. Love and friendship to my editor, Lorna Lynch; her advice made this manuscript come alive. I am very grateful for all the input from my first readers: Michael Canavan, August Cornell, Bill Cross, Sheila LeGacy, and Sherri Winters. My most important first reader—my husband, Paul—deserves his own sentence; his ability to put up with me and catch so many of my typos borderlines on heroic. I want to thank my friend, retired Captain James A. Muraco, for his advice in police matters and for being one of my biggest fans. The Onondaga Sheriff's Department could not have been more accommodating. Undersheriff Warren R. Darby and Sergeant Kevin J. Mahoney were so gracious answering all of my many questions and showing me around the Onondaga County Justice Center. This story would not exist in its present state without the invaluable help of defense attorney Edward Z. Menkin, who met me for coffee very early in the morning and made me understand how it all goes down. I'd like to thank my long-time friend, Dr. Donna Violet, for sharing her veterinary knowledge regarding dogs and chocolate. I am grateful to the members of my writers group, The CNY Creative Writers Café, who have given me so much support and fellowship. I must thank Fred Wooley for allowing me to steal his last name and for snapping such an amazing author shot of me. Thanks go out to my publicist, Mary Bisbee-Beek, for believing in me and this manuscript. Heartfelt thanks to my NAMI (National Alliance on Mental Illness) family, whose members have helped make me the writer and advocate I am today. And lastly, I thank my readers who have added that final key element and truly made *The Chocolate Debacle* a book!

ABOUT THE AUTHOR

Photograph by Fred Wooley

Karen Winters Schwartz was born and raised in Mansfield, Ohio. She wrote her first truly good story at age seven. Her second-grade teacher, Mrs. Schneider, publicly and falsely accused her of plagiarism. She did not write again for forty years.

Educated at The Ohio State University, both Karen and her husband have shared a career in optometry in Central New York's Finger Lakes while raising two daughters together.

Karen is the president of NAMI Syracuse (National Alliance on Mental Illness), a strong advocate for mental illness awareness, and a sought-after speaker at health association events and conferences across the country. Karen knows firsthand the devastation that mental illness can wreak on a family. She has talked to hundreds of families who have dealt with the frustration of a broken mental health care system. She has experienced the price of stigma and has felt the isolation that ignorance, misunderstanding, and judgment can inflict on everyone involved. She knows how these misconceptions delay and thwart necessary treatment—at its best leading to loss of jobs, productivity, and relationships, at its worst leading to tragedies such as suicide, violence, and mass murder. She has also experienced the joy of the recovery of a loved one, stressing early detection and treatment as the key to this success.

Her widely praised novel on mental illness, *Reis's Pieces: Love, Loss, and Schizophrenia* was released by Goodman Beck Publishing in the spring of 2012. The follow-up to her critically acclaimed debut, *Where Are the Cocoa Puffs?: A Family's Journey Through Bipolar Disorder*, *Reis's Pieces* is not only an honest and engaging story but an advocacy tool, an educational tool, and a comfort to those dealing directly and indirectly with mental illness.

Through her books, Karen opens up discussions about the need for empathy and the impact of the negative stigma associated with these neurobiological brain disorders. Through literature, she educates while entertaining, elicits empathy while telling a great story, and advocates by reaching those who just don't "get it."

The Chocolate Debacle is her third novel.